I0658518

Taken

A Detective Al Warner Novel
by
George A Bernstein

Award-Winning Amazon Top 100 Author

Gnd Publishing LLC

GnD Publishing LLC
Palm Beach Gardens, Florida 33418

Author's Note: This is a work of fiction. Names, characters, and incidents are a product of the author's imagination. Locales and public names are sometimes used for atmospheric purposes, but details about those locations may have been altered to meet the demands of the story. Any resemblance to actual people, living or dead, or to businesses, companies, events, institutions, or locales is completely coincidental.

Cover Design by Paradox Book Covers

Ordering Information: Quantity sales. Special discounts are available on quantity purchases by corporations, associations, bookstores, and others. For details, contact the publisher.

Taken/George A Bernstein
1st edition

ISBN 978-0-9894681-9-0

Other 5-Star rated novels by **George A Bernstein**

AL WARNER SUSPENSE

Death's Angel, Book 1
Available in eBook, audio book, and print at:
www.amazon.com/dp/B00P2V63X0

Born to Die, Book 2
Available in eBook, audio, and print at:
www.amazon.com/dp/B016V6P7EK
Soon available as an Audio book

The Prom Dress Killer, Book 3
Available in eBook and print at:
www.amazon.com/dp/ B0743LCVCH

White Death, Book 4
Available in eBook and print at:
www.amazon.com/dp/B07DGVDW6S

Sniper, Book 5
Available in eBook and print at:
www.amazon.com/dp/B08LZJ7C1Y

STAND ALONE

Trapped
A Parapsychological Romantic Suspense
Winner in "The Next Great American Novel" contest
An Amazon Top 100 Novel
Available in eBook, audio book, and print at:
www.amazon.com/dp/B00GLX1EKU

A 3rd Time to Die
A Paranormal Romantic Suspense
Available in eBook, print, and audio at:
www.amazon.com/dp/B00D962DL6

Praise for Bernstein's Novels

Sniper (5*) *Amazon* reviewer 3/16/21 An Exciting Story
"Miami Detective Al Warner has a bad feeling about the first three people shot by a sniper. He has a feeling there will be more killings and he is right. The sniper strikes again, but one victim is left barely alive. Then it happens again. The sniper leaves no clues, no evidence and the motive is unknown. At the same time, readers learn that Charles Seagrave and his girlfriend are on a mission to find a liver for his dying nephew. They are racing against time. The author brings to readers an exciting and fast-moving thriller. The narrative is brought to life by the vivid details of the investigation and the pursuit of the sniper. There is tension, violence and action-packed scenes. Shocking secrets are revealed as the story races to a conclusion. Perfectly paced and well plotted, Sniper is a real page turner. Highly recommended."

White Death (5*) Kindle Customer - A must read book
"This was a great book you don't want to put down. I really enjoyed it can't wait until the next one."

The Prom Dress Killer **(4.5*)** Dr. Cynthia L Clark, Psy.D., Ph.D., Diplomat Homeland Security
"Young auburn-haired women are killed and left in a frilly prom dress. There is no sign of trauma. Al Warner is the detective assigned to the case. With few clues, he must profile this killer. Why red heads? Why this age? Why pose them? Why put them in prom dresses? Working alongside the FBI, Al works hard to capture the serial killer who eventually messes up. But that leaves Al with a decision that will affect his entire life. What will he do? THE PROM DRESS KILLER is a look at how a serial killer is evaluated

and then hunted. It is an intriguing and fascinating read. Enjoyable."

Born to Die (5*) Readers' Favorite Mag, by Tracy Fischer

"Whoa! Just, whoa! That's exactly what I thought when I got to the end of the fantastic new book by George A. Bernstein. This book grabbed me from the very start and had me obsessively reading all the way through until the very end. I loved it. How's that for a review? Well, it's definitely how I felt about this book. Author George A Bernstein has done a fantastic job in creating realistic and interesting characters, a fascinating and sympathetic story line, and a simply great read in general! I highly recommend this book to any reader who loves mysteries or just loves great fiction."

Death's Angel – Midwest Book Review, 12/16 magazine

"A masterfully crafted suspense thriller from beginning to end, *Death's Angel* is a terrifically absorbing read and very highly recommended."

K. Lintneron (5*) 12/14 A "Keep You Up All Night" Read

After reading Death's Angel, it is easy to see why George Bernstein is a top selling writer on Amazon. The story is ripe with suspense and action. All of the characters are excellently developed and bring the story to life with dialogue that feels natural and never forced. Death's Angel breaks out of the formulaic police procedural/serial killer genre and excels above its peers. Al Warner could easily be the next Alex Cross. A thrilling murder mystery with a surprise ending no one will guess!"

Trapped - (5*) Angie F –Amazon review - Paperback

George Bernstein has done a wonderful job with his novel, 'Trapped.' Imagine if you went in for routine surgery and were trapped in a coma - seemingly unresponsive, but you're fully aware of what's going on around you. Imagine you find you also have "awoken" with a psychic ability to KNOW how others are feeling. Imagine if you determined that your "accident" was no accident! "Trapped" is a wonderful, gripping thriller that grabs the reader's attention from the first page and refuses to let go."

A 3rd Time to Die (5*) Dianne O'Keefe - A thrilling ride - don't miss it.

Bearing in mind that I like paranormal romance novels, I was pretty convinced that I would like this novel, especially since I also like horse riding. The big surprise was that I never expected it to be comparable to great writers of this genre such as Dean Koontz or Stephen King. "*A Third Time to Die*" really delivered, providing an intriguing storyline and very believable characters. As I reached midway in the book, I was turning pages almost as fast as I could read to find out what would happen next. I enjoyed it immensely and am glad I tried it out. I look forward to more, and am delighted the author already has another book out. Time to download it to my Kindle!

DEDICATION

For the law enforcement professionals, whether local or federal, who seek justice for those often mowed down by the powerful, "entitled" elite. Little appreciated, these often-maligned heroes stand strong for everyday Americans.

Taken

Prologue

The blue Maserati GT convertible shot the too narrow gap between a Honda SUV and a Ford pickup. At 115 miles per hour, only a light rap by the F150 on the GT's rear bumper sent it spinning across the Palmetto Expressway. It tumbled over four times, careening off the concrete median strip and showered the pavement with sparks and blood spatter.

The mangled vehicle skidded to a final stop, upside down and straddling two lanes. Luckily, late evening traffic was light and further collisions were avoided as all traffic screeched to a halt.

The driver of the Ford and another man leaped from their vehicles and hurried to the $200,000 pile of wreckage, peering inside in the unlikelihood there were survivors. No one was visible, but blood began to pool on the macadam.

Seven minutes later, the police had blocked off the expressway, and an ambulance was transporting the single DOA victim to Jackson Memorial, and eventually the Medical Examiner. He had been IDd as Anthony Stirling, of Coral Gables, a prominent banker and philanthropist. A tox screen would prove negative for alcohol or drugs. The clearly wealthy man had been intoxicated only by speed and power, and probably a life of imagined invincibility.

He'd been wrong.

~ 1 ~

Chief of Homicide Detectives, Al Warner, glanced up from the report he was scanning and grinned. A flurry of applause from the bullpen announced an arrival he had expected. He pushed up from his desk and strode to his doorway where he paused and took in the scene.

A diminutive man bowed, then curtsied to the laughter of Warner's detectives who gathered around him, shaking his hand and patting his back. Detective Olvida's attempt to run fingers over the man's salt-and-pepper goatee earned him a friendly jab on the arm.

Warner moved into the room, hands in his pockets, and tried to screw a frown past his smile, but it didn't succeed. "So, Harris, ya finally decided to quit lollygaggin' and come back to work."

"Yeah, Boss." Harris offered his hand for a shake. "It was that, or you'd have to arrest Doris for Murder One."

"Wife had enough of ya, Jack?" Warner pulled his ex-partner close and squeezed his shoulder. "Seriously, how're ya feelin'?"

"Eager to get back to work, that's how." He caught Warner's eyes, the corner of his lips ticking down. "You're gonna strand me at a desk, I suppose."

"That deadly bitch cost ya a lung, and almost your life, partner, and you ain't gettin' any younger." They turned together and ambled toward Detective Jack Harris's cubicle. "You're damned valuable on a desk, but give it six months and we'll see what happens. Meanwhile, we kept your spot open."

"Thanks, Boss." He settled in his chair and ran hands over

the mica-topped desk. Harris opened a drawer and withdrew his 9mm Beretta and his detective's shield. His eyes misted as he glanced at Warner.

"You're still a homicide detective, Harris. Desk or not, that comes with a weapon and a badge."

"Right." His voice a bit choked. "So, what now?"

"What d'ya think? Work is waitin'." Warner pivoted and headed for his office. "C'mon. We got two murders in Little Havana that have drug cartel undertones. I need ya to dig into them and figure out what's what. It's Beck's case, so hook up with him."

Harris rose and trailed Warner, his fingers absently finding the spot where the very deadly *Shadow* had put a .40-cal through the small opening in his Kevlar vest. Six months to recover, and the ache remained. Desk duty didn't look that bad. If they got another big case, he could lobby for more.

But, right now he was where should be . . . back to work and out of Doris' hair.

"I married you for better or worse—but not for lunch," she'd said. "Get back to work before I kill you." She knew that was his best route to recovery.

So, he had two murders to help solve, and no more time for self-pity.

He felt better already.

~ 2 ~

Maggie Bagwell exited the dressing room and headed for the noisy, smoke-filled lounge. CiCi was doing her thing on stage, wrapped around the dancer's pole, eliciting hoots and hollers from the rowdy male crowd as they stuffed dollar bills into her gold lamé garter.

Maggie, aka Kristal Mounds, made a wry chuckle and shook her head, wondering how she, a nice Irish girl from Boston's tenements, had sunk to this.

She was pretty, but never beautiful. Still, her five-foot-eight buxom figure, topped by a round, emerald-eyed face and waves of shoulder-length Gaelic red hair, drew more attention from guys than most of the other senior girls at South Boston High. Her natural athleticism propelled her to squad leader on the school's pep team. She dreamed of culinary school and her own boutique pastry shop. The only thing missing were the funds to finance that fantasy.

So, when the guy approached her after the season's last game, she was ready to take the bait. His natty suit and fancy business card proclaimed him a Miami Dolphin talent scout. That set the hook.

The Dolphins were holding cheerleader tryouts, and he said she was a natural. Two years performing on the sidelines would earn her enough to start her bakery, and he knew just the site for that, right in the heart of South Beach.

Maggie had nothing to keep her in Boston. Just the opposite. Her dad had deserted his family when she was twelve, and her mousy, clinging mom had taken in an abusive boyfriend a year later. The bastard sucked up what little her mom had left to give, and was less than shy in his attempts to bed her already voluptuous teenage daughter.

So, when the Florida guy pitched the cheerleader gig, she didn't think twice. He'd even supplied a Greyhound ticket to get her south after she graduated high school in June.

Jack West met her at the Miami bus terminal that summer three years ago, set her up at a Quality Inn, and told her she needed head shots and a portfolio. Those ate up the last of her funds, but he promised to help, with the implication their sleeping together was "all she needed" to make things work.

Maggie refused at first, but looming poverty had stacked the deck. She considered going home, but after a whispered conversation with her thoroughly cowed and fearful mother, who implored her to stay away, she'd eventually relented. As a modern teenage girl, sex had no taboos and she wasn't a virgin. She, as with most of her girlfriends, was already experimenting by sixteen.

It took less than two weeks to figure out she'd been lured into unscrupulous hands. The bastard had promised her the world but meant to use her up and discarded her without a thought. When she finally accepted there would be no Dolphin tryouts, she split, toting her few personal things in a small backpack.

Her dreams crushed and now penniless, and home no longer an option, Maggie had nowhere to go but down.

Office jobs were scarce, and she had no portfolio other than cheerleading. Never having waited tables in a restaurant, good tipping server jobs weren't available either. The best she could find was a counter gig at Burger King, and that didn't even pay the rent for a room in a shared apartment.

So, when a college girl she met while at work revealed what she was doing to pay her way through school, it wasn't a stretch for Maggie to start stripping at The Wolf's Den. She was never self-conscious about her body and had the moderately loose morals of a millennial. It was certainly a better, safer choice than hooking on the streets, which she had no interest in.

She often got generous tips from horny guys who salivated over her firm, full breasts, and she allowed a very few persistent, upscale admirer intimate contact with her boobs during private lap dances, and even offered some light French kissing. This fed and clothed her, but not much else. Maggie had one short affair with an older client, and while sex ignited the Irish flame in her, she never found any guy to feel serious about.

Somehow, despite her sordid environment, she avoided anything more dangerous than smoking an occasional joint, but for the last thirty months her life had sucked. It was a year since her last attempt to reach her mom, but the phone was disconnected, and two friends she called in Boston had no idea where she'd gone. Maggie suspected the worst, and vowed never to return.

She sighed and stepped into the lounge, clad in a lacy bra and brief panties, and scanned the boisterous crowd. Where were the two guys who had repeatedly tipped her during her last ten minutes on stage? They seemed sure bets for an executive room lap dance.

There, the biker-type, at the far end of the stage, ogling her. Maggie smiled, and he circled the platform, coming her way.

A hand on her arm sent an icy shiver slithering down her spine. She turned and saw the other guy, clean cut, dressed in a sharply pressed, striped sport shirt and tan, creased chinos.

"Hi, beautiful." His quirky grin made an average-looking face kind of cute. "You up for a lap dance in the private room?"

"Sure, handsome." She glanced at the leather vested, bearded guy who had stopped ten feet away, hands on his hips. She winked at him, hoping he'd stick around, and turned back to her new companion.

"Fifty bucks for the usual, and a generous tip if you want something more... exciting."

"No problem, baby. Let's go." He offered her his arm, and they strolled across the room, headed for a heavily curtained-off area in the back, guarded by a stereotypical hunk of muscle.

"You good, Krystal?" the bouncer asked as they approached.

"Perfect, Buck." She patted the bulges rippling under his shirt's sleeve. "We'll take the room on the left."

"No prob, babe." He parted the curtains. "Enjoy."

They slipped inside and pushed through a second set of drapes into a smallish room, containing a cushioned but threadbare, armless chair, and a loveseat in no sharper condition. Maggie guided him to the chair, pushed him down, and straddled his lap. Her firm, lace covered natural D-cups teased his face as she leaned in, nipped his ear, and whispered, "So what'll it be, handsome. I can give you a *very* good time for a C-note."

"That sounds exciting." He pulled down her face and brushed her lips with his. "But how about something more for three hundred after you get off tonight?" His hazel eyes probed hers.

She arched back and studied his face, searching for anything dangerous. A Cop? *No, that would be entrapment.*

"What d'ya have in mind, sport? I'm not a hooker or into anything kinky or drugs."

She wrinkled her nose, detecting the barest hint of some strange, acrid odor wafting off him. She couldn't place it.

"No, nothing like that. Just a chance to make three Benjamins... and maybe a lot more. It'll be worth both our time." He slipped her another fifty and nuzzled her breasts.

Maggie undid her bra and offered his tongue unlimited access. "Okay, but we still need to do this lap dance. The house expects its vig."

She pulled his face into the luscious heat of her warm, soft mounds and wiggled her bottom, sensing his growing response. She loved turning guys on, and this might prove to be a very profitable evening, depending on what he expected. Maggie hadn't slept with a man in months, and self-gratification was getting old, but she wasn't about to begin hooking.

Fifteen minutes later she'd arranged to meet this classy

fellow, whose name she'd learned was Bret, in about an hour in the lounge's parking lot. They'd go somewhere to discuss his "proposition," but it wasn't going to be a hotel room for a cash fuck. She'd see to that.

With a fifty in her garter and another in her tiny makeup bag, they returned to the main lounge. Bret gave her a peck on the cheek and whispered, "In an hour. I'm driving a tan Chrysler Pacifica—sort of a SUV. I'll be looking for you."

"Can hardly wait, sweetheart."

She winked, then watched him depart and wondered if she could get the dough when he realized fucking wasn't included. She'd have her pepper spray ready, in case things got out of hand.

She glanced around, searching for the biker, hoping for one more lucrative lap dance before she was up for her last set on the stage. Spotting him settled at a small table, nursing a beer, she strolled over and laid a hand on his shoulder.

"Hiya, big guy. Looking for a trip to the private lounge and a really hot session?"

He snagged her wrist and spun her down on his lap. "Yeah, baby. Can't wait ta wrap myself around those beautiful jugs of yours." He drew her against him, but she arched her back.

"Easy, slugger. Get too aggressive out here and Buck," she nodded at the fast-approaching bouncer, "will put you on the street." Maggie braced her arm against his chest and waived off her protector. "Save the action for the back room. It's gonna cost you fifty bucks for the dance, but I guarantee you'll be happy."

"Let's go, then." He rose, still holding her wrist, and she slipped off his lap onto her feet.

"Gotta see the fifty before we go anywhere, hon. House rules." The bouncer lurked nearby, arms folded, but she shook her head. A few minutes later, another fifty in her garter, they headed for the back.

She ground her teeth and fought off a grimace. She hated

this life, especially with guys like this, but after nearly three years, it was something she'd gotten quite good at.

A long way from the little custom bakery she wanted to set up with the money and connections she had expected to make as a Dolphin cheerleader, but that dream had long since flopped.

This tawdry life seemed her only way to survive.

~ 3 ~

Warner tucked in his shirt, cinched his belt, and retrieved his Glock and shield from the nightstand. As he exited his bedroom, he cocked his head and inhaled the rich aroma of brewing Jamaican coffee and frying bacon. Eva had wasted no time in getting to the kitchen to prepare breakfast.

Warner glanced at his watch and shrugged. His redheaded lover's unexpected morning passion had put him behind schedule, but luckily, usual run-of-the-mill homicides were his only current problems. Nothing like the frantic hunt for that deadly sniper, the Shadow, six months ago, and it's totally unexpected conclusion.

Warner stepped into the kitchen and paused to savor the sight of this beautiful woman, draped in one of his long-sleeve, cotton shirts—and nothing else—as she plated a second omelet next to three strips of crisp bacon.

Eva spied him at the entry and nodded toward the breakfast nook. "Your coffee and biscuits are waiting for you." She smiled. "I'll bring the rest along in a moment."

"Biscuits, too?" He grinned and strode to her, hooking her with one arm. Their lips—hers soft and yielding, his firmer—clung together for a moment. "You spoil me, ya know."

"That's my job, lover." She spun free and returned to the stove. "Sit and eat. You're already late."

"Yeah, well if we're gonna have more of these early morning parties—I'm not complainin', by the way—" He kissed the back of her neck, then settled at the table. "I gotta set an earlier alarm."

Eva's lips ticked up as she set his breakfast in front of him, complete with slices of grilled tomatoes. "Seems like my hormones are on a rampage lately." Her fingers trailed across his cheek before she retrieved her own plate and perched beside him.

Warner shoveled a fork full of omelet into his mouth, his eyes catching hers as he snared a buttermilk biscuit from a bowl. "Like I said, ain't complainin'." He slathered butter on the biscuit, took a bite, then eased back in his chair, studying her. "Still tryin' to figure out what we're doin' here, though."

"What? Eating breakfast?" Her eyebrows arched, and she chuckled.

"Ya know what I mean, Eva. We've been together now for—what—more'n two years?" He took her hands as she nodded.

"I love you more'n I know how ta say, but despite all that time, I still find it hard ta wrap my mind around you feelin' the same for me. We got so little in common."

"Why is that, Al?" She raised his fingers to her lips.

"Our backgrounds. Our educations, our—"

"Oh, I see." She shook her head. "I've a PHD in psychology, and am from a long line of educated professionals, while you *only* graduated from a community college, with a family scrambling to make a living. Is that it?"

"Yeah." He shrugged and dropped his eyes. "Partly."

"*None* of that has anything to do with who you are, Al." She tugged at his hands, drawing back his gaze. "Your intelligence isn't measured by your education, and you are a lot smarter than most anyone I knew in college. Plus, under that hard bark exterior, you're a warm-hearted, sensitive, and caring guy." Eva leaned back and released his hands. "There's no question why I love you."

"Okay." He chuckled, shoved aside his empty plate, and rose, pulling her up and into his arms. They shared a tender kiss, then separated. "You made your case, and I'm sold. Still pleasantly confused, but definitely sold."

He picked his jacket from a nearby sofa, shrugged into his shoulder harness, and holstered his Glock before slipping on the sportscoat.

"Now I gotta run, Babe. Late, late, late." He planted a brief, tender kiss on her lips and started for the garage.

"Al." Eva trailed after him. "We need to talk when you get

home."

"Oh?" He spun around, brow wrinkled.

"Nothing bad, darling. Just some things on my mind I'd like to talk about."

He folded his arms and studied her face. "What?"

"It can wait. You'd better get going."

Warner shrugged, turned, and disappeared through the door. A moment later, the rumble of his souped-up Dodge coupe followed the squeal of the rising garage door, and he was gone as the door closed behind him.

Eva resettled at the table and sipped her now cold coffee. *How will he react when I tell him I still want to have his baby? My time is running out on that.* She sighed, stood, and retrieved her purse. She too had appointments, a patient coming in less than an hour.

Eva couldn't shake a lingering cloud of tension. A baby wasn't going to be an easy subject after what happened with that crazy bastard, Ron Bachelor. It'd been two years since his attack caused her to miscarry, and she desperately wanted to try again.

She hoped he would, too.

~ 4 ~

Maggie slipped into a pair of satin shorts, tucked in her cotton blouse, and collected her personal things into a small backpack. She glanced at her watch, wondering if the guy had waited, as she was running fifteen minutes late.

She exited the lounge and spotted the Chrysler Town & Country, idling on the drive. She approached the passenger window and peered inside. Bret gave a small wave and the window spooled down.

"Hey Kristal, get in and let's go."

"Where are we going, Bret?" Her hand rested on the door handle, but she hesitated and wondered what she was letting herself in for.

"The Hilton Inn on Brickell. I'm staying there, but I don't expect you to come up. We'll just talk in the parking lot." He stared at her, still lingering outside the car. "You coming or not?"

"Three hundred, you said?" She opened the door but remained outside. "What d'ya expect from me for that dough? I told ya, I'm not a hooker."

"I know. The three hundred is to come with me and hear an offer that's worth a lot more to you than that." His eyes held hers.

"Sure, I'd love to have sex with you, babe, but that's not what I'm paying for. No pressure, I promise."

"Yeah, sure. Let me see it. The greenbacks, I mean."

She leaned in as he drew three Benjamins from his pocket and fanned them.

"C'mon, mount up, and I'll give them to you now. No need to worry about getting cheated." He patted the passenger seat.

She sighed and climbed in, settling on the plush leather bucket seat.

"Nice car." *What the fuck am I doing?* Her fingers curled

around the small can of pepper spray in her pocket.

"Thanks. Buckle up." He handed her the money. "It's just a short ride, and we've got some things to talk about."

"Talk?" Her eyebrows arched. "That's usually free."

"Call it a marketing incentive, okay?" He exited the lounge's parking lot, heading south. "How would you like to find a way to never have to flaunt your lovely body again? For money, I mean."

"You're kidding, right?" She studied his face. "Who do I have ta kill?"

"Nothing like that." He chuckled and gave a sidelong glance.

"I'm talking about getting clean of drugs, if necessary, free health care, good food and clothes, a nice place to live for a year...and a hundred grand, tax-free and clear. Go your own way and live your dreams when the job's done." He patted her arm. "I'm guessing you've got those too, Kristal. Dreams, I mean."

"Yeah, I had those once." She sighed and thumbed away a tear. "And it's Maggie."

"Huh?" He turned into the inn's parking lot.

"My name. It's really Maggie. Margaret, actually." She gave a nervous giggle. "Kristal seemed more appropriate for that gig at the Wolf." She looked at the Hilton's entrance.

"So, you got a room but we're *not* going up?"

Bret unbuckled his seatbelt and hitched around to face her. "I'd love to. You're a beautiful, sexy woman." He took her hands in his. "But my offer has nothing to do with paid sex. Whatever you do is your decision. No one will force you into anything."

"And what *exactly* am I supposed do to deserve all these wonderful benefits?" She studied his face.

There has to be a catch.

"We want you to do one task for us. Nothing dangerous or illegal. You may even find it fulfilling." He rubbed her palm with his thumb. "When that's finished, you'll be free to go your own way. Clean, healthy, with a nice wardrobe, and a pile of cash to do whatever you want."

"That sounds great, but I gotta think about it. What's this 'task' you're talking about, and how big is that pile of cash—a hundred grand? Really?"

He patted her arm. "That's the deal. I'll explain everything once you decide you're interested. Take whatever time you need."

Maggie's eyes flared. *What the fuck. A hundred G's!*

"Okay, I thought about it." She grinned. "I'm probably in, depending on what this 'task' is. Gotta be an upgrade from where I've been." She squeezed his hand.

"So, are we gonna use that fancy hotel room, or what?"

"Only if you want to, Maggie."

"Not for three hundred bucks, but a legal way to earn a hundred big ones is a real aphrodisiac." She released her seatbelt and caressed his cheek, then leaned over for a sloppy, tongue-fencing kiss. "This whole thing's got me really turned on."

They slipped from the car and hurried across the drive.

A new life loomed promisingly in her future, and since she really *did* love sex, this would be a great way to start it.

Free choice! And health insurance. When was the last time she had that?

She slowed for an instant, remembering an adage her mom favored: *If it sounds too good to be true, it probably is.*

Well, her life couldn't get much worse, so what the hell!

~ 5 ~

Jack Harris pushed out of his chair and scurried to head off Warner as he strode toward his office.

"Got a minute, Boss?" He panted softly as he touched the Warner's arm.

"Yeah, Jack. What's up?" He studied the short detective. "You still gettin' physical therapy? You look winded."

"Some, but this job doesn't provide much free time. I've got—"

"Cut the crap, Jack. We need ya here, but in good workin' order. I want ya to see the therapist four times a week. Make a schedule and stick to it." He laid a hand on Harris' shoulder. "Got it?"

"Yes, Boss." His cheeks pink-tinged as he studied his shoes.

"Okay." Warner nodded toward his office. "Ya waylaid me for a reason. What's up?"

Harris tapped on his pad. "I got a call from Damian Torres."

"The Miami-Dade Sheriff's detective?"

"Yeah. A Seminole brave found a woman's body in Big Cypress, near the Collier County border." He glanced at his tablet's screen. "The sheriff's M.E. IDed her as one Ada Funck."

"And they called us why?" Warner, followed by Harris, entered his office and perched on the corner of his desk.

"Apparently, she's got a record as a Miami hooker... a street walker from the Miami Springs area." Harris pocketed his tablet. "He figured since she was one of ours, we'd be interested, especially since it was so unusual."

"Unusual?" Warner rose and circled his desk "Why?"

"Well, she had the expected track marks on her arm. Most of those babes are users, but they were old and well-healed, and her tox screen was clean as a whistle."

"Huh." Warner looked up from the report he'd begun to scan. "Any info she was in any kind of rehab?"

"Nope." Harris settled on a chair. "And she looked healthy. Or at least she was before she croaked."

"What d'ya mean, 'healthy,' Jack?"

"Well fed, decent haircut, nicely trimmed nails. Nothing you'd expect from one of those babes."

"So," Warner scratched his chin, "someone was takin' good care of her. Cleaned her up, fed her, maybe made a concubine outta her. Then what? Dumped her like trash?"

"Maybe. And one more thing, Boss."

"Yeah, what?"

"The sheriff's ME says she'd given birth right before she died. It was a Caesarian delivery."

"Weirder by the minute. Not uncommon for a hooker ta get knocked up, but I'd guess it would be rare for taking it early." Warner slouched back in his chair. "They sendin' the vic up to our ME? I'd like the Hawk and his CSU unit to go over her, too. See if they missed something."

"Figured that's what you'd want." Harris stood. "She's on the way to his lab right now."

"Good." Warner selected another file to review. "Give it to Dean Beck, and you run all the follow-ups. Keep me posted."

"On it, Boss." Harris headed for the doorway.

"Hope this ain't the beginnin' of some new, nasty creep on the prowl," he muttered under his breath.

It'd been six months since the unsatisfying conclusion of the Shadow affair. A non-conclusion at this point, and still a bone the FBI was chomping on. It was out of his jurisdiction now.

Seems like we can't go a full year without some major loony poppin' up. His gut had the uncomfortable feeling more bad stuff was coming, sooner rather than later.

He sighed, and began scanning a batch of action reports.

Warner's thoughts drifted to Eva. Something was on her mind. Well, she'd spill it when she was ready. His lips arched into a small grin. What a lucky bastard he was for a woman like that to actually love *him*.

~ 6 ~

Warner pushed through the swinging doors of Miami-Dade's Crime Lab and spotted Jack Harris huddled together with Moe Gold, CSU's legendary Hawk.

"So, guys, what d'ya got?" Warner asked.

The Hawk glanced up and grinned. "Ah, The Hero graces us with his presence." He shook Warner's hand and chuckled.

"Been over four years, Moe. You ever gonna get tired of that lame moniker?"

"You keep refreshing it, Detective, case after case. *The Baby Butcher, The Angel of Death,* all the way up to the *Shadow* killings. It never gets stale." His brown eyes twinkled over the beak-like nose that had earned him his nickname.

"You're some piece of work, Hawk." Warner gave a friendly squeeze to the back of the neck of the round-shouldered, almost dwarfed CSU wizard. "So, clue me."

"Not a lot that seems to add up to anything, Detective." He glanced at his notepad. "Ms. Funck was twenty-three, and despite a field of track marks on her arm, had a sterling clean tox screen." He slipped off his stool and beckoned the two detectives to follow him to an array of color photos on a white board.

"Despite some critter predation, we determined she was unusually healthy and well-groomed for someone in her line of work. Still verifying the COD, and we found no trace evidence that will tell us about her killer, or where she'd been prior to death."

"Clothing tell ya anything?"

"I've been checking that, Boss." Harris accessed his Android. "Looks like her clothes came from Target, and the one shoe we found was a Sears closeout. Thousands of identical things everywhere." He pocketed the tablet. "I got Tech accessing security footage of all the local stores using a facial rec program to see if we can pick her up doing the shopping, but it's a long shot."

"Yeah." Warner scratched his neck. "And it won't tell ya much unless she was with someone we can ID."

Warner scanned the photo array. "Musta been a pretty gal before the critters got at her." He turned to Harris. "So, where are ya goin' with this?"

"Beck and a couple of patrol cops are canvassing hooker alley in Miami Springs, looking for someone who knew her, and anything else he can learn."

"Good luck with that." Warner chuckled. "Rare to find anyone there who'll talk ta cops. Maybe the local patrol guys might have more of a connection."

"I'll write up what I've got and send it to your computers," the Hawk said. He laid a hand on Warner's forearm. "I'll print your copy, too, Detective. I know you like things on paper."

"Thanks. Old school's always worked for me, pal." He turned to leave with Harris. "Let's hope this is a one-timer, and not some new nut with an obscure agenda."

The Hawk perched on his stool and picked up a file. "But those are where you shine, Detective."

"Don't mean I gotta like it, Moe. Let's go, Harris."

The two detectives exited CSU, going separate ways.

~ 7 ~

Maggie carried a small duffle bag as she hurried down the steps of her rooming house. She spied Bret, parked in his Chrysler van, and waved. He leaned over and opened the front door.

"Whatcha got in the bag, Maggie? I told you we'd supply everything you need."

"Yeah, I know." She slid into the front seat and tossed the duffle into the second row. "Just a few personal things I didn't want to leave behind." She leaned over for a perfunctory kiss, then fastened her seatbelt.

"Where are we going, Bret? I'm kinda excited to see this great place you described."

"You'll see." He shifted into gear and pulled away. "It's quite a bit west, in a kind of secluded area."

"Secluded? You guys hiding something?" She turned on the radio, which was tuned to a Sirius country channel.

"We just like privacy, where we can keep our girls safe."

"Girls? So, I won't be the only one?"

"Just one other for now. She's been there for five months, so I'm sure she'll love company."

"Why?" Maggie twisted in her seat. "Is she alone there? I thought—"

"Oh, no." Bret reached over and patted her thigh. "There's plenty of staff there: a manager, cooks, housekeeping, maintenance, etcetera." He gave her a sidelong glance.

"Like a posh resort. You'll love it." He turned his attention back to driving. They'd been on I-95, but he exited onto US 41, the famed Tamiami Trail, and headed west.

"Sit back and relax. We've got a good forty-five minutes to go."

"Wow." Maggie tilted back her seat and closed her eyes. "You weren't kidding when you said secluded."

~~~

"We're here." Bret touched Maggie's arm.

She blinked awake, sat up, and peered through the windshield at a long, curving driveway lined with towering live oaks. Their minivan swept out of the path into a small plaza, fronted by a sprawling, two-story brick edifice.

Bret parked to one side, under a porte cochère, a protection for guests against the elements. A buff-body guy, probably late twenties, wearing tan Bermuda shorts and a short sleeve safari shirt, came out and opened the van's passenger door.

"Welcome to Cypress House," he said and took her hand as she slipped off the seat onto the crushed stone drive. "I'm Sam. You got any luggage?" He peered through the second door's window.

"I'm Maggie." A small smile tweaked her lips, and she nodded toward the second-row seats. "Just a small duffle of personal things and one change of clothes. Bret said that's all I'll need."

"Right." Sam opened the sliding door and retrieved the plaid bag. "I'll show you to your room and give you a few minutes to clean up. Then you'll come down to our shop so we can get your sizes and let you pick out some outfits." He started toward the doors, glancing back as she followed. "You'll be fully stocked in two days."

"Great." *Wow. This seems almost too good to be true. Gotta be a catch in here somewhere. Hope Mom's wrong.*

"Maggie."

She turned and spied Bret sitting in the Chrysler. She waved.

"I gotta split." He restarted the engine. "Get settled in, pick out some clothes, and get some rest. Sam will square you away, and there'll be an orientation meeting after dinner."

"Hey." She paused, feet spread, hands on hips. "You still haven't told me exactly what you expect of me."

"Relax now. You'll learn everything after dinner." The passenger window spooled up, and he drove off.

She pivoted back and found Sam waiting. "And what if I don't like what you guys want me to do?" *Idiot! Should have asked more questions first.*

Sam shrugged and continued through the doorway with her trailing.

"Then someone will take you back to Miami, and you can keep the clothes." He peered over his shoulder. "No one's gonna make you do anything you're not comfortable with. But, when you learn everything, and what's in it for you, I think you'll be happy."

Yeah, a hundred grand is worth smiling about, if it's real.

They passed through a lobby, empty except for an unmanned concierge desk, and hurried up an elegant mahogany-railed, curving staircase. In the hall at the top, she spied four raised panel mahogany doors with magnetic key locks. Sam fished a card from his pocket and swiped it on the second door's lock. A green LED lit after a small beep, and it opened. He stood aside and gestured for Maggie to precede him.

Maggie took a tentative step through the entrance and paused, her eyes flaring.

"Wow!"

"Pretty nice, huh?" Sam followed her inside. "A three-room suite. This is the living room, and the bedroom is through those doors on the left. Over there," he nodded toward the right, "is a study with a desk and lap top." He set her bag on a pale green suede sofa.

"That's a 70-inch" HD TV with full cable, Netflix, and Amazon Prime. And there's a cabinet full of CD and DVDs of movies and music." He strode over and pulled open a drawer full of discs.

"Let me know if you want anything else."

She thumbed over the discs but looked up when Sam summoned her.

"Here's the bedroom, Maggie."

She giggled and hurried toward the opened double doors,

then jerked to a stop at what she saw.

Holy shit!

The room was so huge, the queen-size double bed, festooned with a half-dozen throw pillows, seemed almost lost. A plush suede-covered reclining chair hunkered to one side next to an avant-garde standing reading light. Across the room stood a matching loveseat fronted by a glass-top coffee table. The fourth wall held two shelves filled with books.

"The bathroom suite is through that doorway." He gestured. "Get settled in, maybe take a bubble bath, and get some rest. Dinner is at seven." He started toward the entrance.

"I'll send up tailor a with a catalog and samples, rather than have you come to the shop. Happy hour is at six-thirty. When you come down, I'll show you where everything is. Okay?"

"Oh, yeah. Definitely okay. I'm just afraid I'm gonna wake up and find this is all a dream."

"It's no dream, Maggie. You're going to love it here."

And he was gone, closing the door behind him.

I'll say. Whatever they want of me, it's gonna have to be pretty damned bad to make me quit this joint.

She flopped onto the bed, arms spread, and sighed.

~ 8 ~

Warner slid his Charger to a stop next to Eva's Jag convertible, and after a moment's thought, rejected pulling into the garage. Eva's schedule had been filled with patients that day, and it wouldn't be a surprise if she were napping.

He exited his coupe and noticed a newspaper in front of his neighbor's stoop. He scooped it up, trotted up the few stairs to Adele Gerber's door, and rang the bell. He hoped the *Trib* had languished there due only to disinterest, rather than the ninety-year-old suffering a fall or illness. A rustling at the door relieved his worries.

"Who's there?" The voice was musical, belying her age.

"It's Al, Adele. I got your Trib."

"Oh, thanks." The door opened, and she relieved him of the paper and took his hand. "Come in and visit for a few minutes, Detective." She was wearing a full apron festooned with tumbling bear cubs.

"I can't stay, Mom." He grinned at her as she blushed at his acceptance of her as his adopted mother. "Smells yummy, though. Baking apple pie again?"

"Blueberry, actually." She set the newspaper on a small table, patted her always well-coiffed gray hair, and tugged him inside. "The girls and I are going to a bridge party tonight, and the pie is our donation." She peered back over her shoulder at the much taller detective.

"I baked a small one for you and Eva." She chuckled softly. "I've got to keep my newly acquired son and daughter fat and happy, don't I?"

"Keep bakin' pie and we'll be fat, for sure. No way ta stop at just one piece. You're too good a chef, Adele."

"Why thank you, sir. Here." Using a hot pad, she picked up a small pie, probably six-inches across. "Still hot, so you'll need the pad."

"Thanks." He leaned down and kissed her cheek. "Now, I gotta run. Eva's probably wonderin' where I am."

"Of course." She trailed him to the door. "Give her my love. You two make a wonderful couple, and help fill my life with pleasure." She gave Warner a short, fierce hug, and it was his turn to blush.

A moment later, he was though his own door, just a few steps away, stealing softly inside in case his woman was asleep. He found her stretched out on the sofa, a Koontz novel spread across her breast. Her steady breathing indicated she slept.

Warner followed his nose after a pungent odor of garlic wafting from the kitchen. He checked the oven, which was off but still warm, and spied lasagna in a Pyrex dish inside. Fluffy garlic rolls sat inside the toaster oven on the counter. He laid the pie beside it, retrieved and opened a bottle of merlot, and poured two glasses.

He returned to the family room and settled on a chair to watch Eva sleep, her hair spread like an auburn halo on the pillow. Her mouth tweaked into a tiny smile, her breath a quiet, steady purr. He slipped to one knee beside the sofa and brushed her lips with his.

"Hey, beautiful."

Eva's eyes fluttered open, and she pushed up on her elbows. "Oh, Al?" The smile morphed into a full grin. "I must have dozed off. What time is it?"

"Six-fifteen." He took her hands, pulled her to a sitting position, and settled next to her.

Eva curled her arms around his waist and rested her head on his shoulder. "Dinner's ready. Lasagna and garlic rolls."

"Yeah, I saw. Adele made us a pie for dessert."

"Oh, yum. Let's eat." They rose together and carried their wine glasses to the kitchen, where he prepared salads while she plated the dinner.

Taken
They ate in uncharacteristic silence.

~~~

Warner mopped up the last of his marinara sauce with the remainder of a garlic roll and popped it into his mouth. He leaned back, chewing slowly and savoring the flavor, his hands clasped across his belly.

"That was delicious." He grinned at Eva, perched across from him, nursing a glass of merlot. "Where'd a Jewish princess learn to cook such great Italian?"

"You know full well I'm no princess." She chuckled and topped off her goblet. "I was raised in lower, middle-class Little Italy in New York. My best friend's mom was a great cook, and she loved to teach. It just rubbed off on me."

"Lucky me." He reached for the wine bottle. "Italian's my favorite, and so it the woman cookin' it for me."

Eva giggled, rose, and stepped around the table, kissing him on the forehead. "Ready for some pie and coffee?"

"How about in a half-hour? Give dinner a chance ta settle."

"Good idea." She tugged at his arm. "Bring your wine and let's sit in the family room."

"I sense a talk comin'." He stood and took her hand as they strolled into the next room and settled on the sofa. "You look kinda serious."

Eva set her goblet on the coffee table and swiveled to face him. "Yes, this is something I've been thinking about for months." She took his hands in hers. "It comes down to this, Al. We're in love and committed to a monogamous relationship, but I know you don't want to get married."

"Yeah, well, what happened with the nut, Ron Bachelor—"

"Right. You think being married to you can put me in danger from some lunatic seeking vengeance, and I get that. But...

"But what, Babe?"

"But, despite being careful, any determined nut can easily discover we're a couple. I still want to have a baby. *Your* baby.

We *don't* have to marry," she hurried on, "but I'm running out of time. I want to have *our* baby, before it's too late."

"Even after what happened last time?" He caught her chin in his hand and plumbed her gray eyes.

"Yes, even that. But I won't go off the pill this time unless you agree."

Warner wrapped her in his arms and stroked her back as she nestled her head in the crook of his neck. "I can't think of anything more wonderful than bein' a dad to our kid, Eva. I'll work hard at bein' the opposite of my pop, that's for sure."

They leaned apart and he tasted her sweet lips. "I got one question, though." He chuckled as her forehead wrinkled. "Is he or she gonna be a Warner or a Guttenberg?"

"I don't know." She stroked his cheek. "Even under Florida common law, we're not married, so probably Guttenberg—or maybe Guttenberg-Warner, or vice-versa. But you should know I'm going to raise our child as Jewish, with a bar or bat mitzvah and everything. My heritage is important to me."

"I got no problem with that. Religion ain't my thing, anyhow." He rose and pulled her up. "Now, let's have that pie."

They sauntered, arm in arm, back to the dining table, each engrossed in thoughts of a new future.

~ 9 ~

Maggie skipped down the stairs, fully refreshed after a bubble bath in the huge tub, followed by a brief nap. The tailor had arrived soon after Sam left, and only ten minutes were required to ascertain her dress and shoe sizes, and for her to select several outfits from the catalogs he provided.

Sam met her at the bottom, taking her hand. "Looking spic and span and well rested. Get in a nap, did you?"

"Yeah, a bath and forty winks. So, when do I get clued in to whatever it is you guys want from me?"

"After dinner." He laid a hand at the small of her back and turned her toward a hallway at the rear of the lobby. "Meanwhile, there's happy hour at the bar. First door on the right, down that hall." He glanced at his watch. "Dinner's in twenty minutes. Gives you a chance to meet the rest of the team."

"Okay, thanks." She started toward the hall and peeked back at him, hands in his pockets, smiling.

All so damned secretive, like a fucking spy novel. What the hell. At the worst, I'm getting drinks, a meal, and at least one night in this beautiful place.

She turned into the lounge and found a twenty-foot mahogany bar, tended by a skinny young Latino. Typical leather stools lined the edge, and four small, individual tables were scattered around the room. A single woman, about Maggie's age, perched on a stool, nursing a tall glass of clear liquid. Maggie slipped onto the seat next to her.

"Hi." She proffered her hand. "I'm Maggie."

"Charlotte." They bumped knuckles. "You just arrive?"

"Yeah, this afternoon. Whatcha drinking, Char? Okay if I call you Char?"

"Sure." She held up the glass. "Club soda and lime."

"Really?" Maggie chuckled. "Not a way to get a buzz on."

"Yeah, but it's part of my current diet. Glad to finally have some company." She waved at the room. "Great place, and they really take care of you, but it gets lonely. I presume you're taking part in the program?"

"Don't know what the program is, yet, but if it means living here, it'll be kinda hard to turn down. Wanna clue me?"

Char shook her head. "They'll explain everything after dinner tonight. At least, that's how they did it with me." She patted Maggie's hand. "You're gonna get the chance to make a bundle of cash and live the good life. I'm betting you'll find it worth the effort."

"What effort?" Maggie's brow crinkled.

"You'll see. Nothing too drastic. I shouldn't say more, in case it's somehow different than mine."

"Okay, but I'm on pins and needles."

Her drink arrived and she took a sip and wondered what was in store for her.

~~~

Maggie settled in an armchair inside a large den, awaiting Sam to explain "the program." Charlotte hunkered in a corner playing a video game on Xbox. Maggie's gentle prying had failed to elicit much of her background.

Dinner had consisted of a shrimp cocktail, Caesar salad, a thick, juicy slab of rare prime rib, and creamy cheesecake for dessert. Even the decaf coffee was scrumptious. Her only dining partners were Char and Sam. All the staff were Hispanic.

Is this place about what I think it is?

Her eyes were drawn to the doorway as Sam entered, followed by a very tall beanpole. The guy's massive, carefully coifed, wavy blond hair topped a face of chiseled good looks—sharp nose, bow-shaped mouth, and high cheekbones. She rose as they approached.

"Maggie Bagwell, please meet our director at Cypress House, Miles Hoek." They shook hands, his grip firm but not tight. "Mr. Hoek will fill you in on why we brought you here."

The man motioned her to sit, and he settled on a chair next to her. Sam perched on a nearby sofa.

"How have you enjoyed your day here, Miss Bagwell? Has Sam taken good care of you?"

"Terrific. A beautiful suite, free booze, a great meal. A girl could get used to this. But I wonder—"

"Why? Why would we do all this for someone we don't know? A girl who maybe lost her way." He smiled.

"Because we want you to see what your life can be from now on. Not just for a day, but your whole future." He took her hand in his.

"We're offering an opportunity for something we believe you may be perfect for. You'll need to pass a physical exam and be entirely free of any drugs, which we believe won't be a problem for you. And once you pass, you'll carry out one simple, legal assignment that will make you and us quite wealthy."

"Yeah? And what's that, exactly?" *Here it comes. Am I ready for this?*

"You'll carry a baby for us."

~ **10** ~

Warner stepped from his office and spotted Detectives Beck and Harris huddled up at Harris's desk, studying his laptop screen.

"You guys makin' progress on the Funck murder?" Warner asked as he approached.

Beck turned from the computer. "Like you suggested, I got some of the Miami Springs patrol guys canvassing their hooker alley." He flipped open his iPad. "Several of the ladies thought Funck was one of four women to disappear in the last six months or so." He paged through a few screens. "Yeah, Renee Red, Hotpants Hillary, and Sheri Sweet." He chuckled. "Those babes love colorful names. And Sheri seemed to go missing in just in last few days."

Warner shrugged. "Any descriptions or things that might tie 'em together?"

"We pulled mug shots." Harris rotated his laptop so Warner could view the screen. "All good-looking gals in their twenties."

"Pimps in common?" Warner leaned down to study the photos.

"Doesn't look that way, Boss," Beck said. "They were fairly new on the strip, and weren't known to be big time druggies, yet, at least."

"There's apparently a lot of street walkers on that strip, Boss." Harris dropped onto his chair. "Maybe they moved on, looking for somewhere with less competition."

"Certainly possible, Jack, but these are pretty attractive gals, and should be the top of the food chain there. More likely, they'd push other gals out rather then move on themselves." He rubbed his chin, eyes cast down in thought.

Taken

"Run their photos through the vice boys. See if anyone's seen these chicks in another locale." Warner turned to leave. "If you can't locate 'em, maybe we got a bigger problem than one dead hooker." He looked over his shoulder as he started away. "Get this to the top of the list. I got a bad feelin' here." He headed for his office.

Harris looked at Beck and frowned. "When the Boss gets a bad feeling, I get a *really* bad feeling."

"Yeah." Beck perched on the corner of Harris' desk. "His instincts on bad guys are uncanny." He pushed to his feet.

"You circulate those photos, Jack. I've got some guys I can talk to in Vice who may be able to help."

"Copy that, Beck. Let's get to work. The Boss is going to want some answers soon."

Harris began formatting the distribution of the mug shots as Beck hurried back to his own desk.

Something smelling bad to Al Warner was all the motivation he needed.

~ 11 ~

"What the fuck!" Maggie lurched from her chair and backed away. She hadn't known what to expect but it sure wasn't getting knocked up, and it rankled her.

"Just 'cause I worked in a strip joint and had one party with Bret, doesn't mean I'm an easy—"

Hoek rose. "Relax, Maggie. No one's asking you to sleep with them. It'll be a medical procedure."

"What d'ya mean, *medical procedure?*"

"It's what's called in vitro fertilization. Our doctor will impregnate you with the sperm of a very wealthy man. You'll have his baby, and that'll earn you a hundred grand." He grinned. "You'll get nine months of pampering, do a little women's work at the end, and come away a rich girl, able to start a new life."

"Yeah? Sounds great." She leaned against the bar, arms crossed. *This asshole thinks birthing a kid is 'a little work.' Wow!*

"Almost too good to be true." She struggled not to sneer.

"Look, I understand your skepticism. Talk to Charlotte. She's six-months pregnant, on the same program. See how *she* likes it."

That explains the no-gin tonic, Maggie thought, remembering Charlotte's drink in the bar.

"Opt out," Hoek continued, "and we'll send you back to Miami, no harm done." He patted her on the shoulder. "There are plenty of women who'll jump at the chance, so it's totally up to you."

Maggie glanced back at Char, seated at a small table across the room. "Okay, I'll do that."

"Fine," Hoek started for the exit, "but we'll need an answer by tomorrow. This deal is time-sensitive."

Maggie nodded and watched him depart, then turned and headed for Char's table. She sighed. *Is this for real? It would give me a chance to get back on track. I wonder why this mysterious guy's willing to pay so much for a stranger to have his baby.*

And half the DNA will be mine.

The eventual answer to that question was not at all what she expected.

~~~

Maggie lingered over lunch: a huge hamburger, crisp fries, coleslaw, and iced tea. It was delivered to her suite because she wanted no distractions while she mulled over her decision.

Charlotte had sung the praises of "the program," extolling the coddling provided by the staff. She received any perk she requested without hesitation. She *did* go into some detail about the extensive medical tests they ran on her before clearing her to carry a baby. They'd even run a DNA scan, which she guessed went to checking the genes she was going to give to the infant. They were, after all, using her egg, and she supposed they'd want to clear her for any undetected, potential genetic diseases.

Another girl named Rita must have flunked the tests three days before, and was gone in the night, probably back to wherever in Miami. Maggie was apparently her replacement.

She slumped back in her chair and shoved away her plate. Maggie's eyes skimmed the room, taking in her luxurious accommodations, and she sighed. Nine or ten months of this certainly wouldn't be a chore, and if things didn't work out at the end, it would be like a nice vacation. It didn't seem like this was in any way illegal, so she wasn't too concerned for her safety if she decided to opt out.

Her thoughts wandered to the baby she would deliver. What would become of him or her? The child would be half hers, genetically. This rich benefactor surely wants the kid, or why do it at all? How would she feel at twenty-four, giving up her baby? Would she retain any parental rights—visitation, and maybe weekends? She wasn't even sure she'd care. It wouldn't be conceived out of love or passion, so how connected would she really be, just because she carried it?

She pushed away from the table, rose, and sauntered to the bed, perching on the edge. The room's phone sat on a nightstand and beckoned her. She shook her head and shrugged.

What the hell. She plucked it off the receiver and dialed the four-number code Miles Hoek had given her. He answered on the second ring.

"Mr. Hoek? It's Maggie."

"Yes. And you've made a decision?"

"Yeah. I'm in."

~ 12 ~

"Boss."

Warner looked up from the file he was reading and found Jack Harris, poised in his entrance.

"Yeah? What's up?"

"I did some follow-up on the three missing hookers." Harris entered, settled in a chair, and studied his Android.

"I got Vice to run down what they could on the one called Sheri Sweet." He paged to another screen. "No one's seen her at the flop house where she bunked for at least four days. Same with the soup kitchen, where she was a regular."

"So, no leads?" Warner stroked his stubbled chin.

"Gone without a trace." Harris looked away from his tablet. "Same with the other two, but they disappeared weeks ago."

"Any connection to the Funck woman?"

"Not that I can find." Harris pushed out of the chair. "Worked different neighborhoods."

"What about the Hawk?" Warner rose and gathered two files from his desk. "He get anything off Funck's corpse?"

"*Nada*, Boss. He said we were fortunate to get an ID, as corrupted as the body was. She'd been out there in the heat and water for maybe four days." Harris shrugged. "It's surprising a big gator hadn't just eaten her."

"Well, she sure didn't go for a stroll in Big Cypress on her own. You at least got a COD?"

"She drowned. The Hawk says her lungs were waterlogged. No signs of blunt force trauma or any man-inflicted wounds, as far as he can tell." Harris pocketed his tablet. "So, are we calling this a homicide or accidental death?" He trailed Warner out of his office.

"Probable homicide, for now. Not likely a Miami Springs tart went into the Big Cypress Swamp on her own. And the other three missin' women only compound the situation." Warner paused to look at his detective.

"Something's goin' on with streetwalkers disappearin', and this may be a connection. I'll tell Beck this case is his top priority, and you keep Vice in the loop. Maybe put out feelers to the tri-counties. See if they're missin' any hookers."

"On it, Boss."

Harris scurried back to his desk as Warner strode off, searching for Detective Beck.

A nagging inner voice pestered him: *This is only the beginnin' of something nasty.*

~ **13** ~

Sheri Sweet moaned as her eyes fluttered open and squinted at bright sunlight. She brushed moisture from them and pushed up on her elbows, trying to orient herself. Her hair rustled in the breeze, and a loud roaring sound exacerbated the pounding in her head.

Sheri blinked, clearing her vision, and she spotted a guy—*the* guy—perched on a bench, grinning at her. He was framed by a huge circular wire housing behind him.

What the hell? They were on an airboat, zipping across some sort of swamp of sawgrass and reeds, flashing by.

"What the fuck did ya do to me, you bastard?"

She struggled to sit up, her back braced against another bench seat. He just sat there, still smiling.

"Last thing I remember was giving you a blowjob in your car." Sheri pressed her palms against her throbbing temples. "Where the hell are we?"

"The Everglades, babe, on the way to your new home."

"My *what?*" She was too listless to do anything more than glare at him.

He reached down and patted her knee. "Believe me, hon, it'll be a real upgrade. You'll be comfy, well fed, and just keep doing what you're doing." He sat back and chuckled.

She wiggled up onto the bench, the breeze from their high-speed flight across the marsh ruffling her bleached blond hair. Her fingers found a sting mark on her neck.

"What did ya do, drug me?"

"Just a little tranquilizer to keep you compliant 'til we get you to your new home." He leaned back and crossed his arms.

"This is kidnapping, ya know." Sheri shivered and rubbed her sore neck.

"Maybe, but no one's gonna miss you, will they? Streetwalkers come and go, and no one cares. Haven't had a problem yet."

"Yet? You've done this before?" She glanced around at the desolate slough flashing by.

"Oh, yeah. You're probably gonna find some of your friends in your new digs. All happy as a clam."

"Oh, I bet. Out in the middle of nowhere. A regular Eden." She wrapped her arms around her shoulders, lips pressed into a knife-slit grimace.

How the fuck did I get myself into this? Twenty-six and the Oklahoma State Fair beauty queen, stuck hooking for hundred buck blowjobs, instead of my big show biz career. She sighed. *I've sunk so low I don't even care if they kill me... especially if I can't get my next fix.*

Sheri shivered, sensing the growing need for a shot of heroin. *Hooked on H and selling my body so I can buy my next shot.* Her eyes swept the endless vista of sawgrass.

"Where the fuck are we going? There's nothing out here but swamp."

"Fantasy Island." The guy chuckled. "Or the Chicken Ranch East may be more proper."

Her brow wrinkled. "Chicken Ranch?"

"Yeah, like Las Vegas."

"Huh? Out here, in the middle of hell-n-gone?"

"That's how we stay safe, babe. Only special, high-class clientele get to come to our little island paradise."

He peeked over her shoulder and shrugged.

"Should be there in a few minutes." He glanced at Sheri. "Relax. You'll be well cared for."

Yeah, I've heard that before. A fucking island, yet, in the middle of the 'gator infested 'Glades. Not likely I can get away from there alive.

The man leaned forward on his seat and pointed ahead to

what appeared to be a large island covered with a thick copse of live oaks and melaleuca trees. They surrounded a string of ramshackle, dilapidated shacks.

"There she is." He waved as two men wandered down to a dock that looked to be on its last legs.

"*That's* Fantasy Island?" *Shit. I'm fucked.*

"Relax, kid. All ain't what it looks like on the surface."

The airboat slowed and slid next to the dock. The two men offered their hands to aid in disembarking.

"Welcome to your new home, Sheri," the taller, angular man said. "I'm Rex, and this is Smokey," indicating the shorter, plump guy who sported a tiny moustache.

"We're your chaperones here, at the Ranch."

His attempt at a smile sent chills down her back.

"Once you get acclimated to our ways, we hope you'll enjoy your stay."

She shuffled across the rickety dock and onto firmer land. Sheri was a good judge of men, which is how she stayed alive on the streets. She saw nothing pleasant about Rex.

"And, exactly how long is that stay gonna be, Rex?"

"Oh, this is your home now." He snickered. "No need for you to go anywhere else in the foreseeable future."

Shit! That's what I feared. Fucked for sure.

Rex took her by the elbow and led her toward the middle of shacks, as the airboat and her abductor roared away.

Whatever they planned for her it couldn't be much worse than the last two years on the street, as long as she could get her regular H fix.

Without that, life would really suck.

~ 14 ~

Detective Damian Torres gunned the forty horsepower Mercury outboard engine and beached his Miami-Dade Sheriff's seventeen-foot bass boat next to the department's airboat. He spotted three deputies clustered together, just beyond the sandy beach on this small, cypress studded island hammock, obscure deep inside Big Cypress Swamp.

Torres stepped ashore and hauled the boat further up, ensuring he wouldn't have to swim home. He tugged down the bill of his MDSO ball cap, adjusted mirrored sunglasses, and swiped away beading perspiration from his brow. The mid-day sun, moisture-laden air, and the stench of decay weren't pleasant, but such was the life of a sheriff's detective. He sucked in a rancid-smelling breath and strode to join his deputies. They glanced up in unison at his approach.

"What'cha got, boys?"

They parted, and he first noticed the two long legs, one missing a foot, sprawled out from under a bush.

"Dead female," the corporal said. "Looks to be mid-twenties. Some animal predation," he nodded at one footless leg, "but overall, pretty much intact. Judging by the bloating, I'd guess she's been here two or three days."

"Who found her way out here?" Torres crouched and shoved aside the brush for a full look at the corpse, as buzzards swooped and soared above, angry at losing their feast.

"I did," said a deputy wearing Fish and Wildlife patches. "I was scouting for pythons and saw the birds. Thought it might be a snake's nest and stopped to look for mama." He glanced at the body. "Not a very pleasant surprise."

"I bet. Not exactly your bailiwick, huh?" Torres, still

crouched, scanned the area around the body. "No apparent COD?"

"No, sir." The corporal squatted beside him. "Nothing obvious and I didn't want to move the body until you arrived."

"Good. So, let's cut away this brush and see if we can roll her over. You get an ID?"

"No, sir. I scanned her prints and took a photo, but we haven't seen her face yet." He glanced over his shoulder. "No signal out here, so we can't run them until we get back to civilization."

"Okay. When you do, send 'em to my phone." Torres lumbered to his feet. "Then get busy clearing the area and look for anything probative." He glanced up at the hills of inky clouds, massing in the west.

"No sense in chasing CSU out here, with that storm coming. Probably been raining every afternoon, anyhow, so there won't be anything for them here." He turned toward his boat.

"I got a body bag in the boat for the transport back to the lab. We figure out who she is, maybe we can assign jurisdiction." He started toward his beached boat. This was the second female corpse to show up in Big Cypress in the last week. He hoped it wouldn't become a pattern.

~~~

An hour later, Detective Torres slouched in his Ford Expedition, engine idling as the A/C wrung moisture from the air and cooled the interior. Once he'd returned the boat to its mooring just off the Tamiami Trail, he acquired cell-phone service and texted the vic's photo to the sheriff's lab in Miami. Prints would wait until the deputy returned to civilization. He regretted he hadn't taken a print reader with him.

He sneezed. Despite the airtight body bag, the woman was declaring her odorous presence, something he was eager to get rid of. He sighed and shifted into gear, heading east. Death in the 'Glades was seldom pleasant.

His cell phone vibrated, and the Ford's camera screen lit up;

"Sheriff's Office." He punched the button, answering with his Bluetooth connection.

"Torres. You got something for me?"

"A facial ID on your vic, Detective," Chuck, the sheriff's department Tech supervisor responded. "Belinda Amato, aka Scarlett. File says she's a hooker who frequented high-end bars in Fort Lauderdale. Twenty-six, with two priors for solicitation."

"You contact Fort Lauderdale PD yet?"

"Thought I'd talk to you first. You want to keep the investigation or hand it off to the local PD?"

"It belongs to the guys in Broward County." Torres paused and tugged at his earlobe.

"But this is the second female vic outta Big Cypress in less than a week, both hookers. The first one is in the hands of Detective Al Warner in Miami."

Torres eased left to peek past an ancient pickup trailing a pram. He accelerated, sweeping past it just before traffic arrived going west. He glanced at his dash.

"Tell you what. Contact both the Broward guys and Warner. Let them work out who'll handle it. I'll bring the stiff to our morgue unless I hear otherwise."

"You got the corpse, Torres?" Chuck was incredulous. "Shouldn't you have called—?"

"Big T-storms were roaring in, and there was nothing for the ME to do out there, other than collect the body. Been so much rain, I doubt there's anything left for CSU either, but they can go if the sheriff thinks it's necessary." He sniffed and shook his head.

"She's beginning to perfume my car, so I'm eager to offload her to whoever wants her. Check with those guys and get back to me. I'm still about thirty out."

"Copy that, Detective. I'll get right on it."

You'd better. This stink is gonna linger.

Torres ground his teeth, lit up his flashing light bar, and

stepped on it. He'd be happy to turn this over to whichever department wanted it. Some cops loved murder investigations.

Damian Torres wasn't one of them.

~ 15 ~

With a firm grip on her elbow, Rex hauled Sheri stumbling along a crushed stone path and through the doorway of the middle of the three shacks. The plywood and timber door opened smoothly, and with the guy called Smokey urging her forward with a hand on her back, he dragged her inside.

Sheri blinked at the brightly lit interior. They were inside a small foyer with a single desk, manned by a beefy matron-type woman in hospital whites. Neat beige tiled floors and ivory painted sheetrock walls belied the building's exterior.

The woman rose, stepped around the desk, and approached them. Her arms folded across an ample breast, her face blank, as her pale blue eyes swept over Sheri.

"Olga, meet Sheri, our newest resident." Rex glanced at the quivering girl. "Olga will care for you while we get you cleaned up, medically checked out, and made presentable to our clientele."

"Cleaned up?" Sheri struggled to pull free, but Rex had a firm grip, and Smokey was tight against her back.

"Yes. Checking for STDs and a thorough detox. Our girls here are drug and disease free. Our clientele expects nothing less."

"Detox?" She shivered, goosebumps ridging her spine. *No heroin fix? I'm gonna die!*

"A necessary evil for you, I'm afraid." Rex thrust her into the iron grasp of Olga as Smokey chuckled.

"It'll be a rough month or so, but you'll make it," he continued.

"You'll find a much happier life here, once free of your addictions." Rex's eyes held hers. "You'll be well-fed, well-dressed, and well-cared for. And you'll be plying your trade with a much better class of men, and occasionally, women."

Olga drew her forward by her grasp on her wrist. "Come, I will get you settled." Her grip an iron vise, she dragged the whimpering woman toward a white metal door.

"A shower first, and something clean to wear. You smell like shit." They disappeared through the door, which closed with the snap of a lock.

Sheri's wail, "Please don't—" was cut off by and audible slap.

~~~

Sheri curled in a fetal ball on her new cot, one of eight in what could pass for a dormitory. She reluctantly admitted the hot shower, her first in nearly a month, felt good. She'd donned a plain, soft cotton knee-length nightgown set out on a stool in the bathroom, and a striped, light terry robe lay beside her on the bed. Shorts, a cotton tee, and lingerie sat next to it. Faux leather sandals perched under the edge of the bed.

She groaned, rolled up, and wiggled onto the cot's edge, feet dangling. Fingers traced her still-smarting left cheek where Olga had belted her into submission.

"Do what yer told and don't cause no trouble, and you'll be happy here. Otherwise, ..." the beefy matron waved a clenched fist.

Sheri shuddered and swiped away tears, then edged off the bunk, slipped on the sandals, and her new robe. For a joint that looked to be falling down from the outside, the interior was clean, modern, and well kept.

Camouflage? She remembered the duck blinds she'd hunted from with her father as a mid-teen, before that heart attack took him. One minute he was sitting there, helping with math homework, and the next instant he was sprawled across the kitchen table, dead before anyone could react. When her mom remarried creepy Calvin, Sheri knew it was time to go.

She took her rodeo beauty queen prize money, sold the

Angus calf they'd awarded her, and left for Florida. Sitcoms, and even some movies, were in production in Miami, and she figured it might be easier to break into flicks there than in LA.

What a pipe dream!

Her looks got her noticed, contacts were made, and beds of *important* men were visited, one after another, until she realized she was just being used. She decided if she were going to fuck guys, it may as well pay.

First it was a high-class escort service, paying well and seeing mostly decent men. Then the agency got busted, and she spiraled down from there, ending up on the street—and now here she was. There were few independent streetwalkers in Miami, and the first thing the pimp who forced her into his harem did was hook her on H.

And now the need for a new fix was beginning to percolate inside her. She approached a girl three beds away, one of two others in the "dorm."

"Hi." She settled on the next bunk. "I'm Sheri."

The girl—thin-waist, full hips, small boobs, and inky black hair—rolled up on an elbow and lay aside a paperback she was reading. Her slate gray eyes surveyed Sheri, and she nodded.

"Mickey." She offered her hand. "You just arrive?"

"Yeah. Not by choice, though."

The dark hair girl grunted. "Don't know no one who came here by choice. Once you're here, you're here, so get used to it."

"No one ever leaves?" Sheri forced back tears.

"Not alive, anyhow." Mickey sat up, legs crossed, and shrugged. "Two girls made a run for it, using canoes or dugouts or something." She sighed. "They ran one down. Posted photos of her body, somewhere in the swamp. Don't know about the other one, but we're miles from hell-and-gone, somewhere deep inside the 'Glades. She surely died out there, probably wandering in circles."

"Jesus!" Sheri knuckled away a tear.

"Yeah. The only way to find your way in and outta here is with GPS."

The other girl, a petite, bright-dyed redhead, strolled over. "Tanya." She shoved out her hand, shook by Sheri. "Renee Red on the street." She plopped down on a bunk.

"Seems pretty scary to ya, right now, kid, but if ya don't make the best of it, ya ain't gonna last. Like it or not, yer part of this harem, and free will don't live here no more." She settled on the bunk next to Sheri. "We got no way out." Tanya sighed.

"They feed us well. There'll be plenty of nice clothes... for the guys, ya know... once they move ya up into the main house. Even got pretty good medical help. If we ain't healthy, we're useless to 'em."

"You been here long?" Sheri's voice cracked, eyebrows arched.

"Five weeks. Mickey's ten days less. I'm finally clean of crack and a mild case of the crabs, and I gotta admit, that mostly feels pretty good. Supposed to start working for my keep next week, so I've been given the indoctrination talk."

"They're gonna force us to have sex with their clients?" Sheri shivered, then gave a wry chuckle. *So, what's new? I'll be working for a cathouse instead of a pimp.*

"Yeah, doing what I've been doing, but in a fancy room in the main house, with a nice bed and high-class guys. No car dates or grubby motels. Supposed to act like lovers and mistresses, not hookers in a hurry for the next guy. We're trapped here, but on the plus side, we should be safer as long as we toe the line, and we got no cops to deal with."

"The main house?" Sheri hugged herself, trying to quell her growing shivers. "Have you seen it? Looked like a dilapidated shack."

"I think that's to fool any cops or feds flying by. Inside it's really upscale. Gotta be top notch for who their clients seem to be."

"You've seen the inside?" Sheri curled her legs under her, fighting the tremors.

"Yeah," Mickey said. "They take ya up there about two weeks

after they start cleaning ya up. Give ya a peek at what ya got ta look forward to."

"No drugs?" A whimper in Sheri's voice.

"Not a chance. They want us clean and alert. What are ya on, Sheri?"

"Heroin." She dropped her eyes.

"Tough stuff. Your pimp hook ya?"

Sheri nodded, trying to repress the building shakes that would eventually rack her body.

"Look." Tanya took her hand. "If it gets bad, there's a buzzer button on the wall by your bed. Olga's a tough bitch, but she cares for what she calls 'her girls.' She'll help you through the worst days, but you're gonna have to sweat it out."

"Look at the plus side," Mickey said, patting her shoulder. "You're gonna be happy ta be rid of that demon. I'm just shed of the same curse, and I feel alive for a change."

"And no fear of getting re-hooked." Tanya stood. "Anyone showing up here with drugs is 'gator bait. Zero tolerance."

"Not even the johns? Most guys I saw liked to run a line before getting started."

"Not even the johns." Mickey shrugged. "They'll eject anyone... even their clients... who get rowdy." Her hand cupped Sheri's chin. "These bastards are tough and mean, but only if ya get outta line."

"Go drink a full glass of water and lie down, kid. I'll call Olga to sit with ya while ya go through this first bout of withdrawal." Mickey hauled the blond up and steered her toward her bunk.

"Believe me, you're gonna be happier once ya get past this. We might be trapped here, but I mighta come on my own if I knew what it was gonna be like." She grunted. "We ain't getting outta here alive, but working the streets in Miami was an eventual death sentence, anyway."

Sheri slumped on her bed, shuddering. "No one ever leaves?"

"Not upright, far as I know. Ya think they'd let you loose to blow the whistle on 'em? No way." Mickey perched next to her. "I'm twenty-six, and I figure if I use the gym they got here and stay fit, I could be good for another twenty years."

"They got a gym here?" Sheri's eyebrows arched.

"Yeah. All kind of exercise stuff. They've got maybe a dozen girls already workin' in the main house, so we ain't gotta sleep with some bozo every night to survive." She felt Shari's brow for a temperature. "Not many streetwalkers live to be forty, so I made my peace with it."

Mickey rose, covered Sheri with a light wool blanket, and punched the buzzer by her bed.

"We're prisoners here, but we were prisoners on the street too, even if it seemed like we were free. Drugs and the pimps were our wardens." She sighed. "I'm hoping this'll be better than that. We'll see." She glanced at the door.

"Olga's on the way."

~ 16 ~

Al Warner set the phone on its cradle and swiveled to face his office computer. He massaged the back of his neck, sighed, and punched ENTER to light up his monitor. His mailbox showed three new e-mails, but only the first, which just arrived, interested him.

Fort Lauderdale Homicide had sent a file on a woman named Belinda Amato, AKA Scarlett, a high-end escort whose corpse was discovered in the Dade County portion of Big Cypress Swamp. The case was referred to that Broward County department because she worked their beat, but Sheriff's Detective Torres clued them in on Warner's similar case. FLPD Detective Jim Hoshi called, explained to Warner what they had, and after a brief discussion, agreed to e-mail their admittedly slim file for Warner's review.

Warner clicked on the link to download the file attached. He had agreed if the cases seemed connected, they could mount a joint taskforce for the investigation. One dead hooker in the middle of the swamp was worrisome, but two hinted at a pattern.

Prostitutes were often targets of serial killer. Jack the Ripper was the most infamous. But transporting their bodies into the middle of Big Cypress Swamp was unusual. Intuition suggested something more sinister, if the deaths of the two victims proved to be murder and were somehow connected.

Warner blinked out of his musing when a beep indicated the completed download. He opened it and found eight pages, including preliminary autopsy findings. He hit PRINT, and turned back to his file on their own victim.

According to his ME, Ada Funck was drowned, and bruising

on her neck indicated it wasn't an accident. The Hawk scoured the vic and her clothing, but came up with very little. Tech was running surveillance video through facial rec from local Sears stores, trying to ID Funck and, hopefully, someone she shopped with when her clothing items were purchased.

Harris assigned four patrol officers to take her recent mug shot to the stores to see if anyone remembered her. She *was* unusually attractive for a streetwalker. The life hadn't had a chance to corrode her looks before she was taken.

Warner retrieved the printed report from his HP laser printer and flipped to the autopsy. Death by drowning, with back-of-the-neck discoloration and a significant bruise at the base of her spine.

A knee in the back to hold her under?

He returned to Funck's file and scanned the M.E.'s report. No mention of additional bruising. Warner snatched his desk phone and hit an auto-dial button, answered on the fourth ring.

"Miami-Dade Morgue." The M.E. himself.

"Warner here, Doc."

"What can I do for you, Detective?"

"I'm lookin' at the Funck autopsy and got a question."

A tolerant sigh. "Yes? Think I missed something?"

"Don't know." Warner hesitated. This guy rarely missed much. "Any chance there was some bruisin' on her lower back? Maybe like a knee, holdin' her down?"

"Hmm." He paused. "I turned it over to an assistant after I found the marks on her neck. Let me check it out and I'll get back to you."

"Thanks, Doc. ASAP, if it's not a problem. Lookin' for a connection to another case from Broward County."

"I'll get right on it, Detective. I won't be happy if I find my staff missed something like that." He disconnected.

Warner replaced his phone and turned to the two files, side by side on his desk. His instincts again told him they were a harbinger of something more sinister than mere homicides. Prostitutes live a potentially dangerous life, but this smacked of serial murder. He'd see what the doc came up with after reexamining the vic.

~~~

Forty minutes later, Warner was still at his desk, reviewing a report on a domestic homicide. Puerto Rican spouses managed to kill each other in what appeared to be a spat over what TV program to watch. Warner shook his head and set it aside as his phone trilled. He snatched it up, hoping for some helpful news.

"Warner."

"It's Doctor Carson, Detective."

"So, what did ya find, Doc?" He eased back on his chair.

"Embarrassed that you had to tell me what to look for."

"You found the lower back bruisin'?"

"Yes, and in fairness to Chester, it was mostly sub-dermal. We needed an incision to make it out. Definitely consistent with a knee in the back, as you suspected." He paused. "Is this good news for you?"

"Mixed, Doc." Warner sighed. "It helps focus two investigations, but may also signal we got another serial nut on our hands. Thanks for the quick follow-up."

"Thank *you*, Detective, for the heads up. It seems I need to do a bit more training with my staff."

They said their good-byes and disconnected.

Warner pushed away from his desk, rose, and carried the two women's files into the bull pen, heading for Jack Harris. They needed to ramp up their investigations, and dig further into possible disappearances of local hookers. He'd have Harris coordinate with the Vice boys to comb the local escort scene too, since this appeared to have expanded beyond streetwalkers. Go tri-county, too. Since the second known vic was from Broward, they should give Palm Beach a heads up.

"Harris."

"Yeah, Boss. What'cha got for me?"

"Looks like a Broward escort vic matches the M.O. for Funck."

"Oh, fuck. You thinking it's serial?" Harris looked at Warner, who dropped into a seat next to his desk.

"Becomin' more likely." Warner dropped the files on his detective's desk. "Copy these. I don't think the one from Broward is on your computer. Now, here's what I want you to do…"

Two dead hookers had become the department's top agenda. Warner *knew* that was only the beginning.

~ 17 ~

Maggie slouched back from the computer supplied by her new benefactors and rubbed dry eyes. No Internet connections and no e-mail available. She could retrieve information somehow, but not from Google. Some sort of in-house data base, and she was unable to send any kind of message, although she had no one to contact.

She'd spent the morning getting her second physical exam in the ten days she'd been at Cypress House, complete with blood and urine tests.

Her DNA had been run from the first exam, and she'd just learned she was healthy and disease free, which was no surprise to her.

Four days ago, she'd gotten her second FSH injection to stimulate her ovaries. Now they were giving her something called HCG to help mature her eggs, and progesterone to make their retrieval easier. Squeaky-voiced, plump Doctor Lee, (Korean, she guessed) explained everything to her as it occurred.

She expected her period in about six days, so ovarian stimulation continued. An ultrasound in three days would verify eggs had matured in something called her follicle sac. If all looked good, they'd retrieve several eggs the next day, apparently done under anesthesia.

After fertilization by the donor's sperm, they'd be incubated for six days to assure viability before being implanted in her womb. A week or so would pass before they'd know if she was officially pregnant.

Taken

They seemed in a rush to get it done. Apparently, they had a time limit on the donor's sperm, which didn't make sense. Her file search showed sperm was usually frozen and good for years. The same with eggs. Would they freeze some of hers for a second try, in case the first pass failed? Probably.

A strange trepidation stirred inside her. Why the rush?

She sighed and pushed out of her chair, wondering why an apparently rich guy needed a secret surrogate to carry his baby? She supposed he was married, so why didn't he use his wife's eggs instead of those of a stranger? Was there a genetic problem? Or was he single and trying to create an heir for his fortune?

She chuckled at an imagination running wild. Whatever the reason, he obviously wanted it kept secret and was willing to pay her a bundle of greenbacks to do the job for him. So, that's what she would do, and it would earn enough to get her out of stripping and into the boutique bakery of her dreams.

Maggie checked her Casio watch, one of her new perks, and saw there was an hour to nap before happy hour. After dinner, she'd spend some time in the well-equipped gym, keeping fit. She was determined not to let this otherwise indolent lifestyle seduce her into becoming soft and flabby.

She set an alarm on the bedside clock and stretched out. She used to do that on her cell phone, but it was confiscated on her arrival at Cypress House. They really prized their secrecy here.

Five minutes later, snuggled under a light flannel blanket, she snored softly, dreaming of her bakery counters filled with frosted cakes and fragrant pies.

~ 18 ~

Al Warner slouched back in his chair, his ankles crossed on the corner of his desk, staring blankly into space. Two weeks had passed since Eva declared her desire to have a baby... *his* baby... and they'd been busy working at it almost daily. Her electric passion elicited performance from his forty-four-year-old body beyond his expectations. Whatever was the magic day of the month, she intended not to miss it.

He grunted and swung his legs down, sliding closer to his littered desk. Becoming a dad raised conflicts within him, eliciting a grimace at memories of his father, certainly no role model. But, the thought of fathering a child with that warm, sweet redhead infused him with warmth. Marriage or not, they'd work it out, and he vowed it would be a happy time. He sighed and turned his attention to his desk.

Warner shuffled through several incident reports and picked out the one he sought. File in hand, he shoved away from his desk and strode into the department's bullpen.

"Harris. You out there?"

"Here, Boss." The diminutive detective's head popped above the four-foot-high blue metal and frosted-glass divider.

"What's goin' on with the hooker murders?" Warner waived the file. "Nothin' here says you're makin' progress."

"That's 'cause we're not, Boss." Harris stepped out of his cubicle. "Beck's run down what little we had on Funck." He took the report from Warner.

"Didn't appear to have any real friends on the street, and the flop house was day rate, so no one missed her." He flipped to the third page. "Tech never found her with facial rec on CCTV's shopping anywhere." He paged farther into the file.

"The higher-end escort, Amato, had gone to a fancy steak joint on Sunrise Boulevard to meet a hookup. Her roomy got worried when she never checked in, but her cell phone was off." He closed the file and handed it back to Warner.

"There's many joints she could've visited along that street. We got four security feeds from that night but never spotted her at any of what we learned were her usual haunts."

Warner folded his arms across his chest. "And?"

"No joy, Boss." Harris shoved his hands into his pockets.

"She either got taken before she arrived or decided to visit somewhere else. The FLPD detective's got patrol cops armed with photos, asking around, but it's been ten days since Amato showed up and two weeks for Funck." Harris nodded toward the file. "We haven't turned a single clue on either case."

"Anything on the other three hookers that went missin'?"

Harris shook his head. "*Nada.* They all seemed to just evaporate into thin air."

"No new girls disappearin'?" Warner's eyebrows arched.

"None since the Shari Sweet. We've got alerts out with Broward, Palm Beach, and Monroe Counties, but no joy."

"Huh." Warner rubbed the back of his neck. "My instincts said this was gonna be another ugly one, but maybe I jumped the gun. But murder is murder, and these two are connected. Keep Beck on top of it for now, Jack. Serial killer or not, we still got the crime ta solve. Amato's Lauderdale's problem unless we find some other connection, or things blow up with more vics." Warner turned toward his office.

"On it, Boss." He started toward his desk.

"And Harris," Warner glanced back, "keep me in the loop. A report at least every other day, even if there's nothin' new. You know how I feel about unsolved murders."

"Copy that, Boss." He disappeared inside his cubicle.

~ 19 ~

Maggie wandered into the lounge and spotted Charlotte at a table, tapping away at a laptop.

"Hey, Char." She paused, a hand on the back of one of the adjoining chairs. "Want some company?"

"Sure, Mags. Grab a seat." She took a sip from a tall glass of clear liquid.

"What'cha drinking?" Maggie settled on the chair, her legs sprawled beneath the table.

"Virgin vodka Collins." She chuckled. "Tonic water with a squeeze of lime."

"Sound good to me." She twisted in her seat and waived at the man behind the bar.

"José. I'd like one of the same," she gestured at Char's drink, "and some bar snack—peanuts and stuff."

"Comin' right up, Red," he replied.

"Off booze already, Mags?" She closed her laptop. You've been here less than two weeks."

"Yeah, but the timing was perfect. An ultrasound for eggs was positive, so I got the shots—something called FSH, and then HCG—and a week ago, they were able to retrieve several healthy eggs." Her fingers subconsciously wandered over her abdomen.

"That's good," Char sipped her drink. "The first try on me produced questionable eggs, so we had to do it all over again a month later. They were real unhappy."

"Ugh." Maggie looked up as José delivered her drink and two bowls of snacks. "Not something I'd want to go through twice." She took a swig of the cold liquid.

"Yeah." Char grimaced, "Hoek seemed like he didn't even wanna try again." She smiled. "But yours was a success, huh?"

"Yep. Fertilized them with the mysterious donor's sperm, and they went right into an incubator for six days. Two were implanted this morning."

"So, you're prego?" She patted the redhead on the arm.

"As of eight a.m., but they said it'll be about two weeks before a blood test will confirm if it took."

"Good luck, kiddo. You're on the way to a big payday. Maybe you'll have twins."

"Jeez, ya think?"

"Nah, not likely. But you got a lot to look forward to: morning sickness, mood swings, crazy cravings—it's a barrel of monkeys."

They chuckled, then eased into a comfortable silence, sampling the bar treats as they sipped their drinks.

Maggie studied Charlotte from the corners of her eyes. "How'd you end up here, Char? You know, carrying a baby for some unknown guy?"

"Me?" She picked up a pinch of peanuts and popped them into her mouth. "I was working a dead-end job as a take-out cashier for KFC." She washed down the nuts with her drink.

"A regular customer invited me to dinner. Figured I had nothing to lose, so I went, and he made the pitch."

"Bret?" Maggie's eyebrows arched.

"Yeah, that was his name. Nice, attractive guy with a strange odor about him."

"Yeah, I noticed that too. Can't place it. You?"

"Not really." Char took another pull at her drink. "Anyhow, I figured it was a ploy to get me into bed, but he never made a move. Said his offer was time sensitive, and anything looked better than what I was doing, so I jumped at it." She patted her swelling belly. "So here I am."

"You mentioned you were stripping, right?" She slouched back, staring at Maggie.

"Yeah, came down here promised a slot with the Dolphin cheerleaders, but it was just a scam." Maggie rotated her drink on its paper coaster.

"Took my money and tried to make me into his private whore, so I split. Discovered stripping paid better than any measly job I could get. I was never self-conscious, so it was an easy move." She shoved away her empty glass.

"Then Bret showed up and made me the same pitch as you, I guess. Like you, this could only be an improvement." Maggie leaned forward, resting her arms on the table. "You having any thoughts about the baby?"

"What d'ya mean, thoughts?" Char signaled José for a refill.

"I did some research on my computer. This isn't a typical surrogate, where you're implanted with a fertilized egg from the couple. You know, she can't carry the kid, so they use her egg and his sperm, and we do the work." Maggie slouched back, studying Char.

"But these are our eggs, so the kids are biologically half ours. It doesn't make sense."

"Yeah." Charlotte folded her hands together. "I thought of that, but so what? I want nothing to do with a brat. I got no interest in being a mom." She watched Maggie with hooded eyes.

"And you? They just knocked ya up, and it got your parental instincts perking?"

"I don't know." Maggie massaged her eyes and sighed. "No, probably not, but I can't help wondering...you know, what's this about?"

"I learned long ago, too many questions can get ya into a pile of shit." Char drained her glass and rose. "I'm in it for the money and a chance to straighten out my life. I'm gonna drop someone's bundle of joy, collect my fee, and split."

She started away, glancing back at Maggie. "I suggest ya take care of business, keep your head down and your questions to yourself. Plan a future without some unknown guy's kid in your life."

"Yeah, you're right." Maggie pushed away from the table. "Whatever they're doing, the details are none of my business. Just can't help being curious."

They parted and Maggie headed for the gym and a thirty-minute session on the stair-climber. She *was* going to be a mom, and she had growing doubts about how she would handle that.

Oh, well. I'll worry about it later.

Meanwhile, she'd enjoy the benefits. This was the best she'd lived in over two years.

~ 20 ~

Warner ambled into his kitchen as he slipped on his shoulder holster, his sport jacket slung over a shoulder. Eva fussed at the stove, looking especially fetching, dressed as she frequently did in the mornings, in one of his flannel long sleeve shirts.

"Pour some coffee and have a seat, lover." She grinned and peeked at him over her shoulder. "Blueberry pancakes and sausage patties on the way. Coffee's just finished."

"I'm runnin' kinda late, Babe." He filled a cup of dark coffee. This was the first morning in weeks she hadn't initiated sex, and he'd overslept.

"Everything's ready, Al." She plated four plump pancakes and two discs of meat. "You can spare the extra ten minutes. You need the fuel in your system."

"Okay, okay."

He chuckled, still trying to acclimate, even after nearly two years, to someone caring for him, something so unfamiliar before Eva. Sharon had loved him, but they'd never lived together, actually relying on each other.

He settled at the table and took a swig of his java as Eva placed the delicious smelling plate in front of him.

"Looks yummy, Red."

He slathered on maple syrup and dug in. Within minutes, the plate was clean except for a smear of syrup and a few blueberry stains. Warner dabbed his lips with a napkin, rose, and leaned in to kiss Eva.

"That hit the spot, but now I gotta run." He cupped her face in both hands, a grin ticking at his lips. "I love ya, Red."

"The feeling's mutual." She smiled. "I'm planning on treating you to dinner out tonight, so, any idea when you'll be home?"

"We celebratin' something?" His eyes held hers.

"Nope." She chuckled. "Too early to know if all our hard work has paid off. I just thought it might be nice to get out for a change."

"Sounds good ta me." He started toward the garage. "I'll try ta make it by six."

"Perfect. I'll make a reservation at Tony's." She stood and followed him. "Call if you're going to be late." She paused, unfastening her apron as he disappeared through the garage entry door.

"Will do, Boss," he said over his shoulder as the door closed. "Have a good day." Anything else was masked by the rumble of the rising garage door.

Yeah, I've got a busy schedule, too. She turned toward the bedroom to dress. Her first patient was due in ninety minutes.

Have to pick up some pregnancy kits. Probably too early for any results, but I'm going to be ready.

Her brow furrowed. Time was running out.

~ 21 ~

Three weeks locked in this joint is getting pretty stale. It's a comfortable life, but it's still jail. And with nothing to do, and nowhere to go, it's driving me nuts.

With Mickey moved into the main house, Sheri's only company was Tanya and occasional check-up visits from Olga.

On the up side, Sheri was through detox, no longer suffering withdrawal. Their little complex provided a lounge with TV, a small kitchen/dining area, and a modest exercise room with a few aerobic machines, some weights, and other miscellaneous devices. Plus, the dormitory and bathroom.

No booze, no drugs, and not a lot of joy. A prisoner, no matter how you looked at it.

She sprawled back in her chair, legs thrust out under their small dining table, and nursed a now cold cup of dark coffee, awaiting Tanya's return from a potty break. One hand wandered over her once again firm breast, and she grinned.

They'd plied her with a healthy diet while clearing her system of drugs. She'd regained some of the twenty pounds she'd lost on the streets, mostly returning her gaunt body to its once full-figured glory. They'd just run her second physical, and even sedated her without her consent for some sort of internal exam. She sighed. As the Borg on *Star Trek* always said, "Resistance is futile."

She groaned and shook her head. Her physical lust for heroin had passed, but not the mental need. That bastard, Chico, had forced himself on her, shot her up with H, and declared himself her pimp. The drug sapped her will to resist.

If she somehow got out of here, she vowed never to go back to that. Maybe she'd find the bastard and kill him. Who'd miss one more pimp?

But, escaping whatever servitude they'd planned for her here seemed very unlikely, considering she was planted in the middle of nowhere.

Sheri glanced up as Tanya returned and plopped onto the next chair. Sheri sighed, casting aside her thoughts, and held up a well-worn deck of cards.

"Wanna play some gin?"

"Might as well. I'm getting jaded with the daytime soaps." She studied Sheri. "Ya look a bit jaded yourself, kid."

"Yeah. Had my second physical this morning."

"They put you under? You look kinda groggy."

She nodded. "Yeah, didn't have a choice. Some sort of internal exam, they said."

"The only choice we got here is go with their program...or die. So, looks like you're getting qualified to move up inta the big house, like it or not."

"I guess." Her eyes welled, and she patted her abdomen "Feels kinda weird."

Tanya grunted. "No one told ya? They tied your tubes. They do it to all of us."

"What? I can't have kids?" Rills of tears trickled across her cheeks. "I'm only in my twenties."

"So what?" Tanya's mouth tightened. "We're never getting outta here to find a Prince Charming, as if that'd ever happen. A knocked-up girl ain't any use to 'em here." She shrugged.

"I talked ta Mickey when I took the tour. Condoms aren't required. What's better for a john than unprotected sex with a hot, healthy babe he knows is STD free? It's one reason they're probably getting big bucks." Tanya cut the deck.

"It's a bitch, making that decision without our okay— forcing us inta their service. But, let's face it, I'm guessing this'll be better than a fucked-up life forcing us to work the streets." She handed the deck to Sheri.

"Maybe," Sheri dealt ten cards each, "but at least out there, I had a choice."

"The hell you did!" Tanya reached over and took one of her hands. "Your pimp controlled your life with drugs and fists. You weren't going anywhere except into an eventual pine box, and that probably sooner than later." She sat back and caught Sheri's eyes with hers.

"We gonna be sex slaves here, no damned doubt about it. But so were we on the streets. At least here we're not hungry, hooked on drugs, and scrabbling for a safe place to sleep." She sighed. "And I'm hoping we ain't gonna get beat up on a regular basis, either." She drew a card and threw a three.

Sheri's eyebrows arched. "You think they'd allow sadistic sex at what's supposed to be a high-class joint?"

"The customer's always right... within reason, anyhow. I wouldn't be surprised if some of their rich and powerful clients don't enjoy physical domination. At least if we get knocked around, we'll get good medical treatment instead of dragging our ass inta an ER." Tanya sighed again.

"Good medical's hard to find for a hooker on the streets."

They sunk into pensive silence as they played their cards, awaiting their next move... a life choice no longer in their control.

~ 22 ~

"Boss." Jack Harris materialized in Warner's doorway.

"Yeah. What's up, Jack?" Warner shoved aside the report he was reading and waved his detective in.

"Looks like we may have another one." Harris settled in a chair and offered his Android tablet to Warner.

He took it and studied the screen. "Another missing hooker?" He handed the tablet back to Harris. "So, our perp is back in business. Tell me what'cha got."

"One Kiesha Swift, and *not* a hooker, but she fits the M.O."

"Really." Warner slouched back and steepled his fingers. "Why's that?"

"She's twenty-one and was Junior Prom Queen at Florida A & M this year."

"A & M? So, a Black girl this time?"

Harris nodded.

"If you're right, we got a perp who believes in diversity, it seems." Warner doodled on his pad. "Why d'ya think she's a vic in this case?"

Harris glanced again at his tablet. "She dropped out of school at the end of her third year. Beck checked with her advisor who said Swift was getting into modeling." He looked up. "Supposedly offered a contract by a Miami agent."

"Startin' to sound familiar. Another scam?"

"Probably." Harris closed his Android. "Best we can tell, she never got a gig. She moved back to Overtown, where she was living with her mom."

"So," Warner leaned forward, forearms on his desk, "get to

the point, Harris. Why d'ya think she's one of the vics tied to the missin' hookers?"

"Beck interviewed her mom who said she left to meet a guy supposed to be an agent and never came back."

"When was this?"

"Two days ago." Harris paged through screens.

"Why so long before we hear about this?" Warner growled and pushed back from his desk.

"It took that long before the old lady realized she was gone." He laid his tablet on the desk. "Swift often stayed out overnight. Got a boyfriend she sometimes shacks up with."

"But not that night?"

"Nope. Never saw her that night. But, this time we mighta gotten a break."

"Yeah? What?"

"The mom told Dean Beck she saw her daughter get into a silver sedan. Unsure of the model, but maybe a Chrysler or Dodge. It had a roof rack."

"So?"

"He recanvased Miami Springs with one of the vice dicks, and a supposedly reliable CI said she remembered a silver Chrysler in and out of the area about the same time our first vics went missing."

"Okay. That may be something." Warner jotted a note on a yellow lined pad. "I got an idea how we can work with that." He eased back in his chair. "Any other details on the car?" He folded his hands across his belly and stared at his detective.

"Four-door, silver, and that roof rack. Florida plate with a manatee on it, but no numbers. That's about it."

Warner grunted and scratched a note on his pad. "So, what do we know about Ms. Swift. Let's be sure we're not racin' off on a wild goose chase."

"Okay." Harris flipped past two pages on his Android.

"But not much else that might help. Obviously, a beauty, and she had good grades at A & M. A Communications major and popular with both guys and girls."

"She was a *modern* girl. I suppose." Warner scratched a note on his pad.

"You mean did she sleep around?" Harris chuckled. "Beck learned she's had two different boyfriends over the three years at A & M. They call it 'liberated' nowadays."

"Okay, so maybe a person of interest." Warner shoved back from the desk. "Have Beck get Vice to check the local escort services, to be sure she hasn't been pressed inta service."

"Vice has closed down a lot of those agencies in Miami, so if it's forced prostitution, she probably woulda got pushed onto the street by her pimp."

"And there's no sign of her there, so she seems to be gone," Warner said, stroking his jaw. "Just like the other gals. So, we either got another serial nut, expandin' past just killin' hookers, or someone's settin' up a private cathouse with an attractive set of professional ladies."

"Human trafficking? That makes sense, Boss." Harris leaned forward. "Could explain the vics in the swamp, too."

"Yeah, girls who resisted too much, or flunked whatever criteria the perp's required." He reached for his phone.

"Get Fish & Wildlife and the sheriff's office to sweep Big Cypress lookin' for a location—something outta place that might fit as a cathouse."

"Already on it, Boss. We've got two Cessna planes crisscrossing the whole preserve, looking for something unusual. It's a big area, and so far, no joy."

"Keep at it. Meanwhile, I'm gonna call Agent Pauletti at the BAU and see if the FBI can run a search on our street cams and CCTVs for a silver sedan that might fit that car. The roof rack and manatee plate'll help." He dialed a cell number he'd long since learned by heart. He glanced at Harris.

"They got that great vehicle recognition app we used to locate that black-market transplant ring last year. Maybe we'll catch a break again."

"Good idea." Harris rose. "I've got Beck and local patrol working the likely areas, keeping an eye out for that car."

Warner looked up, nodded, and waved for Harris to go, just as the call was answered.

"Agent Pauletti? It's Al Warner." A pause, then, "Yeah, everyone's back to work here. How's the Shadow chase goin'?" He listened, then sighed. "I know it's still hard to accept the bastard got away, and the loss of Agent Dalwin." Another pause, and he listened before responding.

"I appreciate that, Agent. Anyhow, got a favor ta ask. Can I get ya to use that vehicle rec program again? We got a situation down here..."

Eight minutes later, a new search began, this time for a silver Chrysler or Dodge sedan, cruising the hooker-patrolled streets throughout the Miami-Dade district.

If these perps made a move on another streetwalker, Warner was gearing up to catch them in the act.

Or so he hoped.

~ 23 ~

Sheri wiggled from beneath the light flannel sheet and sat up in bed, knuckling sleep from her eyes. The sound that awakened her was an airboat arriving. She glanced at the clock/radio on her bedstand: 7:50. Too early for horny clients, so either supplies, or a new girl for the harem. She'd been dragged out here before eight a.m. too.

Sheri's eyes swept toward Tanya's bed and found her still asleep. The woman was about to move into the main house, so Sheri hoped this would be a new girl. She hated the thought of banging around in there alone. She grimaced, realizing she was hoping bad luck for another girl, snatched off the streets against her will.

She slipped off the flowered cotton teddy and donned a pair of khaki shorts and a sleeveless cotton blouse, sans bra and panties. She stepped into the kitchen, turned on the already prepped coffee maker, and poured a bowl of Cheerios. Blueberries and a carton of 2% milk from the fridge completed the breakfast as she settled at the table to eat. Coffee was in the final stages of brewing.

Halfway through the meal she cocked her head at the bang of the outer door, scuffling feet, and muted voices from the lobby.

"What's going on?" Tanya, fastening her robe, joined her and dropped into a nearby chair.

"New girl arriving, I think." Sheri glanced at her, then back at the door. "Another addition to the harem, from the sounds of it." She keened softly. "How the fuck did we get caught up in this?"

"Bad luck with bad choices. How d'ya think? Yer never

safe on the streets."

"Yeah, I know, but I mean, how'd we get out there in the first place? I was raised in a good, middle-class family."

"Like I said, bad luck, bad choices." Tanya sighed. "We were innocent enough ta think our looks would take us somewhere good, and we got played. But here is where we are, so we gotta make the best of it."

They looked up as their door rattled, and a plaintiff "No-o-o" echoed from the hall. A moment later, Olga bulled through, dragging a tall, mud splattered Black girl behind her.

"Shut yer mouth bitch, or I'll belt ya again."

She hauled her newest charge to one of the beds and shoved her down. The girl sprawled backward onto the mattress and mewed softly, her hands covering her eyes.

Olga strode to a cabinet and withdrew a plain cotton nightgown, a terry robe, and underwear. She returned to the new arrival who had scrunched into a fetal ball, and laid the items on the bed.

"Strip and take a shower." She yanked off the girl's ragged blouse and tugged at her mini skirt. "Wash yer hair, too. Ya smell like crap." She brandished the woman's outfit, torn and covered with mud. "I'm gonna burn this shit. I'll be back in fifteen minutes." She headed for the door.

"Be sure yer clean and dressed when I get back." She glanced back over her shoulder and shook a clenched fist.

"Don't fuck with me, bitch. You ain't the first one I gotta teach who's boss. You ain't gonna like it, if it comes ta that." She stormed through the door, which slammed shut, followed by the click of the lock.

Sheri and Tanya moved over and perched on the cot beside the whimpering woman. The blonde reached out and touched her leg. The girl flinched and jerked back, her wide, dark eyes flooded.

"Easy, sweetie." Sheri knelt next to the bed. "We're not gonna hurt you."

"No," Tanya pitched in, "we're trapped in here, just like you, kid."

"Where—where the fuck am I?" The woman sat up, scooted backward, and scrunched against the wall.

"In Hell," Tanya said, glancing at Sheri. "Kinda a fancy, upgraded version, but Hell, none the less."

"I'm guessing we're the same as you." Sheri rose and sat beside her. "Girls who fucked up and ended up on the streets, selling ourselves to stay alive. Right?"

The new woman cowered, arms wrapped around her knees, and shook her head. "I'm no hooker!" Tears trickled over round cheeks.

"Really?" The blonde's eyebrows arched. "That's a surprise." She glanced at Tanya. "They trying to upgrade their staff?"

The other woman shrugged and turned to the new arrival.

"I'm Tanya, and this is Sheri." She nodded at her blond companion. "What's your name?"

"Kiesha." Her deer-in-headlight eyes swept from Sheri to Tanya. "What d'ya mean, Hell? What the fuck is this place?"

"The Chicken Ranch East." Tanya grunted and shrugged.

"Huh?"

"It's a bordello." Sheri reached over and brushed long, silky, black hair from her face. "An apparently *very* high-class house, and we've been invited, totally against our will, to service their clients."

"What the fuck...?" Kiesha drew her knees tighter against her ample breasts.

"Yeah." Tanya leaned closer. "How'd they get you?"

"I...I was supposed to be going to a modeling interview." Her voice a broken whisper, she whimpered and brushed droplets from her eyes. "I remember we pulled into the studio's lot, and Kris—supposed to be my agent—leaned over to adjust my collar...and next thing I remember is two guys dragging me from some kind of boat and through the mud."

Sheri took Kiesha's chin in her fingers and swiveled her head, noting an inflamed red dot on her neck.

"He knocked you out with an injection, just like they did with us."

"But why? I don't belong here. I gotta—"

"Ya think we do?" Sheri grunted and looked away.

"Look," Tanya took Kiesha's hands, "we're here, out in the middle of hell-and-gone, and there's no way out. Those what tried ended up dead. You're gonna have ta make yer peace with it if ya want ta survive."

"This may be tougher on you that it is for us because you aren't a professional like we were," Sheri said, "but I'm guessing you're no virgin, either. You're gonna have to perform with the johns...or die. No one's getting outta here alive."

"The good news is, they're gonna feed ya well. I'm guessing you're probably not hooked on drugs, which is how they seem ta want us." She sat back, her eyes holding Kiesha's.

"Whether ya like it or not, we're trapped here. We're gonna do what we were doing on the streets, and maybe what you were doing with some guy back home. For us," nodding at Tonya, "it'll hopefully be an upgrade, in fancy rooms with a much higher-class john, and a nicer place ta live." She shrugged. "The end of free will, but I'm gonna have to make peace with it." She patted Kiesha on the knee.

"Best you do too."

"No-o-o. They can't do this to me." Eyes clenched, she shook her head. "Shit, I was a college beauty queen. I was going to be a famous model, not a piece of meat for some guy's pleasure."

"Yeah." Tanya rose, arms folded. "We all had dreams." She nodded at Sheri. "Ours ended up dumping us on the street, scrabbling to stay alive. At least you avoided that shit hole before ending up here."

"It is what it is." Sheri also stood. "You can make the best of it and survive, or get the shit beat outta you, and eventually get discarded in the swamp." She shrugged. "And you won't be the first to die out there."

Kiesha sniffled as she slipped off the bed, her arms crossed over her breasts.

"You're saying I was kidnapped, and I'll be forced to have sex with strangers? Jesus! Why me?"

Tanya shrugged and glanced at Sheri. "Good question."

"My guess is because you're a Black beauty. They wanted...?" Sheri's forehead wrinkled. "Diversity, I guess, and most of the Black street hookers are pretty shopworn."

"Most of *all* street hookers are shop worn, Sheri. You and I were unlucky enough ta be newbies, and not yet ground down by the life."

"Yeah, maybe." She took Kiesha's hand and led her toward the bathroom and a shower. "Whatever the reason, if you gotta accept what you can't change. Focus on staying alive, and hope somehow we find a way outta her someday." They paused in front of the shower stall.

"We're just tools for these bastards, and if they think you won't cooperate for their use, I'm betting they'll toss you away without another thought. Think about that while you're getting cleaned up."

"You ain't gotta detox or put meat back on your bones like we did," Tanya leaned against the door jamb, "so yer probably gonna be put to work pretty quick. Do the job, and if ya do it well, maybe there'll be some perks."

Tears still streaming across her high cheekbones, Kiesha

stepped into the tiled enclosure and turned on the water, adjusting for as hot as she could bear.

Shit! How the hell did I get into this? Well, I'm here, and I guess there's no way out... for now. I gotta be a compliant girl, and hope something happens to help me get away. Good old step-dad taught me what it is to be used and the dangers of making a fuss. I suppose I can do it here, too, for now.

She stepped under the steamy water, soaking her long, silky black hair as she reached for the shampoo. An A student, and always a practical problem solver, her sharp mind began mulling her current realities. Despite what the two girls said, there ought to be a way out of this.

If there were, she was determined to find it.

~ 24 ~

Warner strolled through his department, looking for Jack Harris, who wasn't at his desk. He noticed Ciro Salinas hunched over a report, looking perplexed.

"What'cha workin' on, Detective?" He dropped into a seat across from his newest detective.

"A Jane Doe murder. Her body was found three days ago out past SW 177th Avenue."

"Her prints not in the system?" Warner reached for the report.

"No prints to check, Boss." He handed Warner the file. "The tips of all her fingers were cut off, and her face was disfigured by acid."

"So, the perp went through a lot of trouble to ensure she isn't IDed." Warner scanned the single sheet of paper. "The Hawk send her DNA through CODIS?"

"Yeah, but so far, no joy. The ME estimates she was mid-twenties so we sent a physical description through NICI for a possible hit in the crime base. So far, nothing there either."

"I see she was suffocated. Any signs of rape?" Warner handed the file back to Salinas.

"No, but," he picked up another report, "the ME saw some signs of non-forced vaginal intrusion, probably shortly before her death."

"Like a physical exam? Weird." Warner rose. "She seemed otherwise healthy, huh? They do a tox screen?"

"Yeah, and no sign of drugs."

"So, maybe not connected to our missin' hooker case. Give what ya got to Harris, though, just in case it somehow ties to the one he and Beck are workin'."

"Copy that, Boss."

Warner stepped away from Salinas' desk and spotted Jack Harris returning. Warner followed his detective to his desk.

"What's goin' on with the missin' hookers, Harris? Any action from the vehicle rec program?" He leaned against the back of a chair.

"Nothing yet, Boss. We also got plainclothes and beat cops in the likely areas, keeping their eyes open."

"Okay. Keep on top of it. If this is a traffickin' op, they'll be lookin' for more inventory, and hookers are the easiest source." Warner rubbed the back of his neck.

"Salinas is workin' a Jane Doe that's probably not connected to your case, but I told him to read ya in anyhow. The perp went outta his way ta see she couldn't be IDed. Follow it up, Jack."

"On it, Boss."

Warner nodded and left, heading for his office. His cell phone vibrated, and he plucked it from his jacket pocket. Glancing at the screen, he saw it was Eva.

"Hi, Babe." He looked at his watch. "Done with clients for the day?"

"Uh-huh. I'm headed home. What time can I expect you?"

"Hopefully, by six. Ya got something goin' on this evening?"

"Remember, I'm taking you out to dinner for a change." A short pause. "I've made a res at Chez Petite at seven."

"Huh. Fancy digs. Ya didn't say if we're celebratin' something?" Warner entered his office and slid onto his chair.

"Why? Does eating out always mean something's up?"

"At a place like that? Yeah, usually." He chuckled. "I'm a pretty good detective, ya know. Good at figurin' clues out."

Eva giggled. "I know. So, yes. Something special."

"Ya gonna tell me now, or keep me guessin'?"

"Well, I wanted it to be a surprise during dinner." Her voice softened into a huskiness that always excited him.

"C'mon, lady. Spill it. I gotta get goin' here, if I'm gonna make it home in time. I'll need ta shower and shave."

"Oh, damn, I guess there's no reason to delay this." Another pause. "It turned blue, lover."

"Huh? Blue? What turned blue?" He stroked his chin.

"I thought you were the great detective." She chuckled again. "The pregnancy test. It turned blue." She paused a moment. "I appear to be pregnant, Al."

"Wow!" He jerked upright and fumbled his phone, securing it before it dropped. "Are ya sure, Babe?"

"Well, those tests aren't infallible, so I've got an appointment with an OB tomorrow for a blood test, but I *feel* pregnant. Are you happy about this?"

"Are ya kiddin'? I know we've been tryin' but I never really thought..." He trailed off, then thrust to his feet.

"Happy don't describe it, Eva. This is what we both wanted. I'm thrilled at the thought of being a dad."

"Even if it's a girl, Al?" Her voice soft, barely a whisper.

"Hell yes. The mirror of her mama, and it don't mean she can't learn ta fish."

Eva joined in with his laughter.

"Okay. Let me get goin' so I can tie up a few loose ends here and head home. See ya soon."

"Al."

"Yeah?" He brought the phone back to his ear.

"Let's keep this to ourselves for the moment, until we know for sure. Okay?"

"Sure, hon, but I'm about ta pop the buttons off my shirt." They disconnected and he headed for the bullpen, looking for an update, but his mind was elsewhere.

He intended to be the dad his father never was.

~ 25 ~

Maggie hunkered over the toilet, arms braced against the seat, awaiting the next convulsion. Morning sickness arrived in her ninth week, and the eight days of throwing up that followed were more than enough as far as she was concerned. After a minute, she eased back on her haunches, suspecting this bout was finished.

She pushed up and went to the sink to rinse her mouth and gargle, trying to expel the acrid taste of bile.

That idiot Hoek called this 'doing a little work.'

She dropped onto the closed toilet seat and propped her head in her hands, elbows braced against her thighs. When no additional waves of nausea swept over her, she sighed and rose, exiting the bathroom. She paused, glanced at the clock on her nightstand, and decided to head down to the lounge. Maybe Char would be there for a game of gin. This total separation from the outside world was wearing on her.

Why is this sperm donor so obsessed with secrecy?

It was the same for Charlotte. They were confined here with zero outside contact, almost like prisoners. But that was *their* bargain, fueled by a big payday. She could have left any time prior to being pregnant. Once that happened, she was locked in until the end.

She slipped on a fresh cotton blouse, ran fingers through her red hair, and exited her room, skipping down the stairs. She blew through the lobby with a wave at Sam, puttering at his desk, and entered the lounge. Char sat at a table playing solitaire and Maggie moved to join her. She caught José's eye, polishing the bar from behind.

"A Virgin Mary, please, and bring some bar snacks," she called before settling on a chair next to her new friend.

"How're you doing?" She studied Char's face. "You look a little pale, lady."

"Yeah." Charlotte sighed. "Had a procedure this morning and I'm bushed."

"What? Everything okay?" Maggie took one of Char's hands.

"Oh, sure." She eased back on her chair. "No problems with the pregnancy. They apparently wanted a sample of the kid's DNA, maybe to see there's no genetic problem, so I was sedated." She chuckled. "Everything wears me out, nowadays."

"Really?" Maggie stroked her chin. "I'd have thought they woulda done that like in the third month. It's getting kinda late in the game to discover a problem, isn't it?"

"You'd think so." Charlotte nodded. "But they seem to know what they're doing." She sighed and glided a hand over her extended belly.

"I'm sure gonna be glad to shed this load, collect my money, and get back to civilization."

"Jeez, Char." Maggie's eyebrows arched. "You don't feel any attachment to the baby—*your* baby—you've carried for eight-and-a-half months?"

Charlotte shook her head. "Why should I? He's not the product of love, or even passion. We share some DNA. So what?" She picked up a deck of cards and started shuffling.

"It's just a nine-month payday." She glanced at Maggie.

"We gonna play some Gin, or what?"

The redhead nodded and took a sip of her Virgin Mary.

"I'm not so sure I'll feel so disconnected. It *is* my baby, too." She began sorting her hand.

"Yeah." Char picked up her cards. "But I signed a contract disavowing any claim to the infant, and I'm guessing you did, too." She drew a card and discarded one from her hand.

"If you cause any problems, you'll probably lose your reward. That hundred G's is more important to me than a brat I got no emotional connection to."

"Yeah." Maggie sighed. "I suppose you're right. Getting my bakery started with a newborn to care for would be a real problem."

"Damned right," Charlotte said. "This is a business deal, and you gotta treat it that way. Letting emotions get in the way can only muck things up."

"Right...only sometimes it doesn't quite feel that way." Maggie picked a card, resorted her hand, and laid it on the table. "Call on two."

"Caught me with a hand full." Char chuckled. "Serves me right for saving kings and tens."

Maggie wrote down her points and shuffled the deck. They wiled away the afternoon with meaningless activities as they both awaited a financial conclusion.

Charlotte would be first, due in less than two weeks, with Maggie six months behind. How would she spend her time once Char was gone? It augured to be a lonely time.

~~~

Maggie yawned, stretched, and glanced at her bedside clock: 8:15 AM.

Her fingers caressed her eyelids, and she plucked up a bottle of artificial tears. Somehow, her pregnancy had brought on dry-eye syndrome. She pushed up and swung her feet to the floor, yawning again. It was getting harder to shake the ennui filling her days.

She sighed, rose, and slipped into cotton workout shorts and a white tee shirt. Undergarments were becoming less frequently used, although she *had* noticed Sam ogling her firm, unfettered C-cups. Visualizing that, her forehead wrinkled, and she sighed again before stripping off the thin shirt and donning a lacy bra. She found a loose fitting, less revealing top before grabbing a novel and heading down for breakfast.

She reached the lobby and shrugged, relieved Sam was absent from his desk. Her eyes swept the room and the hallways leading to the lounge and gym. Empty, much like her life had become since her arrival at Cedar House. It was a very big place, but other than staff, the only two visitors were Charlotte and her. It would seem a lot emptier once Char had the baby and left, and that should happen in about two weeks.

Maggie shook her head and set her jaw, then headed for the breakfast buffet, set up daily in the lounge. She scanned the room, but other than a cook setting out a large steamer tray of scrambled eggs, no one else was around.

Maggie wandered over to the Belgian waffle-maker and found a pitcher of batter. She poured a dollop onto the open grid, closed the top and rotated it as extra batter oozed from the edges.

"Shit. Overfilled it again," she muttered.

The white aproned cook was quickly at her side. "No problem, Miss. Get some coffee and whatever else you want, and I'll bring this to you when it done."

"Thanks." Maggie wandered over to the hot tray and filled a plate with eggs, crisp bacon, and a pork patty. *I'm eating for two, I guess. Better watch it or I'll become a blimp.*

She settled at a table and wondered where Char was. The cook arrived with her waffle and a cup of maple syrup.

"Thanks." She touched his arm. "Has Miss Colman eaten already?"

"Haven't seen her, Miss Bagwell. Not since yesterday, after lunch."

"Really? I hope everything is okay with her."

The man nodded and turned to leave.

"Hey! If you see Sam, ask him to stop by," she called.

"I'll have him paged. Miss." He disappeared into the kitchen.

Maggie mopped the last crumbs of egg up with a flaky buttermilk biscuit just as Sam sauntered into the lounge.

"You wanted to see me, Maggie? Everything okay?"

"Oh, sure. I'm swell—except for puking my guts out every morning. Today was the first in over a week I didn't do it."

"Yeah." Sam chuckled. "One of the lesser perks of pregnancy, I hear." He dropped onto a chair. "So, what can I do for you?"

"I was wondering if Char's okay? Haven't seen her since yesterday."

"Oh, you didn't know. She's having the baby as we speak."

"Really? I though she wasn't due for—"

"Well, there was a small problem. Nothing very serious, but the kid's coming early." He rose. "She's at the hospital, just in case of any trouble, but it all looks good. Anything else I can help you with?"

"No, thanks. So, will she be back afterward?" Maggie leaned back, her eyebrows arched quizzically.

"No reason for her to return here. Her contract will be completed, and we'll forward her things to her new address." He smiled. "I'm sure she'll want to move on...start her new life with the funds she's earned."

"Oh, sure. I just thought we might get to see the baby—"

"No. She won't get to see the infant either." He stood, arms folded over his chest. "This is a job you've signed up for. Better not to have a chance to become attached, and the donor will be there to take immediate possession of *his* child." He leaned over and patted her shoulder.

"It's best for everyone this way. No emotional complications."

"Yeah" She sighed. "I guess. I just thought..." She trailed off, unsure of what to say next.

Sam nodded and left.

How do you avoid emotional attachments with a person you've carried around with you for nine months? Not sure I'll be able to do it. Don't see any other path, though. I gotta think about this. Do I really want to jeopardize my hundred G's?

A small groan slipped between her lips as she stared blankly into her cup of black coffee.

Somehow, she wasn't sure she was as happy as she should be over her hefty coming payday.

Well, she had nearly five months to figure things out. Meanwhile, she was going to be a mom, one way or another.

~ 26 ~

Sheri exited the bathroom after a morning pee and a warm water face rinse. Her eyes found Tanya hovered over her cot, stowing her few things into a large cardboard box. The girl was no longer Renee Red, as all the dyed hair had grown out and had been sheared off, her natural brown locks now styled in a pixie cut. Olga watched, standing nearby, beefy arms crossed over her massive bosom.

Sheri groaned softly, her blond, shoulder-length curls dancing to a small head shake. Tanya was about to move into the main house, so Kiesha would be her only companion. That was expected, but still depressing.

She moved to her new friend's side and peeked inside the box.

"Not much to take with you, huh?"

"Nope. Just my personals, PJ's and the like. They fix ya up with sexy daytime outfits, for when ya mix with the johns."

"Nervous?" Sheri touched her arm.

"A little." Her glance shifted from Olga to Sheri. "I keep telling myself I'm just gonna be doing what I was doing before. I'm trying to get over that I got no choice here." She shrugged. "I do believe life's gonna be a lot safer than it was, tricking on the street for a pimp."

Kiesha, eyes red and swollen from two days of crying, wandered over to join them. She stared at the two girls, her forehead wrinkled.

"You getting out of here, Tanya?"

"Yeah, but nothing for you to get excited about. Just going

next door to start earning my keep." She side-glanced at the girl and muttered, "Just keep your head down and don't cause trouble." She touched the Black girl's hand. "The quicker you accept there's no way outta here—not alive, anyway—the easier you'll have it."

"But this is wrong. I'm not a prostitute." She whimpered.

"You think it was our first choice?" Sheri shover her hands into the pockets of her shorts. "Life happens, and you try to survive. Girls like us get the short stick all the time."

"Look," Tanya closed her box and turned to her, "you're probably not a virgin, so sex ain't gonna be anything new to you. Likely you'll only have to see two or three guys a week, so make the best of it. I hear some of the clients have favorites, so try to be a girlfriend to them, and maybe they'll treat ya right."

"Okay." Olga grabbed Tanya's arm. "Enough chit-chat. I gotta get ya moved and get back here for other jobs." She towed Tanya, cradling her carton, toward the door.

Kiesha plopped down on the empty bed and glanced up at Sheri, her eyes welling.

"Now what? With Tanya gone, there's only you and me, and I know you'll be moving out any day now." She dabbed at her tears. "I'll go crazy if I'm stuck alone here."

"Relax, hon." Sheri patted her shoulder. "I'm up for an orientation visit tomorrow, and while I'll probably get moved later in the week, you should be close behind." She dropped on the bed next to the softly sobbing girl.

"I know this seems like the end of the world, but it's the hand we've been dealt, with very few options. They didn't have to clean you up and get you off drugs, so I'm guessing they'll be bringing you over pretty quick." She grasped the girl's chin, meeting her eyes.

"Look, I know this is tough to wrap your head around, especially since you weren't 'in the business,' as we say. But the only chance you got in here is to go along. If you can really give yourself to the johns—act like a lover—you'll survive." The blonde took Kiesha's hand. "If you fight it—well, I've heard the rumors." She rose and stared down at her.

"They ain't gonna send you back to Miami. Resist and you die." Sheri sighed. "It's a helluva thing, knowing you got a life sentence on this funky little island in the middle of nowhere, but it's live it their way or..." she trailed off.

Kiesha nodded, still weeping and slipped back on the bed, pulling a pillow over her face. Her body shook as she vented her sorrow.

Sheri shrugged and returned to her cot, slumping down, depressed by her own comments.

Life sucks.

~~~

With a bear trap grip on Sheri's left forearm, Olga led her through the doorway and on the way toward the main house. This was her to be orientation visit prior to moving in at the end of the week.

The blond peeked back down the path. The roar of an airboat probably announced the arrival of clients, and there they were, fifty feet behind them: three men, all wearing Mardi Gras-type masks.

"C'mon, move it." Olga jerked her along. "They ain't none of yer business yet." She hurried along, opening the distance between them and the arriving guests.

Sheri peered over her shoulder at the airboat, which was unloading supplies. It was considerably bigger than the one that hauled her groggy body out here to hell in the 'Glades. This one had a sizeable enclosed cabin, probably for the comfort of their pampered clients. Nothing too good for the wealthy. Might there be some way to slip away and hide aboard for an escape back to civilization?

She stumbled as Olga jerked her arm, and returned her attention to what was to soon be her new home. Sheri sighed, knowing escape was a pipe dream. Security was tight, and there'd be no way to sneak off and board a boat without being seen.

Time to take her own advice and make the best of what was left for her. Despite being a prisoner, there would be no abusive pimps, and hopefully, no psycho johns who took pleasure in dealing out pain...or worse.

They pushed inside, entering a spacious, dimly-lit, ornate lounge. Plush red velvet sofas and deep armchairs clustered around small tables. Sheri spied an ornately masked pair, huddled with three of the girls. One patron, apparently a woman, caressed the thigh of her recent friend, Mickey, dressed in an erotic halter and shorts. Two other girls draped themselves in sensual poses on nearby settees, and a third lounged at a long mahogany bar, awaiting the arriving clients.

Olga hustled Sheri up the stairs where they passed a brunette descending, her unfettered, perky breasts draped in a diaphanous robe and wearing gilded panties.

"Newbie?" She smiled at the blonde and winked.

Sheri nodded, but was quickly drawn away, hustled to the second floor.

"No time for chit-chat now, cunt. The girls are working, and we gotta get you set up so ya can start payin' your keep." She shoved Sheri into a room, and found a wall lined with racks of sexy outfits, all displayed by size, from petite to large.

"Pick out six what work fer ya, and them drawers over there," she nodded toward another wall, "have undies and such. You'll. find some loafing clothes and slippers in those." Olga indicated a second set of dressers. "Ya got ten minutes. Then you'll see where ya'll live and yer new roommate, if she ain't working right now." She released the girl's arm. "Then yer goin' back to the ward for a medical clearance before comin' back here, permanent."

Sheri glanced around, shrugged, then went to the ornate display and started rummaging around, impressed by the quality of the goods.

Twenty minutes later she was back in her dorm, preparing to go for a physical exam. She took time to comfort Kiesha and explain what she had to expect.

She was surprised to find the girls lived two to a private room instead of in a dorm. There looked to be ten of those on the second floor, and she wondered if she'd be allowed to trade roommates, once ensconced in the main house. She'd developed a friendship with Tanya, and life might be a bit easier if they were together.

Whatever; a new chapter was about to begin, and it included a life of forced prostitution... something she never expected when she moved to Florida. She was trapped now with no apparent options so she intended to make the best of it.

To do otherwise might be fatal.

~ 27 ~

Al Warner shuffled through several reports, shook his head, and dropped the small stack onto his desktop. He pushed out of his chair and headed toward his door.

"Harris, you out there?"

"Yeah, Boss. "He grumbled a reply. "Stuck on desk duty, where else would I be?" The wiry detective appeared in the doorway.

"Don't get grouchy on me, Jack." Warner chuckled. "You're doin' important work for us."

"Yeah, yeah. I know." He scratched at the hidden scar on his chest. "But I'd rather be in the field."

"Sure, but it ain't gonna happen 'til the medics say you're one-hundred-percent." Warner laid a hand on his shoulder, giving a friendly squeeze. "You coulda died on that boat."

The shorter man shrugged. "Yeah, lucky me." He shook loose and slid onto a chair. "So, what d'ya need, Boss?"

"You got any follow-up on the hookers case? We got two bodies and at least four missin' girls. These aren't high profile vics, but they're just as dead or missin' as some bigwig babe."

"We're not ignoring them, but so far the only thing we got is a silver Chrysler in the vicinity when some of them vanished."

"No new vics that you know of in what...two weeks?"

"Sixteen days, Boss, and no new leads either. We may not get anything until another girl disappears."

"That's what I'm afraid of, Jack, so let's try ta see the next one snatched is one of ours."

"Huh?" Harris's eyebrows arched, as Warner slid behind his desk.

"Get two or three undercover female detectives to work the most likely streets, actin' like hookers." Warner eased back. "Good looking babes, tasked to look for that silver Chrysler. Have Tech build 'em a background, and maybe arrange for plainclothes cops to pick 'em up a few times to lend legitimacy."

"Good idea, Boss, but it could be a dangerous assignment. The perp probably knocks them out after they get in the car."

"Yeah, well, ya need volunteers that know the score. Arrange tracking devices, maybe in a lipstick tube or something. And a coded text they can send when they think they're on stage. We need ta get ahead of these perps before we lose any more women." Warner rose.

"Problem is," Harris said as he also stood, "we don't know if the perp—or perps—is a serial killer or a trafficker."

"Either way, we gotta get proactive. Let's spin our own web."

"On it, Boss." Harris turned toward the door. "I know at least one undercover lady who'd be perfect for the job."

Warner nodded and returned to the never-ending paperwork littering his desk.

~ 28 ~

Warner headed for his office after assigning new cases to three of his detectives. He picked up his pace when he heard his desk phone ringing. He hoped it wasn't a harbinger of another new case, as his plate was currently overflowing: a drug-related gang assassination in Little Havana; two car-jackings, with one fatality; a deadly home invasion in Doral...and the murdered/kidnapped hookers. With Jack Harris still confined to a desk, he was getting thin on investigators.

He snatched up the receiver and punched the winking red button as he circled his desk.

"Warner." He slumped onto his swivel chair.

"Al. It's Charlie Seagrave."

Warner perked up and slid up to his desk. Was this news about the elusive Shadow?

"Hey, Charlie. Been a while. Heard from your girlfriend?"

"No." Charlie emitted a restrained chuckle, then a sigh. "Don't think she'd be dumb enough to call after all that went down."

"No one could ever accuse that deadly dame of bein' dumb, Charlie." He settled back on his chair. "So, is this a social call? How's the kid?"

"Hunter's doing great. The rejection meds are working fine. We're back to fishing offshore. But there *is* something..."

"Spit it out, pal. If it's something I can help with—"

"I've got a friend who needs help." Another short sigh. "The wife of a deceased friend, actually."

"Okay." Warner drew over his lined yellow pad and clicked a ballpoint. "What's the problem, and why are ya comin' ta me?"

"Looks like she's being blackmailed. Her husband, Tony Stirling, died in a traffic fatality about nine months ago..."

"Stirling? The big-time banker and philanthropist who racked up his Maserati? Ruled an accident, wasn't it?" Warner jotted the name on the pad. "No one else injured, as I remember."

"Right. This isn't about looking for victim compensation." Another pause and some throat-clearing. "I'm not sure I should be bothering you about this, Al."

"Me, either, unless there's a claim the accident *wasn't* an accident. What are ya lookin' for, Charlie?"

"Look, Tony was a straight arrow who worshiped his wife. He never even visited men's clubs with clients. Always sent one of his guys if a client was looking for action."

"So...?"

"So, out of the blue, there's this guy, alleging a fast-food cashier he was representing and Tony had an affair. Tony was supposedly hightailing down the Palmetto to meet her when he was killed."

"And they want money to protect his rep, huh?" Warner doodled on the pad. "Got any proof?"

"Yeah, a baby." Seagrave groaned softly. "Even supplied a DNA match."

Warner grunted. "Well, that sure seems like proof enough." Warner sat back. "Look, it sounds like he did the deed. The woman can make a case for child support, and with his wealth, it could be substantial. What's the real problem?"

"I knew Tony, Al. He was like a brother to me. We hunted and fished together. There's no *way* he'd have shacked up with this woman." He grunted a soft curse. "To quote the Bard, something rotten in the state of Denmark."

"Okay, I'll take you at your word, but what do ya want me

ta do? It's not homicide."

"Yeah, but you're the best detective in this town... or any town, for that matter. Let me buy you dinner and go over what I got. His wife's totally distraught. He's got two young kids, and I don't want to see all their lives ruined by some bogus claim. If, after you've gone over everything, you don't feel you can help, I'll accept that. Ashley, his wife, is banking on me."

"Dinner, Huh?"

"Yeah. How about Embers, in Miami Beach, tomorrow night at seven?"

"Embers? Mind if I bring Eva? Her psychology background might lend some insight...and she loves their roasted duckling."

"Doesn't everyone? Sure, I'd love to see her again. You're luckier than me, Warner."

"Hell, I'm luckier than anyone when it comes to the sweet redhead." He chuckled. "Okay, so I'll check with her, too, but I'm pretty sure her calendar's open for Embers duckling. See ya tomorrow night at seven." Warner hung up, stared at his sparse notes, and shrugged. He turned back to his desk, where real crimes awaited his attention.

An evening out at a great restaurant with a somewhat unlikely new friend might be a pleasant diversion.

He just didn't know what he could do to help the widow.

~ **29** ~

Maggie slouched in her chair sipping a tonic and lime, her romance novel laying face-down on the table. She struggled with thoughts she didn't want to have.

Twenty days had passed since Charlotte disappeared to have her baby two weeks early. They'd developed a real friendship, and Maggie missed her.

She glided her hand over her extended belly, seeking a twitch of motion. Yesterday was her first experience of fetal movement; physical proof she carried a living thing inside her uterus. It ignited a ripple of shivers down her spine.

Maggie moaned softly and shook her head. *Maybe it's the hormones.*

This is *her* baby, conceived with a man she didn't know; someone without any connection, other than his sperm. She knew a surrogate usually carried the fertilized egg or embryo of a couple. It was their kid with their DNA. But this was different. She was one of the two genetic parents of this infant.

Why hadn't the donor used his wife or partner's egg, instead of hers? Maybe he had no one and was a rich guy, looking to create an heir. Whatever, she realized now, it was going to be painful to just give away her baby, contract or no contract. She wasn't sure she could do it, but what options did she have? Once in the delivery room, she'd be at the mercy of the doctors, Hoek, and the donor. No representation for her and *her* baby.

She sighed and turned at the sounds of approaching footsteps. Miles Hoek materialized at her side and laid a hand on her shoulder, firing a shiver down her spine.

"So, Miss Bagwell, how are you doing? Still having morning sickness?"

"No." She shrugged away his hand. "At least, not the last two days. I think I'm past that now."

"Good. You're due for a physical end of the week, but everything seems to be going along swimmingly. Any questions?" He settled on a nearby chair, crossing his long legs.

"Will they do an ultrasound?" She crossed her arms over her belly. "Too early to know the baby's sex?"

"I believe we'll save that for the next exam after this one." He interlaced his fingers, resting on the table. "Current science recommends keeping those to a minimum." His dark eyes held hers.

"The sex of this child is of no concern of yours, you know. We will avoid anything that may create an emotional attachment." He reached out and took one of her hands. "You've contracted to do a job, Ms. Bagwell, not become a mother. We must keep that in mind."

"Of course. I understand." She eased back in her chair. "Just normal curiosity, I guess."

Can't let this guy in on my doubts.

"No news about Charlotte? I thought maybe—"

"No, and you shouldn't expect to hear from her, either. She delivered a healthy baby a few weeks early and fulfilled her contract. She has moved on, substantially richer and apparently eager to start her new life." He rose.

"We discourage any attempts by our contractors to develop friendships. Confidentiality and privacy are a bulwark of our services, and our clients expect no less. Fraternization between contractors could jeopardize that, and it could cost you loss of your fee. Best to forget Ms. Colman and concentrate on your own project." He started for the entrance, glancing over his shoulder.

"I can understand a need for companionship, however. So, speak to Sam about that if you wish." And he was gone.

She stared after him, slouched back, the only comfortable way to sit nowadays. She huffed softly, fingers exploring the spot on her belly just receiving a tiny thump, and smiled. The kid was becoming active, just over five months pregnant.

The corners of her mouth dipped into a small frown. *This is my kid, too. Maybe the guy and I can work something out so we can* both *be its parents.* Would she really risk losing that hundred G's on an emotional whim?

She wasn't sure, but she had nearly four months to figure that out. She sipped her now flat tonic and picked up her novel.

Plenty of time yet to decide what to do then.

~ 30 ~

"Boss." Jack Harris stuck his head through the doorway. "The BAU team just arrived."

Warner pushed away from his desk and rose. "I wasn't sure this case warranted the FBI, but I asked 'em to come down anyway."

"Good. We need all the help we can get," Harris said, stepping aside and then following Warner into the bullpen. "Same team as usual, but looks like they got a replacement for Dalwin."

"Hard shoes to fill," Warner muttered as he strode toward the six agents.

"Special Agent Pauletti." He shook hands with the shorter, olive-skinned man. "Glad you could make it." His gaze swept over the FBI team, noting the tall, lean Black man, its apparent new member.

"Always happy to work with you, Detective." He turned toward his five coworkers. "You know everyone except for our new member, L'Shawn Swift." Hands were shaken all around.

"Still chasin' the Shadow, Lon?" Warner, along with Harris, ushered the group toward the conference room.

"You bet, especially with the death of Agent Dalwin." He grimaced and shook his head.

"No leads, I take it?"

The eight took seats around the oblong table.

"Not a peep. Became as invisible as ever."

"No surprise there." Warner opened the file he'd carried. "So, the captain invited ya in at my request, but I'm not sure this is an FBI matter."

"There's two reasons we're interested, Detective." Agent Pauletti fished a folder from his briefcase. "When you asked for our vehicle recognition software to surveil streetwalker neighborhoods, Agent Swift made a stunning connection no one else had put together."

"Which is...?" Warner's gaze shifted to the Black agent.

Agent Swift drew the file in front of him and dished out four reports, fanning them in front of Warner.

"None of these jurisdictions actually asked for our help, but I was doing research on missing girls and discovered multiple hooker abductions in all these cities."

"Atlanta, New Orleans, Richmond, and Chicago?" Warner stroked his chin. "That's a pretty wide net. All low-level streetwalkers?"

"Six of the fifteen were escorts." Agent swift reclaimed the files. "Two others were college girls, but not prostitutes. All gone without a trace."

"So, you're thinkin' a national human trafficking ring?"

"That's why we're here, Al," Pauletti said.

Warner looked at Agent Swift. "What tipped ya to hookers disappearin', Agent, if the locals weren't askin' for help?"

"It wasn't the hookers, Detective; it was a college girl. My niece, Kiesha, vanished right here in Miami. That's what I was researching when I discovered all the other girls."

"Right. Swift. Shoulda tied it together." Warner leaned back and crossed his arms. "Kiesha Swift was the last of five girls to go missin'. Nothin' to really tie her to the hookers, except for gut instinct." Warner studied the agent. "She's your niece, ya say?"

Swift nodded. "She was supposedly interviewing for a modeling gig, but the whole thing was bogus. The two other college girls I found," he tapped his file, "were supposedly going to casting calls for parts that didn't exist."

"So," Jack Harris piped in, "you believe all three were lured into a honey trap and snatched? We were unsure our vics weren't the results of a serial killer."

"You've had more than your share of those," Agent Ina Yeager said, "but we're convinced this is human trafficking."

"From what we've been able to put together," Agent Harry Ashkin interjected, "we believe these women have been taken precisely because of their vocation." The shortest of the agents extracted a twenty-page report from his briefcase.

"From chatter we've been able to monitor, and two dark web sites we're still trying to crack, it sounds like there are high-end—*very* elite—bordellos operating under the radar in all these cities." Ashkin ran a finger along his prominent, hooked nose.

Agent Anita Solto slid over the report and flipped through its pages "Our investigation suggests these women, almost all of them young and still attractive, are being pressed into the service of clandestine bordellos for the exclusive enjoyment of some rich, decadent people."

"And the three college girls?" Warner skimmed through the file's pages. "Why them?"

"All some sort of beauty queens." Blond Amazonian Agent Ina Yeager gestured at the file. "None of the three likely virgins, which is no surprise nowadays. What could be more exciting for some entitled wretch than a gorgeous twenty-something there to fulfill his every sordid fantasy?"

"Right," Agent Ansel Whitehead added, "and I'm guessing if they don't conform, they're not released back on the street. Not alive, anyhow."

"Yeah." Warner pushed to his feet. "And that probably explains the three female vics we found floatin' in the 'Glades. "We figured there may be some secret venue out there, but so far, no joy in findin' one."

The six agents and Jack Harris rose in unison.

"Detective Harris will help ya get set up in here." Warner

glanced around and chuckled. "By this time, this oughta feel like a second home."

"Our sixth case in as many years," Special Agent in Charge Pauletti said.

"Yep." Warner patted his shoulder. "All the way back to the Baby Butcher." He paused. "And the first one without Agent Dalwin to lead the way." Warner held the man's dark gaze.

"Yes." Pauletti looked away to hide the mist in his eyes. "And we'll miss him, but life goes on."

Warner nodded. "Okay, I'll leave ya to it." He glanced at his watch. "Meet ya back here in two hours to get coordinated. Then we gotta find those missin' babes."

Warner had three female undercover detectives working the streets, trying to lure out whomever is snatching hookers.

He didn't want to see any more dead bodies before they put an end to this.

~ 31 ~

Sheri surveyed her image in the mirror and shrugged, unable to suppress a small grin. The transparent tent-like shroud she'd donned did little to hide the skimpy lacy bra and form-fitting silk panties underneath. All her luscious curves were clearly visible for the appreciation of the johns below, and she grudgingly admitted she never looked anywhere near this good on the street.

Two buzzes on the intercom signaled it was time to go—her first day on the job.

She sighed. It wasn't as if she was about to do anything different than she'd been doing, but that had been *her* choice, albeit forced upon her by circumstances. This, however, was being forced upon her by overlords not of her choosing, and despite being the same work, it *felt* different. She had no option here, but in reality, neither had she one on the streets. There her pimp ruled with an iron fist and the drugs he'd made her reliant upon.

She glanced again at her reflection, ran fingers through her yellow hair, and exited the room, heading for the stairway to her new hell. The gossamer cloak clung to her as she glided down the stairs, eliciting wolf-whistles from two of the men lounging below.

Sheri's eyes swept the room. Five other girls were already there, competing for the four men's attention. Sheri learned from her roommate, Evelyn, a girl not attracting action from "clients" was a ticket to oblivion. This was her life now, and if a guy treated her well, she'd do her best to make him happy.

She strolled to the bar, where three girls snuggled against

two of the men. The women sipped what Sheri knew were Shirley Temples. Actual liquor was reserved for the paying customers. Tipsy working girls were of no use to the house.

She pressed a breast teasingly against a taller, middle-aged guy, her fingers lightly brushing the back of his neck.

"Buy a lady a drink, handsome?" She cocked her head and winked.

He appraised her and smiled. "Absolutely. What'll you have, gorgeous?" He wore a black eye-mask, probably to obscure his identity from other customers. Good luck with that.

"What do I call you?"

"Cassandra." Apparently, her keepers felt Sheri wasn't exotic enough. "Cassie for short."

"Beautiful name for a beautiful woman." He signaled for the bartender.

"You're so sweet." She leaned in and kissed his cheek, then turned to the server. "The usual," code words for tonic and lime. Water, poured from a vodka bottle completed the charade.

Sheri, like all the service staff, was instructed to make the clients court them—create a real girlfriend experience. Rushing a guy to bed, no matter how eager he may be, was discouraged.

Many streetwalkers were illiterate, coming from poor backgrounds, and the art of seduction might be unfamiliar to them. Apparently, the bosses here knew this and took care to only acquire girls like Sheri, from better circumstances but who had fallen on hard times. How they knew this was unclear.

She sipped her drink as they chatted about weather and politics, which sounded like his bailiwick. They touched, teased, and shared gentle kisses, until time came to retire upstairs to complete the reason he was there.

Sheri hugged the man, who told her to call him Jack, kissed his cheek, and nipped at his ear as he left her room two hours later, two Benjamins pressed into her hand. She guessed she'd better squirrel away the money someplace secret, not sure how it would ever come of use.

She had always enjoyed making love in her "old life," rather than just having sex, so this could have been worse. The guy, probably in his forties and reasonably fit, was a passionate kisser. They'd made out like teenagers, and she teased him into a near-frenzy by making his lips chase hers before submitting to serious tongue fencing and roaming hands.

She eventually pushed him onto the bed as she did her version of the Dance of Seven Veils, despite only having three things to discard. She made him wait to shed his clothes, with her doing the deed, slipping in and out of his reach as she removed one piece of his at a time.

Her earlier orientation emphasized these encounters were to be as slow and sensual as possible. The johns paid top bucks not to be rushed, and this made the encounter more like an act of love than cheap sex, which was okay with her. The longer this took, the less likely she'd have to repeat it with another guy that afternoon.

As Jack descended to the lounge, Sheri returned to her room and settled on the bed. She leaned over to smell the pillow, still radiating the odor of their sex. She sighed, pleased she wouldn't need to see another guy any earlier than later that night, if at all. Different from the usual scramble when she worked the streets to hook up with as many fifty and hundred-dollar quickies as possible so she could satisfy the pimp and still eat and pay rent.

She sighed, rose, and headed for a shower. If this were to

be her life, captive here probably forever, it could be worse. At least she was safe from the dangers of the mean streets, well fed, and nicely dressed when she wasn't "working." She hoped there were no nasty surprises on the horizon, but the last few years of very hard knocks seeded doubt about that.

Whatever; she vowed to make the best of this and survive until some way out presented itself...if ever.

Meanwhile, she had to clean up and clear the room in case her roommate, Evelyn, returned with her own catch of the day.

~ 32 ~

Warner slid the silver Jaguar convertible into the valet parking area in front of Embers Restaurant. They were in Eva's car because Warner never left his with valet, and parking spots were rare in the restaurant row of Miami Beach.

He jumped out, darted around to the passenger side to help the redhead out, and handed the keys to the attendant. He offered Eva his arm and headed for the entrance, pausing for a moment before the large plate glass window to admire the view of succulent ducklings and bubbling racks of ribs rotating on spits over flickering flames.

"Looks good, huh?" He grinned at his love.

"Yum. Got my insides percolating already." She squeezed his arm. "Let's go." She tugged him toward the door. "From what you've told me about Charlie, he's probably already inside."

A greeter opened the door for them, and they approached the maître d's podium.

"We're here to join Charles Seagrave," Warner said.

"Of course. They're already seated." He handed two menus to a waitress. "Table forty-six."

They followed the woman toward the rear of the restaurant, and the odor of roasted duck and pork fired their salivary glands. Seagrave and an attractive fortyish woman were ensconced in an isolated alcove. Seagrave rose as they approached, offering his hand.

"Thanks for coming, Al." He turned to Eva. "Happy you could join us, Doctor Guttenberg." He gestured toward the empty chairs.

"Nice to finally meet you, Charlie." Eva settled on her seat and glanced at the dark-haired woman.

Seagrave nodded and touched his companion's hand. "This is Lois Sterling, Tony's widow. I'm going to let her tell you her story...after we order some drinks, and the detective updates me on his investigation."

"The Shadow, you mean?" Warner eased back in his chair. "Not my bailiwick anymore. It's in the hands of the FBI again. Special Agent Pauletti and his team are here on another case, and he said they have no current intel on Public Enemy Number One."

Conversation paused as they ordered drinks, then Warner turned to the other woman.

"So, Mrs. Stirling, Charlie seems to think I can help with your problem, but I'm not sure how." He glanced at Eva. "Dr, Guttenberg is a psychiatrist and may also be able to give some aid." He looked back at Seagrave.

"Charlie says you're bein' blackmailed."

"I suppose that's what it is, Detective." She interlocked her fingers and rested them atop the table. Stress lines crinkled the corners of her eyes. "And frankly, I'm conflicted about the whole thing."

"So, tell us about it."

"A man came to my house last week, saying he represented this woman, Charlotte Colman, who he claimed had a protracted affair with my deceased husband...and she's had his baby."

"And he offered proof of this?"

"Yes. He had a DNA match, done by what appears to be a very reputable lab, showing the baby was Tony's."

"Where did they get your husband's DNA for the match?" Eva reached across the table and took one of her hands.

"Apparently, court-ordered samples were procured from

the morgue. It was positive proof the infant was Tony's." She sighed, sat back, and ran fingers through her hair.

"And they're lookin' for money to keep it private?" Warner's eyes held hers.

"Yes. We are...were...active donors to our church and women's crisis protection organizations. It would be a terrible blow to Tony's legacy." She leaned forward, her dark eyes glittering. "One of my problems is, DNA match or not, it just wasn't like Tony to cheat on me—especially with a fast-food cashier." She sighed again.

"Not to disparage the woman, but Tony was the ultimate pragmatist. If he were to have an affair, there were a dozen lovely, married women in our circle who would have relished a tumble in the sheets with my handsome husband. Much safer and more discreet for him than a common waitress." She thumbed away tears. "He couldn't know this Ms. Colman well enough to actually love her."

"Yeah." Warner grunted. "But you know what they say about a guy's blood supply." He folded his arms across his chest. "Not enough to fill two organs at the same time."

Eva glared at him and pinched his thigh.

The widow whimpered, and Warner sighed.

"Sorry. That was kinda insensitive. I'm sure your husband was better than that."

They paused, leaning back as the waiter arrived with their drinks. Warner took a sip of his scotch. "So, you said 'one of my problems...' Is there another?"

"Maybe." She paused and rubbed her palms together, dispelling nervous energy. "The million dollars she wants is inconsequential if it were to protect Tony's legacy. But *we've* never had children. Unfortunately, I'm...not fertile, but this infant girl is as much my daughter as Ms. Colman's. I'd love to be in her life."

"Okay. You'd think the woman would jump at your

involvement," Eva said. "Both she and the baby would benefit from a two-parent household."

They looked up, conversation grinding to a halt as the waiter arrived again.

"Ready to order, folks?"

No surprise that each selected the roasted duckling for which the restaurant was famous. After he departed, all eyes were again on the widow.

"As a condition for the money, I offered her, through her surrogate, residence in the house and full access to any services I could provide; nurses, nannies, everything."

"And?" Warner's eyebrows arched.

"Flat out refusal." She retrieved a tissue and wiped at her nose. "She wants the money and a guarantee there'll be no interference by me, or she'll go public. I don't know what to do."

"Sounds like a job for an attorney rather than the cops, Mrs. Stirling."

Another pause as the waiter arrived with their salads. Warner took a fork full and glanced at Charlie.

"I don't know, Al." Seagrave picked at his greens. "It just feels like something crooked is going on here."

"I agree." Eva touched Warner's arm. "I've dealt with abused and deserted women a lot. This girl may be from a lower or lower-middle class background. Any I've worked with would jump at a chance like this, despite a million-dollar payday: a beautiful home and most importantly, someone to help raise the child with love."

"That's what I thought...what I hoped." Tears filled the woman's eyes again. "Some piece of Tony to hold onto. A way to have something meaningful from this tragedy." She sniffled. "A child I could never have on my own."

Warner nodded and went to work on the salad. Eva knew

his mind was in gear, sifting probabilities. Their dinners arrived: crisp half-ducklings with orange sauce. All ate in silence for a few moments. Then Warner sat back, his eyes sweeping from Seagrave to the widow.

"I dunno. Not much to go with here, but my gut agrees—something doesn't smell right." He looked again at Seagrave. "Give me whatever ya got on the girl and the guy who's representin' her, and I'll see what I can come up with." He bit into a duckling leg, chewing as he thought.

"On the surface, it looks like a plea for child support. Nothin' illegal there, if in fact that's all it is. If there's more, maybe I'll find it."

"Legal or not," Seagrave said, "it's all pretty rotten, threatening to smear a good man's name. And withholding the child from a second loving mother."

All nodded in agreement as they dug into their fragrant dinners, eating in silence except for the crunch of crisped duckling skin and smacking lips.

~ 33 ~

The platinum blonde leaned over and ran a hand through the Honda's driver's wavy hair, as her lips brushed his cheek.

"Thanks, handsome," said as she tucked some bills into her bra. "Come see me again soon." She slipped out of the car and waved as it drove off.

Detective Nicki Unger tugged down her faux leather miniskirt and strolled across the walk to lean against the wall. That was her second fake "john," a plainclothes detective, during her three days as a newly minted Miami streetwalker. If she didn't make contact with the driver of the mysterious silver Chrysler soon, she'd have to hook up with another undercover cop to keep her cover viable.

She glanced at the three other girls lounging around the entrance of the seedy bar. All pretty run down and used up, so none would be competition for Nicki if the perp showed. At five-foot-six and a curvy one-hundred-thirty-pounds, Nicki filled the profile of the girls Detective Warner felt these traffickers sought.

A gold Chevy slid to the curb, the passenger window spooling down. Nicki watched as two of the hookers sidled up and leaned against the car. After a bit of verbal give and take, the uglier one, but with bigger boobs, slid inside as the other girl turned away, frowning. The sedan pulled out, probably heading for the deserted under-building parking lot, a popular place for quick car sex.

Nicki sighed and wondered why she let Jack Harris talk her into this gig. If the perp arrived, she had to be willing to give him a covered blowjob. *Under over work can really suck.* She grimaced at the unintended pun. She sighed.

Nicki tapped her ear, reassured her tiny, intra-canal mic was operational. At least four surveillance cars were patrolling the general area, searching for that silver sedan. She'd get a heads-up if it were spotted so she could be first to the window, hoping to make contact.

She removed the tracker-enhanced lipstick from her little cloth clutch bag and put it in a pocket of her skin-tight skirt. If she *were* snatched, they'd likely relieve her of the bag but might miss the little gold metal tube.

Another "john" arrived and whisked away a second girl, leaving Nicki with only one for competition. This was getting very ...

Static crackled in her ear.

"Okay, Unger," the voice said, "possible perp in a silver Chrysler 200 coming your way. Be ready, and good luck."

Nicki pushed away from the wall, tugged at her blouse to show maximum cleavage, and eased toward the curb. Hands on hips, she scanned the avenue in both directions, searching for her prey.

There. A silver sedan, turning south, heading in her direction. She steeled herself, preparing her pitch. She'd spent half her career at Miami-Dade PD as an undercover cop, so she'd learned to subvert fear when she was about to go into action. Her tension was all about the performance art. Pulling this caper off right could lead to a Detective First Class shield.

Do it wrong and she could end up in a body bag.

Nicki sidestepped to the curb, thrust out her right hip, and lit her pretty face up with her very best smile. She sensed the other remaining hooker, Carmen, edging up behind her.

Shit! blue Ford F-150 slid to the curb and the Latino driver leaned across the seats. "Hey, *chica.* You workin'?"

She swiveled her head and nodded to the other woman.

"You take him, Carmen. I got something else going on."

The pudgy little hooker sidled to the truck's open window, trying to look sexy, and stuck her head through. After a short negotiation, she slipped inside and they drove off.

Nicki sighed, relieved she'd be alone when the silver car... if it were *the* silver car... arrived. Carmen was no competition, but her vying for attention could muddy up the waters. She watched the Chrysler approach, less than a half-block away now, cruising slowly, close to the curb.

She stood, arms akimbo, and realized she was holding her breath. She exhaled, struggled to quell her thumping heart, and freshened her smile. The sedan coasted to a stop beside her and the passenger window slid down. The driver, dressed in denim shorts and a cotton sport shirt, didn't appear dangerous, but Nicki knew that could be deceiving.

"Hey, Hon," he said, "what's a pretty girl like you doing out here on the streets?"

"Outta work for over a month, handsome." Nicki leaned against the metal door, her face in the opening, her cleavage well displayed. "Nothing else coming my way, and a girl's gotta pay the bills." She winked.

"Lucky me." He chuckled. "But why this?"

"Not so different from my old gig with an escort service, but the cops closed us down. I *am* picky who I go with, though." She grinned. "You look like you qualify. Interested?"

"Damn right." He clicked the unlock button. "You're the best thing I've seen out here for weeks. I'm picky, too." He crooked a finger. "Wanna get in, babe?"

"Let's discuss what you're looking for, and what it's gonna cost you." She knew not to seem too eager after proclaiming she was cautious.

A minute later she was in the car after agreeing to a covered blow job and maybe some physical play. That was one of the qualifiers for this assignment. Nicki had spent nearly two years deep undercover with a Cuban drug cartel and had done some despicable things to prove her worth. If this *was* their perp, she needed to get inside their operation, no matter what it took, and hopefully, call in the troops.

She tucked a fifty into her bra and laid her hand on his thigh.

"This will only get you a blowjob, Babe. You want more, it's gonna cost you." She'd been prepped during her orientation for this gig on how a hooker acted—be proactive, limited to a covered blowjob, or pass on the assignment. She'd agreed to make it real.

"We'll see how it goes." He gave a sidelong glance. "Where you from, sweetheart?"

"Detroit." Not a lie. She swiveled to look at him and leaned against the car door. "I was a cheerleader for two years at MSU," also not a lie, "and I was told the Miami Heat were looking for a new squad." They actually had been, but that wasn't why she'd moved to Miami.

"I met a guy who said he was a scout," and the fiction began. "A college degree didn't seem like it was gonna get me anywhere, so I gave it a shot."

"Didn't pan out, huh?" He turned into the shadowy, under-building parking lot frequently used for "car dates."

"How'd you guess?" Her chuckle had no music in it. "Introduced me to a couple of so-called execs who were only interested in shacking up." She sighed, really getting into her role. "By the time I caught on, my stash was gone and my single mom had lost her job, so there was nothing for me back in Michigan." She peeked out the windshield and gestured for him to park in a darker corner of the lot.

"No work for anything more'n peanuts, so when I met this gal at Starbucks who said she was an escort and told me what she was making, I signed up." Nicki unbuckled her seatbelt and nestled against the guy.

"That didn't work out, like I said, so here I am making a handsome guy like you happy." She gritted her teeth and unzipped his fly. "Ready, honey?"

"Boy, am I ever."

He reclined his seat as she opened a condom. Subverting her disgust, she hoped this was their guy.

I'm gonna be pissed if this is a waste of time.

As she leaned over to get started, she sensed he was fumbling with his center console, but she was blocking everything from her mind.

Then she felt a sting in her neck.

And everything faded to blackness.

~ 34 ~

Warner was studying CCTV footage reports regarding a search for one of their undercover cops who had disappeared. The four unmarked cars in the area had been admonished not to press too close and chance spooking their quarry. They were counting on Detective Unger's tracker, but it never pinged.

By the time they became alarmed, she was gone, and a frantic sweep by the scout vehicles was fruitless. Traffic cams picked up the silver Chrysler heading west in NW 45th Street, and then it disappeared.

Warner was shaken from his concentration by a knock on his door.

"Got a minute, Boss?" Jack Harris stood in the doorway, grasping a file.

"Sure, Jack." He sat back. "Good news?"

"About Unger? No. Well, maybe, indirectly." He entered and settled on a chair.

"Patrol found another Jane Doe." He plopped the folder on Warner's scarred oak desk and flipped it open.

"Actually, they were called to the scene by a construction crew in west county." He plucked out a page and slid it in front of Warner.

"They were about to pour a foundation for a three-story office building in a new strip mall when one of the crew noticed a big, black plastic garbage bag in the hole." He handed Warner a photo.

"That's what was inside. Pretty gruesome, huh?"

Warner studied the photo of what appeared to be a woman, her face almost totally burned away, and her legs broken and folded over her torso, probably to make a smaller package.

"Yeah." He shoved the photo across his desk. "The Hawk able to make an ID?"

"No face or prints to match." Harris withdrew a two-page report.

"The tips of all her fingers were cut off, too. The Hawk's running DNA to look for a match, but it sure looks like no one wanted her IDed."

"Okay, give it to Olbredo. Seems like a good one for a new guy to cut his teeth on." He leaned back and folded his fingers together over his lean belly.

"So, ya said there might be some good news about our missin' undercover cop, Detective Unger?"

"Huh? Oh, yeah. It isn't her."

"What isn't?"

"The Jane Doe." Harris closed his file and rose. "It isn't Unger, thank god." He stared at his boss. "You know, I'm the guy who recommended her for this gig, and—"

"Don't start the guilt trip, Jack." Warner pushed away from his desk and stood. "I checked her file before assignin' her. She's a tough, clever cop who can take care of herself. Hopefully, she'll get that tracker on and we'll jump on it."

"Yeah, hopefully. Meanwhile, we got nothing new on the missing hooker caper. All the missing babes had DNA on file from earlier busts, so Moe'll check this new Jane Doe against them. It's not the Swift girls because the vic isn't Black."

"I got a feelin' she'd not connected. All of the hookers offed were found in the 'Glades, so this doesn't fit with their MO. At least, not so far."

Warner patted the smaller man on the back as they exited his office together. "I know your itchin' to get back into the field, but you're doin' a great job on the desk, partner. The best we've had since Harry retired. Keep it up."

Taken

"Meanwhile, I'm countin' on ya to organize a very discreet search around where Unger went missin'. No CCTV footage on the corner where the girls ply their trade, and that's probably by design."

"I know." Harris sighed. "I got Tech working the traffic cams in the area to see what they can find. One of our scout cars spotted a silver Chrysler heading toward Unger, but they were told not to follow and chance spooking the guy, if he was the perp." Harris paused at his desk and turned toward Warner. "Then the fucking thing disappeared, probably with Unger onboard. I just hope—"

"Easy, Jack." Warner squeezed his shoulder. "Let's not go off the deep end yet. It's been less than two days. She may not report in until she's got the bastards nailed. Stay loose."

Harris sat and placed the folder on his desk. "Yeah, yeah. Stay loose." Warner left and he snatched up his phone and placed an internal call. "Olbredo? I got a case for you."

He then texted Olvida and Beck to organize a serious but covert search for Detective Unger. He knew Warner, despite his unconcerned comments, was damned worried too.

Harris' finger slid over his shirt, tracing the extensive chest scar, thanks to *the Shadow*. He knew what it was like to nearly die at the hands of a perp, and he hoped for better than that for Nicki Unger. He'd never forgive himself if she …

He shook his head and groaned. Can't think negative thoughts. He hunched over his desk, reading a file on another case. Life must go on.

~ 35 ~

Nicki Unger groaned, and her eyes squinted open. Her body rocked and bumped as she struggled to roll to her side but was restricted by something. She shook her head and her vision cleared. Craning her neck, she realized she was bound hand and foot, sprawled on the floor of a car's backseat.

She drew in her feet, wiggled onto her butt, and tried to clear her head. Her neck felt like it was stung by a bee.

Shit. The bastard stuck me with some kinda tranquilizer. Where the hell am I?

Digging her heels into the carpeted floor she shoved back and managed to shimmy up and work herself onto the seat. Gazing through the window all she could see was the blur of sawgrass, palm fronds, and a few live oaks. Classic Everglades. Two men, a driver and another very large guy, were in the front.

"Whatcha do to me?" Her words raspy from a swollen tongue and sandy throat.

"Finally awake, are you?" The driver glanced at her. "Relax, babe. We're almost there."

"Where's 'there,' and what the fuck's going on?" Nicki ran a dry tongue over cracked lips. "You're going through a lot of trouble for a blowjob and a little hand action."

This was a lot more than that. She'd scored whoever was snatching hookers. *Need to alert the team.* But she was too tightly bound to work her hand into the pocket containing her lipstick-tube tracker.

"You're going to have plenty of time for that, babe, once you're situated in your new home." He chuckled.

"What are ya talking about? I got a home."

She'd play along, pretending to be innocent, but this was getting hairy. If she couldn't fire up the tracker, she could be in serious shit.

Nicki gave up trying to get a hand in her pocket, and stared out the window. Nothing but endless 'Glades. Could the Tech boys back at HQ even pick up a signal this far out? Maybe with a plane.

"There's the turnoff."

The hulk in front gestured at a rutted opening through a wall of six-foot high sawgrass. The driver slowed and pulled onto the path. They bumped and swayed along for a hundred yards before breaking into a small clearing alongside a narrow canal.

Nicki spotted a twenty-foot airboat perched on the bank with two men seated aboard. The sedan pulled to stop and her two escorts stepped out.

"Gotcha one pretty package, wrapped up and ready to go." The bigger thug opened the rear door and hauled her out, pitching her onto his shoulder like a bag of wheat.

One of the men stepped off the boat. "I'll take her." He took Nicki's arm and appraised her as the big man set her down. "Nice lookin' chick. She'll fit right in."

"Fit in where?" Nicki regained her voice. "What the hell are you guy's talking about?" She realized Jack Harris was probably right. This was human trafficking—sex slaves.

The boatman ignored her. "This fills our quota for now," he told the driver as he handed him a fat envelope. "We won't need another girl unless we lose one for some reason." The second boatman grabbed Nicki and dragged her, kicking and cursing, toward the airboat. "You've done good work, and we're relying on you to keep it close to the vest."

His eyes riveted the driver. "Loose lips will sink *your* ship, buddy, so keep that in mind." He turned toward the boat and looked back. "We got powerful people you don't want to make angry. Got it?"

"Sure. I've got no reason to talk about this. No matter how you slice it, this is kidnapping, and that's Federal." He checked the envelope and fanned a thick wad of greenbacks.

"I'm not going on any spending spree either. This, and the four other contracts, are all headed for a discreet account in the Caymans." He grinned at the boatman. "My future retirement fund."

"Smart guy. And your partner?" He nodded toward the bigger man.

"My cousin, and don't let his size fool you. He's as smart about money as I am." He patted a bulging bicep. "We both got day jobs, but you know how to reach me if you've got any new requirements." He glanced at Nicki, now strapped to a seat in the middle of the airboat.

"Must be one helluva joint you're running out there. Might like to pay a visit myself."

"Invitation only for high rollers. Best keep your fees for that retirement." He spun and strode toward the airboat, its engine coughing to life. Looking back, he yelled over the growing roar, "Be safe. I'm sure we'll need your services again sometime down the road.

He stepped aboard the craft and climbed to the raised driver's platform. A quick wave and the engine thundered, skidding the boat off the grassy knoll and onto the canal. The decibel level skyrocketed as it gained way and sped off into the Everglades, quickly disappearing among a forest of tall grass.

Thirty minutes later, the airboat slowed and coasted onto a gravely beach beside the dilapidated remnants of a pier. Nicki was hauled ashore and thrust into the hands of a beefy matron. Noise-canceling earplugs were removed and the woman gave her a onceover.

"Pretty lady, I am Olga. I take care of you for now." She

removed a switchblade and cut the zip-tie around her wrists. Her feet had been freed once aboard the boat.

"Be good and all is fine. Cause trouble, you regret it." She rummaged through Nicki's cloth pouch that was handed to her and pocketed the seventy-dollars she found. The rest was rouge, eyeliner, a pouch of peanuts, and a few tissues. The woman grunted, then tossed the bag into a wire trash can.

"You need nothing there. We give you better." She snatched Nicki's arm in a vice grip and ran her hand through her pockets, coming out with a lipstick tube. She plucked off the cover and touched the coral-red wax to a finger.

"Pretty. I keep."

"Try it," Nicki urged. If she would just turn the bottom of the tube... "It would look good on you."

"Later." She recapped it and slid it into a pocket. "Now I take you inside. Get you ready for your tests."

"Tests?" Before she could ask more, they were interrupted by the ear-numbing boom of a large airboat arriving. It skidded ashore and as the engine dwindled to silence, three men, each wearing elaborate face masks, exited a small cabin. They stepped ashore where they were greeted by a formally dressed man and a svelte blond woman, poured into a tight red dress.

After a brief exchange of greetings, they headed up a path under camouflage netting toward a large ramshackle building that looked ready to collapse.

No wonder aerial surveillance never checked this place. It looks like a deserted wreck.

"Come." She stumbled as Olga yanked her into motion. They moved off to the right toward a second decrepit shack. "Time to clean you up for the doctors."

Her eyes swept from one structure to the other. Two messes out here in nowhere. *Wonder what's insides?* She was about to find out. And somehow, she had to get Olga to use that lipstick.

~ 36 ~

Maggie trudged slowly up the stairs, seeking solace in her suite, as disparate thoughts cascaded through her mind.

She'd just finished her seven-month physical, complete with blood work, an ultrasound, and an uncomfortable internal exam. Returning from taking a quick pee in the lab's bathroom, she overheard the medics talking. She paused in the hall and grinned, learning she was carrying a girl, but that morphed into a grimace from what else she overheard.

Maggie scrunched beside a watercooler as the younger medic, a plump, mousey woman, complained about not seeing any money yet.

Money? For Char's baby? Were the employees here on commission instead of salary? They spoke softly, but she heard everything.

"It seems the woman is stalling over making the payment," the older male said.

Woman? It was supposed to be a guy who had no woman to carry his kid.

"Really?" the female said. "She'd risk everything for a million bucks?" She snorted. "That's chickenfeed for the bitch."

A million dollars? What the hell are they talking ...?

"Yeah, well, Hoek says she wants the mistress and infant to move in with her. Wants to be in the kid's life, too."

"Huh, good luck with that." She finished putting instruments into a sterilizer, and both stripped off their latex gloves. "Maybe that's something to consider in the future."

"Not possible to keep the surrogate around. Too many

questions with all the wrong answers." He glanced toward the hallways. "Where the hell is Bagwell?"

Maggie edged backwards before rising and striding into the room.

"Wow, that was a relief. Really had to pee." She forced her eyes to find theirs. "We done here?"

"Yes," the male responded. "Everything looks fine. You've got about seven weeks to go."

"But you won't tell me the sex of the baby?" She'd play dumb.

"You know that's not allowed, hon." The female medic patted her shoulder. "The less emotionally attached you are to this infant, the easier it'll be for you in the end."

"Yeah, so you keep telling me." She shrugged. "So, next visit in two weeks?"

"Right, unless you're experiencing any problems," the man said.

"Okay." She waved and hurried off, eager to be away and have time to digest what she'd heard.

Maggie entered her rooms, locked the door, and sprawled across the bed, arms and legs flung wide.

What the hell did I get myself into? Nothing added up. They said seven weeks, but she'd calculated it was really nine. *Hmm.* Char delivered in what seemed two weeks too early.

And where *was* Char? The way they talked about her sounded kind of... kind of ominous. Why did they call her a "mistress?" And why were they negotiating with a woman for the baby when the donor was a man? Wasn't everything paid for in advance when using a surrogate? And a million bucks? No surrogate should cost anything near that.

If my donor had a wife or a partner, why hadn't they implanted one of her fertilized eggs instead of using mine?

Maggie groaned and pressed her palms against her

temple. So many questions! What was going on? Nothing sounded as it should. Had something bad happened to Charlotte? Did *they* do something to her after the baby came?

Are they gonna do something to me too? She should have been suspicious about all the secrecy, but the big payday was too good to pass up. Despite their warnings not to become emotionally involved, this was *her* baby. Half anyway, with some unknown father. Could she just move on and never be a part of her daughter's life?

Much to her surprise, the maternal instinct stirring within her made that seem unlikely.

Who woulda thought?

Maggie chuckled despite her growing angst. She wiggled back, propping up on her elbows, and stared vacantly at the wall. She shook her head and struggled to dispel gloomy thoughts.

Seven weeks to figure out what's really going on here, and maybe make a plan...to do what? Escape? Seven months pregnant and on the run? If that's in the cards, I'm gonna need help.

With Charlotte gone, who could she count on? José, the bartender, was the only one she felt wasn't part of the organization. From their conversation, it seemed he was just hired to tend bar and manage the lounge. But still, could she trust him. That was something to explore.

I got some time to figure what I need to do. Coming up with 'how' may be the challenge.

If she were going to plan an escape, should it be before or after the baby came? She'd come to believe her life may hang in the balance, and that was damned scary. If they were the heartless monsters she began to suspect, how long would she survive after giving birth? Once they had her baby, they'd have no need for her.

So, if she were to do this, it had better be soon, while she could still get around. A seven-month pregnant woman wasn't someone quick on her feet.

Maggie slipped off the bed and dressed for dinner, donning a tent-like flowered frock. She'd ply José to get an idea where he stood in all this. Without his aid, she would be helpless. Caution was her by-word.

If Sam Gregory or Miles Hoek got a sense of what she plotted, she'd be dead in the water.

She shivered, hoping that was only a metaphor.

~ 37 ~

Warner pushed through the door of the crime lab and spotted the Hawk at a table, hunched over a microscope. The odor of gunshot residue hung in the air, the probable result of a test fire. It appeared the Hawk was comparing rifling marks on two slugs.

"Hey, Moe." Warner laid a hand on the short man's shoulder. "Ya got something for me?"

"Yeah. Just a second, Detective." He fiddled with two dials, aligning the bullets, then sighed and sat back. "Not a match."

"What's the case?" Warner leaned against the table.

"Liquor store robbery." The head of Miami-Dade CSU rolled his shoulder as he swiveled to face Warner.

"Yeah." Warner nodded. "One dead and one wounded." He glanced at a Smith & Wesson 9mm, laying on the bench. "Not the weapon, huh?"

"No. Detectives found it in a trash bin a half-block away, but it wasn't used for this shooting." He slipped the slug from its perch and bagged it. "I'll run it through the system to see if it ties to anything else."

"Okay." Warner pushed away from the table. "But I'm guessin' that's not why you called me down here."

"Oh, right." The Hawk turned and strode to his desk where he plucked up a manila folder.

"Finished the DNA test on the Jane Doe found at the construction site, and I ran it against all the missing prostitutes."

Warner flipped open the file and scanned the first page.

"No match with any of them?"

"No. It's also being run through the NCIC data base, but so far, nothing there either."

"So, no other way to ID that poor woman?" Warner handed back the file.

"Not here. Maybe autopsy will find some sort of medical marker."

"Like a serial number on an artificial joint or something?"

"Yes, our last hope, but she was in her twenties, so that's a slim chance." He dropped the folder on his desk.

"At least we know she wasn't Detective Unger."

"That was never really in question, Detective. Her death preceded Unger's disappearance by at least three days. I only ran that match for Jack Harris because he seemed so panicked."

"Okay. Anyhow, we're turnin' out the troops in force, tryin' to find our missin' coal mine canary without alertin' the perps as to who she is."

"Harris said she's got a tracker." The Hawk settled behind his desk. "No signal from it?"

"Not yet." Warner turned toward the doorway. "Lots of reasons she may not have used it, but I hope it isn't because it's inop... or that *she's* dead."

He glanced over his shoulder as he exited. "Keep me posted it you get anything off the Jane Doe."

And he was gone.

~ 38 ~

Nicki tried to size up her surroundings but was hampered by Olga's vice-grip as she dragged her across the path toward the smaller, ramshackle hut. A hurried scan revealed two dilapidated shacks on a sizable island dotted by scrub and a thatch of tall live oaks. Gravel paths to each structure hid under camouflage netting strung across several trees. Nothing there but deserted ruination if spotted in a flyover.

Nicki stumbled over the door's threshold as she was hauled inside.

"Move, bitch, or I carry you." Olga growled, and yanked her though the opening.

Nicki blinked and tried to wipe moisture from her eyes with her zip-tied hands. She was stunned to be in a well-lit, white tiled vestibule, where everything seemed clean and orderly, belying the crumbling wreck outside.

"Sit." Olga shoved her into an armchair and lumbered behind a gray Formica-top desk. The hulking woman snatched keys from the center drawer, and turning, retrieved a bag from a cupboard behind. She circled the desk and dragged Nicki to her feet, the bag clamped under one arm.

"Come." She produced a switchblade and freed Nicki's wrists.

Nicki was hurried by a hand in her back toward an inner door, secured by a large, keyed deadbolt. The matron unlocked it and shoved her through, closing the door behind them.

The detective scanned the room, which appeared to be a dormitory with four bunk beds lining each side. She spotted movement from one of the cots. An attractive young Black woman rose and stood near a wall, gazing at her, wide-eyed.

Must be Kiesha Swift, the most recent abductee. Positive verification Nicki was in the right place. So, how to get Jack Harris and the Miami-Dade PD out there to take them down.

We're five miles past nowhere. If I can't activate that tracker, no way anyone will find us. She plopped down on a bed, her eyes on the other girl. *Even then, we're outta range of any receiver, unless it's picked up during a fly-by.*

"You get outta those rags. This you wear in here." Olga dumped the bag she'd carried onto the bed, spewing out a green one-piece jumpsuit, some lingerie and a pair of sandals.

"First a shower and wash hair." She gestured toward an open doorway. "I come back in thirty minutes. Be done then."

Lips pressed thin, hands on hips, and eyes in full glare mode left no doubt for Nicki of the need to comply. She'd earned a black belt and had competed successfully in several karate competitions, but she had no desire to tangle with this female hulk. The role she was playing didn't fit with those skills, either.

She watched Olga clump away, locking the door behind her. Nicki pushed off the bed and took a few tentative steps toward the other woman.

"What the hell is this place?" She gestured around the room.

"The River Styx," the Black girl muttered.

"Huh?" Nicki glanced around the room and saw no one else. She would play dumb for now and decide later whether to clue the woman in as to why she was there.

"Ancient Greek legend." Kiesha stepped away from her bed and approached Nicki. "You must cross the River Styx to get to Hades."

"So, you're saying that other bigger building is our Hades? Jesus!" She offered her hand. "I'm Nicki Unger."

"Kiesha Swift." She gave a soft handshake. "Yeah, and I'm

~ 140 ~

scared silly." Her eyes welled. "It's a whorehouse, and we're gonna be servicing their clients."

"Christ!" She ran fingers through her hair. "You weren't working the streets?" She knew better but had to play along. "I wonder if some of my friends who went missing were snatched like me?"

"They were." Kiesha settled on the edge of Nicki's bed.

"Two were here—Tanya and Sheri—and they said two others had been moved up to the big house after they arrived. She knuckled moisture from her eyes. "And no, I wasn't doing tricks. I was a junior in college and thought I was headed for a modeling career."

"So, how're they gonna force us to do this we if refuse?" Nicki knew the obvious answer but wondered if Kiesha realized it.

"From what I heard from Sheri, it's submit or die. She thinks they've killed at least three girls—maybe more—who either didn't perform or tried to get away."

"You mean we're gonna be trapped here...forever?" Nicki's head swiveled, sweeping the room. This was worse than she'd suspected.

"Yeah. There's no escape, unless you've got an airboat and a GPS to find the way out." She rose and absently straightened the blanket. "Unless the cops find us, and how could that happen? We're in the middle of nowhere, and from the air, I'm sure the place looks deserted. We're screwed!"

"Hang tough, kid." Nicki squeezed her shoulder. "Maybe we'll get lucky."

"Not likely." She sighed. "Tanya and Sheri made their peace with it. Said it was probably a better life than they faced out on the streets, but that wasn't me." She grimaced.

"I'm trying to psych myself up, because it's coming soon. From what I've heard, you can't just lay there." She started to tear up again.

"They require their girls to act like they're in love.

Apparently, their clients are upper-upper and aren't just looking for a quick hookup."

"So, if you can't pull it off, what? They kill you and find someone else?"

Kiesha sniffled and nodded. "I think so. It looks like they treat you well if you cooperate and perform, but they can also be damned ruthless."

"We're just property to them, I guess. From what I've heard, these kinds of guys hook you on drugs to make you compliant. Not here, though, huh?"

"No." She wandered to her bed. "Sheri said they want us clean and healthy. She spent two months in here, detoxing." She sat and hugged her knees.

"I'm scared, Nicki. I'm not sure I can do this."

"Yes, you can, 'cause you gotta. Somehow, we're gonna get out of this, and you got to hang in there until that happens." She began to strip and headed for the shower. Olga would soon return, and somehow, she had to get to that lipstick tube.

A lot of women were counting on her, even if they didn't know it.

~ 39 ~

Warner absently reached for his trilling desk phone as he continued studying three action reports. Glancing over, he punched the winking Line 2 and answered.

"Warner." He wedged the receiver between his shoulder and ear as he stacked the files and laid them aside.

"It's Charlie, Al. Hope I'm not disturbing you."

"Things are always hummin' here, Seagrave. I'm in the middle of a hot search goin' nowhere at the moment." He had the phone in hand now. "What's on your mind?" He slouched back on his chair.

"Just wondering if you had a chance to look into the Stirling thing we talked about?"

"Sorry, friend." He sighed. "We're in the middle of an urgent investigation, and I haven't had time. Any new developments?"

"Yeah. The birth mother's agent, or whatever he is, is pressing the widow for money. Claims the woman wants to take the infant and move on to somewhere new to raise it." He paused and cleared his throat. "She called today and asked me what to do."

"Has she talked to the other woman?" The detective sat up, elbows on his desk.

"Never met her. Everything's been through this guy."

"That's strange." Warner paused. "Has she seen anything? Maybe a photo with the baby?"

"Yes. She's got two or three photos."

"And the DNA results? She's seen the so-called proof?"

"Yes," Seagrave said. "She's got all that."

"Okay." Warner scribbled notes on a yellow lined pad. "Can ya e-mail the photos and test results?"

"Sure. What's the address?"

Warner recited his personal Gmail account ID, which he could read on his phone.

"Like I said, we've been swamped here, Charlie, but I promise to look into this today." His cell phone on his desk buzzed for an incoming message.

"Thanks, Al. Just sent everything."

"Yeah. I heard it come in." He picked up the android phone and opened the file. "Can't make any promises, bud. I'll call ya if I've got something or have more questions."

"That's all I can ask, Al. I know you're busy, and this may amount to nothing. I appreciate anything you may come up with."

"Okay. I know this is time-sensitive for Mrs. Sterling, so I'll try ta make some time. Gotta go now. Bye." He hung up.

Warner studied his phone, and then opened the first photo. An attractive woman, probably mid-twenties, was holding a small infant.

Hmm. A *really* small infant. Newborns' sizes varied, but this one looked especially undersized. Maybe even a bit premature? Scrabbling around his desk, he found his notes from their dinner when Seagrave told him about this. Scanning his scribbles, it appeared Stirling must have knocked up the gal just days before the accident.

Timing-wise, this so-called agent approached the widow a week after the baby arrived, if it were in fact full-term. Something didn't sit right with his famous instinctive gut.

He clicked on the "share" function on the phone, and sent all three files to his printer. He grinned as he pocketed the Android.

I'm getting' ta be a regular techno geek. All this electronic stuff was great, but he still preferred paper and pen.

He pushed away from his desk and strode to his open doorway.

"Harris. C'mon in here and bring whatever ya got on our search for Unger."

"Coming, Boss."

Zilch so far, he knew, but they'd better come up with something because that cop's life hung from a thin tread.

Seagrave's problems took a backseat to their missing detective. He'd go over his files at home. Maybe see what Eva thought about the photos.

Warner returned to his desk as Detective Harris hurried in, a small file in hand. By its thinness, Warner knew there wouldn't be much new.

He gritted his teeth. *Ain't gonna lose another cop if I can help it.*

"Not much here, Boss." Harris dropped the file and they huddled over it, searching for some missing bread crumb.

What they needed was for her tracker to come alive. Without that, things looked pretty bleak.

~ 40 ~

Maggie reached the bottom of the stairs and took a surreptitious peek at the entry desk. Sam was on the phone and wasn't watching her. She ambled toward the front doors and pushed quietly through.

Morning sunlight engulfed her in a steamy embrace. She glanced over her shoulder, but before she could start down the steps, a shout echoed from inside.

"Hey!" Sam charged through the doorway. "Where are you going, Mags?"

"Just thought I'd get some air." She turned toward him. "I haven't been outside for weeks." She twirled on her toes, catching her balance as the distended belly threw her off. "It's a beautiful day for a stroll."

"You should stay inside, hon." His sudden grip on her forearm was light but insistent.

"Hey!" She pulled free. "This isn't a prison, is it? I volunteered for this gig." She planted fisted hands on her hips. "You can't lock me up if I want to go for a walk."

"No one's locking you up, sweetie. I'm just concerned for your safety." Sam folded his arms across his chest. "You *are* seven months pregnant and there's nowhere to go, out here in the boonies."

"I'm not *going* anywhere, Sam. I only wanted to take a little walk and get some air." She smiled. "Pregnant women are supposed to get some exercise, you know."

"Yes, yes, I know, but—"

"Look, if you're so worried about my safety, maybe José

can accompany me."

"Good idea. He's doing some stocking now." He took her hand. "Come inside, and we can schedule your walk after lunch." His eyes caught hers. "How's that sound?"

"Perfect. After lunch is fine." He dropped her hand, and she followed him back inside.

A lengthy survey of her surroundings was needed if she did decide to try to leave. Certain her hosts would be unhappy about that, she had to proceed with caution. The conversation she'd heard about Char and her baby convinced Maggie she wasn't safe after the infant came.

If she were to escape... *escape?*... as if a captive? She groaned softly, convinced that's what she was.

Anyway, I'm going to need help, and José may be my only option.

Conversation with the man over the months convinced her he wasn't actually part of their organization. He was a tradesman, hired to tend bar and manage the lounge...and he *liked* her. A tiny spark smoldered between them.

Maggie entered the lounge behind Sam, who went to look for José. She settled at a table and opened the suspense novel she'd been reading.

Better not rush this. Feel José out and plant a seed to gain his aid. I can't get outta here without help, but it's gotta happen soon. Ten to twelve weeks left, and it's gotta happen while I'm still reasonably quick on my feet.

She scanned the room, then sighed. Things had gotten a lot more complicated than she'd expected. She was supposed to provide a paid service for a childless couple, but it had somehow become a lot more.

She sensed her life may depend on what she did next.

~ **41** ~

Nicki looked up as the outer door opened and Kiesha came through, followed by a stern-lipped Olga. The girl glanced at Nicki, gave a small shrug, and went to her bed, perching on the edge.

"So," the hulking matron stood, arms folded, "physicals done. We get results in one, two days. If both healthy, you go soon to main house. You the last two bitches we need there." She nodded toward Kiesha.

"Pretty Black cunt gonna be real popular, I think." Her lips drew into a wicked smirk as she turned to leave. "With no new bitches coming, I finally get rest." And she was gone, the door locked behind her.

Nicki's eyes were pulled from Olga's exit to the whimpers of her companion. The complete reality of the captivity had descended upon her: a life of sexual servitude.

"Oh Christ, I can't believe this." Kiesha's voice quavered. "I'm a decent, educated girl whose family struggled so she could go to a good college." Tears trickled in tiny rivulets across her cheeks. "And now I'm going to be a sex toy for a bunch of rich dilettantes?" She shook her head. "How will I do that without barfing all over them?"

"I hate it too." Nicki moved over and settled next to her. "This isn't my life, either, and I'm plenty scared." She lay a hand on the girl's forearm.

"But if we want to survive, we gotta suck it up and do it with a smile. From what I heard between the Russian bitch and one of the guys, we were snatched to replace two girls who 'didn't perform.'" She took Kiesha's chin, turning her face toward hers.

"It seems pretty obvious... you don't perform, you're replaced... permanently."

"You mean they'll... they'll *kill* us?" Her eyes flared, big as quarters.

"In a heartbeat, I'm afraid." Nicki sighed. "We're just replaceable trash to them. Plenty more where we came from." She shrugged. "Like me, anyhow." Still playing the streetwalker. "You, not so much. You may be one-of-a-kind here."

"Lucky me." Kiesha blotted her eyes with a tissue and blew her nose.

"Yeah; me too. This isn't what I signed up for, going on the streets." She grunted in her mind, knowing this was *exactly* what she'd signed up for when she took this assignment. She just never expected it to go so badly.

"Look." She took both the girl's hands. "I'm guessing you were never on drugs and didn't have a venereal disease."

Kiesha shook her head.

"Me either. So, that's what they seemed to be checking us for." She rose. "They do an internal exam on you?"

She nodded, lying back on her bed. "Sedated me and I've got this little incision on my lower belly. Maybe some kind of arthroscopic procedure. Whatever they did in there, it hurts inside."

"Me too." Nicki pulled an earlobe. "Wonder what that was about. They wouldn't talk about it, but the ache eased up in three days." She wandered to her bed. *We're just possessions to these bastards, to do with whatever they want.*

"Anyhow, I'm guessing we passed our exams and will soon be over there," she nodded in the general direction of the bigger building, "so, you gotta start psyching yourself to do what's needed, and do it with a smile."

"Have sex with strange men? How do you do that?"

"Hookers do it all the time. Normally, I'd say disassociate...find someplace pleasant to visit in your mind. I don't think that'll work here." Nicki lay back and propped her head up with a bunched-up pillow.

"Sheri, one of the girls from the bordello, dropped by while you were getting your physical. She was looking for a locket or something she may have lost here." Nicki stretched and yawned, still tired from the anesthesia and her physical exam, four days before.

"Anyway, she said you can't just have sex with these guys. You gotta treat them like lovers. If they get two complaints about your attitude, you're gone."

"Gone?" Kiesha sat up. "Jesus! You mean like *dead* gone?"

"That's the impression I got." She rolled over and sat again on the edge of her cot. "She knows of at least one girl with a so-called bad attitude who just disappeared."

"Oh, god, how will I survive this?" Her sobs were punctuated with small hiccups.

"By being tough and knowing the consequences of failing." Nicki sighed. "The good news—if you can call it that— is Sheri said so far all the guys have treated her really nice. Two keep coming back to see her, and have even given her gifts."

"Gifts? Really?" She stared through her tears.

"So she says. Once settled in, she said life here was better, and safer, than hooking on the streets, despite being a prisoner." Nicki snorted. "Said she was her pimp's prisoner on the streets, anyway, so this is actually a step up, despite being forced on her."

"Sounds like a bunch of crap to me," the girl said, dabbing her eyes.

"Yeah, well that's called making the best of a lousy situation and surviving."

Nicki paused, battling with herself over whether to clue

Kiesha in about her being an undercover cop, and that help may be coming. She sighed and settled back on the bed.

Better not to give her a chance to slip up and expose me. Somehow, I gotta get that Russian bitch to use that lipstick. The guys are never gonna find us out here without that tracker to home in on.

She glanced at her companion. "I told you I got friends who are certainly looking for me, so don't give up hope."

"From what I saw during my airboat ride out here, we're smack in the middle of the Everglades." Kiesha shook her head. "No way anyone's going to find us here. We're screwed."

"I never quit hoping," Nicki muttered, lying down again.

And I'm afraid you're right, kid. We're gonna get literally screwed by a bunch of rich bastards, but I can live through that.

I gotta! I hope you can too, Kiesha.

~ 42 ~

Warner followed Buff up the stairs to his duplex, the golden retriever's tongue hanging breathlessly from the corner of her mouth, her tail sweeping a wide swath. The detective paused on his stoop, then side-stepped to the door on his left and rang the bell.

"In a moment, Al." The voice clear and musical, despite its age, came through the video entry camera. Adele Meyer had recently celebrated her ninetieth birthday, and as was his custom, Warner felt compelled to check on his substitute mom.

The door opened revealing the trim, petite woman in a flowered house dress covered by a full denim apron. "Come in, Detective." She stooped to scratch the dog behind the ears.

"You too, Buff."

She straightened and patted her silky gray hair, wound in her usual bun. The aroma of cinnamon and cooking pastry wafted through the doorway as they entered, setting Warner's stomach grumbling.

"What are ya bakin' today, Adele? Smells scrumptious."

"Brownies for my bridge girls." She turned toward the kitchen. "Have a seat in the den, and I'll be right there."

"With chocolate chips, I suppose." He chuckled as he perched on the edge of her love seat.

"Of course," she called from the kitchen. "And chopped walnuts." An opening oven door sounded a familiar creak. "Brownies are nothing without chips and nuts, you know."

"Yes, I know. No one does it better than you, Mom."

"I love it when you call me that, Al, but it probably ought to be grandma, at my age." She chuckled. "You don't need to lay on the charm. I'm making a plate for you and Eva too."

She arrived in the den, wiping her hands on a towel. She settled next to Warner and stroked Buff's head which she'd laid in her lap.

"No need for you to cajole me, either, pup." She snickered. "I baked some special doggy biscuits for you yesterday." She glanced at the man who filled the void of her son, an Army captain killed in the last days of the Viet Nam conflict.

Warner leaned over and wrapped an arm around her pulling her close. "You're the best mom I've ever had, Adele, and age is no factor." He released his grip and swiveled toward her. "Mine never had time or energy to bake cookies or pies.

"Can't stay though. Eva and I have the dinner plans I told you about. Just thought I'd check on you before we went out." He patted her hand as he rose.

"Well, I don't want to keep you from your sweet lady on this special day." She came spryly off the sofa. "Just a minute and I'll make you a plate of brownies... for later." She hurried into the kitchen. "Then I'll be baking the cake we talked about for this evening."

~~~

Warner closed the door behind him and carried the plastic-wrapped plate of aromatic brownies into his kitchen.

"Mmm." Eva came out of the easy chair in the den where she'd been reading notes from her last patient's visit, and followed him.

"Smells delicious. Adele's, I suppose."

"Yeah. For after dinner." He slid the plate onto the kitchen counter. He turned to her. "Sorry I'm a little late. Just stopped in to check on her. You ready to go?"

"Of course." She slipped into his arms and kissed his neck. "Carlo will hold our reservation, even if we're a bit tardy." They were headed for their favorite Italian restaurant, *Il Bistro*.

"Okay. If you'll feed Buff, I'll take a quick shower and change. We had a nice run together, and I worked up a pretty good sweat."

"No problem. That'll give me enough time to finish my notes on my last patient, too."

He nodded and kissed her on the tip of her nose, then turned for his bedroom.

~~~

Warner inhaled the aromas of oregano and cooked tomatoes as Eva and he followed Carlo to the rear of the dimly lit restaurant. He'd held their usual booth in a secluded nook in the rear despite their thirty-minute late arrival.

"Here we are." He distributed two menus and gestured for Eva to slip in on the left side, giving Warner his preferred view of the entry. The detective wasn't paranoid, but he wasn't careless either. His years of success in homicide had earned him more than a fair share of enemies.

"You are as lovely as ever, Madonna," Carlo said with a small bow before turning to leave.

"Everyone loves a beautiful redhead." Warner chuckled and gave her hand a gentle squeeze. He shoved aside the menu, knowing what he would order: lasagna with a side salad. His Dewar's on the rocks and Eva's Chablis were already on the way. He leaned back, sighed, and massaged his eyes.

"Tired, Al?"

"Mostly frustrated." He watched a waiter deliver their

cocktails.

"No progress on the missing detective?" She swiveled to face him.

"Nothin'. Still hopin' she'll get a chance to turn on her locator, and the whole team's on high alert. Sheriff, state troopers, everyone." He withdrew an envelope for his inside jacket pocket.

"Meanwhile, I've been lookin' inta Seagrave's friend's problem." He slipped two photos out of the envelope. "Here's pics of the so-called mistress and the newborn."

Eva studied the photos of an attractive mid-twenties woman, one cradling the baby, and the other holding it up as if for inspection, apparently in a hospital room, possibly shortly after giving birth.

"Hmm. The infant seems kind of small. Was it premature?"

"Not that I know of. And that wouldn't fit with the supposed timeline, her gettin' knocked up just before the auto accident. She'd have ta have gotten pregnant *after* Stirling died if the kid's a preemie, so that don't work."

A waiter returned to take their order; Warner the lasagna and she veal Marsala. Eva's attention focused on the photos after he'd left.

"Has Mrs. Stirling spoken to the mother? Charlie said she'd invited the woman to live with her so she could be in the baby's life."

"Never met her, and this guy declined the invitation without givin' her the option." Warner gathered the photos and slid them back into the envelope. "Charlie said she's only had contact with the agent, the excuse bein' the mother wanted ta remain anonymous."

"Strange." Eva eased back, stroking her chin. "You'd think a young, unmarried woman would jump at the chance at being a part of all that money."

"Yeah, ya'd think." He glanced up as their salads arrived. He started to pocket the envelope, then paused, withdrew a photo, and studied it, his brow knit.

"Ya know, guessin' the height of this gal, based on the door behind her, she's about the probably size of a dismembered Jane Doe we found at a construction site." He continued studying the image.

"Seagrave said this agent guy supplied DNA proof the kid is Stirling's." His eyes caught Eva's. "I think I've got a copy of that test at the office." He pocketed the envelope. "I'm gonna have The Hawk run it against the Jane Doe, 'cause the kid's mother's DNA is in there too."

Evan grabbed his hand. "You think they murdered the mother?"

"Yeah, it's possible. The whole thing smacks of extortion, and with the woman not around..." He trailed off, eyebrows arched."

"And the baby?"

"If it's a strictly criminal operation, they may want a double prize—extort the widow and sell the kid on the adoption black market."

"Jesus! What heartless bastards." Eva hugged herself.

"That's who I deal with every day, babe. Just something to add to the stress of a missin' undercover cop."

A clatter of dishes drew their attention as the waiter delivered their dinners. Warner finished his salad and shoved the plate aside. They ate their meals in silence, but he sensed something else was on his lover's mind.

He glanced at the redhead. "Ya got something else ya wannna talk about, Babe?"

She hesitated, picking at her food, the raised her eyes to hiss. "We've discussed trying again for a baby of our own, Al."

"Yeah, I know." He sat back and sighed. "Just things have been so hectic..."

"The sands of time are running out, sweetheart. I'm

almost forty, and if we're going to do this, hectic or not, now is the time." She took his hand again in both of hers.

"It's just I worry about nuts like Bachelor..." He touched her cheek.

"Yes, that was traumatic, physically and emotionally devastating, but with therapy, I've gotten mostly past it. I can't live my life in fear that some other lunatic will attack me to get at you. I love you, and I want to be a parent with you."

"I love ya too, Red." His face now serious. "I can only think of one thing better than havin' a baby with you."

"Really?" She drew back, still holding his hand, and chuckled. "What could that be?"

He slid across the booth's bench and folded her in his arms. "Havin' a kid with my *wife,* instead of my girlfriend." His lips brushed her cheek, and then across both eyes.

She wiggled free, her gray orbs riveting his. "Detective Alan Warner, are you...?"

"Proposing?" A grin split his rugged face. "That's why I set up this dinner. It just took a little different turn than I expected." He fished a small velvet box from his front pocket.

"Al?" Her eyes wide, the corners of her lips ticking up.

"Can't make it onto a knee here, Babe, but, Eva Guttenberg, will you do me the honor of becomin' my wife."

He flipped open the box, exposing a one carat blood red, oval ruby, bracketed by two small, faceted diamonds mounted on a platinum band.

"The one good thing I got from my mom."

"Oh, Al!" She cradled the box in both her hand as tiny rills of tears trickled across her cheeks.

"The last time we tried this, Eva, fate got in the way." He cupped her face in his hands. "I *really* want to be your husband and proper father to our kid. So?" His eyebrows arched.

"Yes! Yes!" She threw her arms around his neck and peppered him with kisses. "There's nothing I want more."

"Hooray!" Carlo appeared, as if he'd been listening in, and popped the cork on an Asti Spumante. "Congratulations to my two favorite people on now becoming one." A waiter materialized with champagne glasses and Carlo poured and offered a toast. Giggles from smiling faces filled the air, and nearby customers offered applause.

"Looks like everyone knew about this except me." She snuggled closer, planting a passionate kiss on his lips.

"Yeah." He chuckled. "Good thing ya said yes, 'cause Adele's bakin' a cake as we speak."

Her grin widened. "You crafty devil. No *wonder* I love you."

The evening went on with no more thoughts of extortion, murder, and missing detectives.

At least for the moment.

~ 43 ~

Maggie leaned against the concierge desk, her eyes sweeping the foyer. *Where's José? I hope—*

Her thoughts were interrupted as the young Latino emerged from the back office. A smile on his honey-colored face eased her concerns, tension slipping away.

"So?" Her brow wrinkled.

"We're good." He paused, weight shifted to his right side, hands in his pockets. "Talked to Sam, and he agrees the walks outside will do you good. Apparently, the doc said it'll be healthy for you and the infant." He took her by the elbow.

"Ready to go?" He drew a peaked cap from his back pocket. "Here. It's pleasant out, but very sunny. I'll get you a pair of sunglasses for next time."

"Thanks." She tucked her hand under his arm and they started for the door. "I'm really eager for some fresh air." She smiled, giving his wiry bicep a gentle squeeze.

With Charlotte gone, her only companionship had been this guy. They'd had many long talks in the lounge, and even played gin rummy on several occasions. They'd developed an easy compatibility, with some mild flirting thrown in. Might something be developing past friendship? Romance, even? There seemed no possible future there.

She'd become convinced of less than honest intentions from this organization, but felt José was no part of it—just an employee hired to fill a need. She asked him a few days ago how he came to work there.

"I was head barista at a cantina on Calle Ocho when I saw their ad for a lounge manager." They were at a table in the lounge, playing cards. "I was going nowhere fast, and this gig paid very well and offered room and board. Gave me a chance to save my bucks, so maybe I could start up a bar or small café of my own. Seemed too good to pass up."

"I get it." She patted his hand and shivered as a ridge of goosebumps erupted down her spine. *What the hell?*

"This is the first time I've had no living expenses since I moved away from home." Her voice now a bit breathless.

"When I drop this bundle," she caressed her belly, "and collect my payday, I plan on opening a small, custom bakery." She was back in control. "I'll give you my number and maybe you'll drop by when your services are completed here."

Thinking back, she wondered at the almost pained look he'd given her then. Had she been too direct?

Oh, well. They were out the door and strolling along the sweeping circular driveway. There was a flagstone path at the end, leading toward the gardens in the rear. Maggie inhaled the floral aromas wafting to them on the gentle, warm breeze.

Maggie peeked at him from the corners of eyes. "Have you heard anything about Charlotte?" They had arrived at the gardens—rows of red and yellow roses, colorful bougainvillea, beds of pink and white New Guinea inpatients. A kaleidoscope of colors.

José looked away at her question and shrugged. "No reason to expect to hear from her after she'd left."

"I… I'm worried about her, José." She tugged him to a halt but he wouldn't meet her eyes. "I overheard a conversation between Sam and Mr. Hoek, and it scared me."

He turned slowly, his face screwed into a frown. "It should, Maggie. It should."

"What… what d'ya mean?" Her grip tightened on his arm. "What's going on, José?"

"I'm sorry." He pulled free. "I shouldn't have said anything. I don't actually *know* anything, anyhow."

"But you got suspicions, and so do I." She grabbed his shoulder, forcing him to face her. "Tell me what you think!"

"Look, Maggie." He shook off her hands. "They don't tell me anything anymore than they tell you. And frankly, the less I know, the safer I feel." He tried to turn away, but she restrained him.

"José!" She had never been so aggressive with a guy she liked. "All this time we've spent together—there's something growing between us." Her eyes drilled into his. "Isn't there?"

He sighed and nodded. "You're the nicest girl I've ever known, inside and out. Any other time, I'd be falling for you."

"So why should this be different." She planted fists on her hips. "I feel the same way." She chuckled. "At first, I thought it just because we're crammed together here, but you're a sweet and caring guy who I think may be as trapped here as I am."

"Yeah, in more ways than one."

His sigh was more like a groan. He glanced at the mansion and saw they were screened from sight by a six-foot tall bougainvillea bush. He gathered her in for a gentle hug and rested his head next to hers, his chin on her shoulder.

She snuggled as close as her swollen belly would allow, and brushed her lips across his ear. "This is nice." Her hands caressed his back.

José drew back his head, his eyes plumbing hers, then he kissed her, their lips separating, fielding her darting tongue with his. After a breathless moment, he shuddered, and pushed away, snatching both her hands in his.

"Oh, shit! Shit! Shit! Shit!" His cocoa brown eyes were watery pools.

"What's wrong?" She looked toward the building but saw no one. "They can't see us here."

"I know. It isn't that." He drew her back into his arms.

"What then?" She kissed his neck. "It's not like I'm cheating on anyone." Her fingers fluttered over her abdomen, and she snickered.

"Oh, did you feel that? This kid's warming up to kick a sixty-yard field goal."

José dropped a hand to her belly just as the baby delivered a one-two jab. He started a chuckle, then his face drew into hard lines.

"How many weeks, Mags?"

"To go? My calendar says six."

"Yeah, but from what I heard, they're gonna do it in three or four."

"Two or three weeks early?" She stepped back. "Why wouldn't they wait for full term?" The smooth skin of her brow wrinkled.

"The same as Charlotte." One hand rubbed the back of his neck and his eyes grew solemn.

"Char? Wasn't there a problem…?"

"Yeah, the problem was, full term didn't meet their timeline." He shook his head, tears growing in the corners of his eyes.

"They're pretty careless what they say when I might hear them. I don't think Charlotte got what she expected."

"What d'ya mean? They didn't pay her?" Maggie's hand crossed over her belly and her lips curled down.

"No." His eyes, full of tears, flitted away from her face. "I think Charlotte is *dead*!"

"*Dead?* I don't understand…"

"Look." His eyes bore into hers. "From what I've been able to piece together, this was *never* about some rich guy looking for a surrogate." His glance swept the grounds but saw no one.

"This is about blackmail to preserve a reputation." His voice nearly a whisper. "These pregnancies—Charlotte's and yours—are tools to squeeze money—a *lot* of money—from rich widows."

"How the hell did they manage that?" She stepped back, her eyes narrowing. "And how do you know all this? I thought you weren't part of their operation."

"I'm *not*." He grabbed her wrists, pulling her back toward him. "Like I said, they don't guard what they say around me, and the rest I've figured out." He sighed and peeked at the house again.

"I don't think you're safe...and I doubt I am, either."

"You think they plan on *killing* us?" She clapped a hand across her mouth. "My god!"

"Makes sense. Get rid of any condemning evidence...us. We're talking about millions of dollars here."

"Sure." She knuckled away tears. "Makes no difference what you hear if their gonna kill you. Aren't they worried you might run off?"

"I don't get paid until the end of my gig here, so I think they figure that'll keep me around. They probably don't think I'm smart enough to worry about *my* life, too."

"So, what are we gonna do?" She sucked in a ragged breath. "I don't want to die." She reached out and stroked his cheek. "I don't want *you* to die either, José." The corners of her lips ticked up, despite a flood of tears. "I like having you around."

"Me too." He curled her again into his arms and this kiss was laced with intensity. They broke, gasping for air, eyes flared at the wonder of what was happening.

"We gotta make a plan." He panted. "Figure out how to escape." He caught her chin in his fingers, their eyes locked.

"These walks they're allowing are the key, but if we're gonna make a run for it, it's gotta happen soon." He pulled at his ear lobe.

"We've gotta get back now, before they get suspicious, but I think there's a way we might do this later next week." He took her arm and guided her back up the path.

"We'll take daily walks, each a little longer, to set a pattern, until I figure out the details." He glanced at her at his side, clutching his arm. He pasted a smile on his face.

"Be brave, Mags, and try to act happy. Be a girl expecting a big payday in five or six weeks. They can't suspect we're on to them."

"I'll try, darling. I'll try."

The grin on his face was no longer forced.

She'd called him *darling*!

~ 44 ~

Warner strode into his office, tossed his jacket onto the back of a chair, and deposited his Glock and badge in a desk drawer. He sighed as he slumped onto his chair, leaning back, his hands clasped behind his head.

His meeting in Captain Santiago's office with Dade and Broward County Sheriffs produced no new intel on the whereabouts of Detective Nicki Unger. Both sheriff offices had small planes patrolling the Everglades and western parts of the two counties, searching for a signal from Unger's tracker. The lack of that contact was driving Warner crazy.

She's sure to be in trouble somewhere, but Harris says she a resourceful gal.

He sighed and slid up to his desk, noticing a yellow PostIt note attached to his phone:

Hector Carrera called

"Shit!" Warner glanced at his wall calendar. Two weeks until they were tentatively scheduled to run another session of their troubled teen boot camp. The press of his current investigation and missing detective had driven it from his thoughts.

Warner opened a lower drawer in his desk and his fingers danced across the tops of files, finally withdrawing a thin manila folder. He slipped it onto his desk and removed a single sheet of paper—twenty-four names, each with annotated comments. He skimmed the list, then picked up his desk phone.

He chuckled softly and muttered, "Am I the last guy who likes old-fashioned land lines?" Three rings and Hector answered.

"Hey, amigo, I was starting to wonder if we're still on?"

"Sorry, Hector. Been really swamped lately."

"Yeah, I heard about your missing detective. Any news?"

"Nada, buddy. We'll talk about that later. You're callin' about the next DCBC session, I guess."

"Right. You gonna be able to make the time, Al? If things are getting too intense—"

"I'll work it out. I got a list from the judge and—"

"Okay, hang on a minute. Let me call you back and I'll see if I can get the other guys on a conference call, so we only have to do this once."

"Good idea. I'll be here."

"Your land line, Al, not your cell?"

"Yeah, I'm in the office."

"You're a dinosaur, buddy. Move into the twenty-first century."

"Thanks." Warner chuckled. "It's what I'm comfortable with. I use the cell when I'm out, but I like the feel of a real phone, just like I prefer to hold a printed book, rather than readin' one from an Android. Call me back when ya get the guys lined up."

"Wilco." And the line went dead.

Warner again scanned the paper he'd received from the juvie judge's secretary, then set it aside, and retrieved his pocket calendar. He smiled at the thought he was probably the only one in the department not keeping his appointments on his cell phone.

He glanced up as the direct line on his desk phone rang, and reached for the receiver.

"Hector?"

"Yeah, with Darnel and Ben on the line. Jorge is in a deposition, so we'll fill him in later."

"Hi guys," Warner said.

He was greeted with a chorus of salutations. He pulled

over a yellow-lined pad of paper for notes. More old school. He grinned and picked up his pencil.

"So, I got a list of two dozen juvies the judge thinks we may be able to make a difference with."

"He knows we only go about a forty percent success rate, Al?" Darnell Franklin was an Overtown detective, working primarily Breaking-and-Entry crimes, and thirteen of these kids were from his beat. His status as a second level high school All American running back made him a great role model for their program.

"I gave him all the stats," Warner said. "I also told him about our successes. They aren't all Carlo Delgados, goin' to college on a full scholarship, but we got some pretty good results.

Anyhow," He scribbled Franklin's name on his pad, "Darnell, ya checked out the camp site? How's it lookin'?"

"Pretty overgrown. Al. It's the 'Glades, after all. Nothing that a half-day's work with our campers can't fix. Sweating their balls off and a bunch of bug bites usually sets the tone."

This elicited a chorus of chuckles.

"Okay." He made a check mark by Franklin's name. "Ben, ya got the tents, cots, and field kitchen queued up?"

"Sitting in a storage locker, Al. If some of those kids are in my beat, I'll spring them from detention on a day pass, and put 'em to work mending a few tears in the canvas and cleaning up the gear. Be a good warm up for 'em."

"Sounds like a plan." Warner scrawled a note. "Hector, what about provisions? Ya got the funds ya need?"

"All taken care of. With the private donations we've raised and a stipend from the county, we've got a twenty-seven-hundred-dollar excess, even after I bought the supplies. Everything'll be waiting for us at Publix when we're ready to go."

"Good. That after ya got funds to Jorge for the pants and

shirts? I gotta get him size info for each kid." Warner snickered. "We're gonna look like a regular summer camp."

"The quasi-uniforms are a clever idea, Al, especially for Jorge's gang-bangers. Gives them a feeling of belonging to something."

"Okay. So, looks like we got the bases covered, and all we need is a starting date. Any suggestions?" Warner eased back and cradled the phone on his shoulder.

"Four consecutive weekend sessions again, Al?" Hector asked.

"That's always been the routine. If we can't motivate these kids to pursue a real future by then, they're probably a lost cause." Grunted agreements echoed over the line.

"How about three weeks from this comin' Friday? That work for everyone?"

He heard a chorus of agreement from his three fellow detectives.

"Okay, so that's it. Hopefully, I'll have this thing with Unger and the missin' and murdered hookers tied up by then. Which brings me to a request." He was greeted by eerie silence.

"This missin' detective is my department, but it smacks of something larger. She's under cover and may be in serious shit. We got the whole department and the Fibbies on it, but I wanna ask you guys to keep your ears open too." He paused. "I'm gonna text you each a radio frequency for her tracker. Get it out to your guys in the field and help us listen for it." He sighed.

"Could be low on battery, so if it pings anywhere, we gotta pinpoint it ASAP. These perps killed at least three hookers we know of, and I don't want Detective Unger added to that list. Okay?"

Each detective answered, promising to get their bosses to

put it at the top of their guys' list. A cop in danger took priority in every department.

After final goodbyes, Warner slouched back and massaged his eyes. Nothing more to do at the moment on their current case, and at least now he could concentrate on something positive: turning juvies and gangbangers into useful citizens.

So far, they'd succeeded with twenty-seven out of seventy-six kids they'd run through their Dade County Boot Camp. Mostly minority kids who were usually the first in their families to finish high school, with nineteen going on to college, and the other eight into trade schools and apprentice programs.

It was tough, often unrewarding work, but kids like Carlo Delgado made it all worthwhile. He sighed again and sat up, addressing a pile of reports clustered on his desk.

He had two other murders to solve besides the hooker case, and they needed to be assigned.

As he jotted detectives' names on sticky notes and attached them to the two files, his thoughts drifted to Eva and their quest to produce a child. It was an enjoyable assignment, making love every day during her fertile period.

His grin slipped away, remembering the last time they tried and the nearly deadly interference of Ron Bachelor, that crazy killer. He shook his head, returning his attention to the two cases he was about to dish out. He could think of no one out there looking to punish him that way again.

Right now, finding Detective Unger was priority number one. He gathered up the files and headed to the bullpen. They were still beating the bushes, but his hopes hung on her somehow activating that tracker.

Without that, they were up the proverbial creek without a paddle.

~ 45 ~

Nicki glanced up, then patted the bed beside her. "Take a load off, Kiesha. Prowling around isn't gonna get you anywhere."

The girl halted her pacing and jammed her hands on her hips, staring at the undercover detective. "What's that Russian bitch doing out there? She makes me nervous." She moved over and settled beside Nicki.

"Yeah, I get it. Me, too." She covered the girl's hand with hers. "I think that's one of the bosses, telling her it's time."

"Time?" Her brown eyes flared. "Time for what?" The pinched expression on her lovely face belied a question she really knew the answer to.

"I suspect we're about to move into the main house and start earning our keep." Nicki saw the girl's eyes flood. "Have you recovered from whatever prodding around they did inside during our physicals?"

"Huh?" Kiesha produced a tissue and dabbed her eyes. "Oh yeah. Pretty much back to normal yesterday." Her eyes plumbed Nicki's. "Any idea what they did to us?" She glided fingers over the small incision.

Nicki shook her head. "I'm afraid to think about it. Maybe not too serious, with only some moderate pain for three days." She hitched around, gathering up both of the girl's hands, not ready to share her suspicions.

"You gotta start psyching yourself up for what's coming, kid. This is gonna be harder for you, 'cause you weren't in 'the business,' selling yourself for sex." Nicki chucked her under the chin, raising her fallen eyes to hers.

Taken

"According to that gal, Sheri, who stopped by last week, we're expected to be eager and passionate lovers...or else! Put your mind with someone you really care about, or you're not gonna last here." She sighed.

"And I suspect, you being Black and beautiful will get a lot of attention from bastards who need to pay for the action."

Kiesha covered her mouth with a hand and mewed.

Nicki ached for the girl's pain, more even than for her own. After all, she *did* willingly sign up for this. She hesitated, then discarded the notion of telling Kiesha who she was and that help may be coming if she could only get that tracker activated. Maybe because she was moving over, Olga would return her lipstick tube. She'd try, anyhow.

A rattle at the door drew both their eyes, and a moment later, hulking Olga lumbered through, a wicked smile curling her lips.

"So, my little sheep, you leave me now for the playpen. Finally, I get some rest." She regarded them, arms crossed over her massive bosom, then reached out and gently pinched Kiesha's cheek.

"And you, our little black sheep, you gonna have lots of horny rams chasing you." She gave a throaty chuckle.

Kiesha's eyes spilled tears, and she batted away the offending hand.

Olga snarled and raised her fist, then hesitated. "*Nyet.* Cannot send over bruised merchandise. Not good for the business." She stepped back.

"But remember, bitch, that's what you are... merchandise. We *own* you." She turned. "Get ready. They come in ten minutes." She waived a hand. "Take nothing, not even tooth brushes. They give you everything... the best stuff." She barked a hoarse laugh.

"Be good little sheep, and life not so bad here. But make trouble—" She looked back, face twisted into a snarl, then shook her head.

"Olga." Nicki edged forward, knowing this might be her last chance to fulfill her mission. *The batteries on the tracker may not last much longer.*

"My lipstick? It's special to me. Can I—?"

"What? That fancy little gold one with the red top?"

"Yeah. It was a gift from my father. Can't you—?"

"Is on my table, looking nice. Is a pretty color, huh?"

"Uh-huh. Did you try it?" *Maybe she already...*

"Nyet. I don't use. Anyhow, I tell you they give you everything over there. Best cosmetics for your dates." She chuckled. "I keep it." Olga smirked and turned toward the exit.

Damn! *I've gotta find a way to activate that tracker, then hope the battery is still good and someone is in range to pick it up.*

The Russian slammed the door behind her, and Nicki turned to a weeping Kiesha, sighed, and gave her a fierce hug.

"Keep your chin up kid and play along. Somehow, we're gonna get out of this."

~~~

The two new arrivals followed a young blond woman up the stairs inside the bigger building, marveling at the luxurious appointments. Nicki conceded reluctant respect for these crooks. The decrepit, falling-down exterior was a clever disguise for this opulent interior. No one flying over or buzzing by in an airboat could possibly imagine what lay within.

Nicki studied their erotically decked out escort and realized she was one of the "working girls." She reached out and touched her shoulder.

"You been here long?"

Her head swiveled, her green eyes unemotional. "Fourteen months. You'll get used to it."

Taken

They'd reached the second level and traversed a long hallway lined with paneled doors, each numbered. She paused in front of "6."

"This is your room. You'll probably remain as roommates." She pushed open the door.

Nicki stepped in and studied their new digs: a mini-suite with a living room and apparently two small bedrooms.

Girls needed privacy if they were going to entertain lovers.

"One of the managers will come by to orient you," the blonde said. "Meanwhile, take a shower, wash your hair, use a little perfume, and then pick out some outfits from the closet." She glanced over her shoulder, then drew them both inside and spoke softly.

"I know you're probably scared, and certainly angry. You're here against your will, to be used as sex toys." She gripped Kiesha's shoulder, sensing her panic.

"The only way to survive here is to act as an enthusiastic lover to whoever you're assigned to." She gave the girl a gentle shake. "Resist, or even be just mechanical, and you'll disappear. Gone from here—and the world—without a trace."

She sighed and released her hands. "Life here is what you make it. Fit in and you'll be well-fed, well-clothed, and mostly well-cared-for."

She paused, hands on her hips. "Surprisingly, some of us have even developed regulars from the clientele... guys you may actually enjoy seeing. Men who treat you like a girlfriend." She started for the door, looking back.

"I don't know what your stories were on the outside, but accept this reality and you'll probably find life here better than hooking on the streets or working some raunchy massage parlor."

"No one ever gets to go outside?" Nicki asked.

"Why would you want to? Not in the summer, anyhow. Hot, sticky, and mosquitos by the thousands." She shrugged.

"Nothing to see, and nowhere to go."

With that, the woman, whose name they'd never learned, was gone.

Kiesha turned toward Nicki, tears sliding across her high cheekbones. The detective gathered the girl in her arms, gently patting her back.

"Be brave, hon, and get tough-minded. You *can* do this. You *must* do this! I really believe we're gonna get out of here, but you gotta survive now if you're gonna have any chance to make it." Nicki pushed back, searching Kiesha's dark eyes.

"I've got a plan I'll tell you about later, but now I gotta figure how to get back into the dorm. I left something there I need."

"What?" Kiesha's voice a panicked squeak. "You can't. They'll catch you and... Whatever it is, forget it. You—"

"I'll be careful, but it's very important." She headed for the bathroom and found what she needed there.

~ 46 ~

Nicki returned and took Kiesha's hands.

"I think I can get out through the bathroom window. No bars or anything because they're not worried we're gonna get away, but it's gonna be a tight squeeze." She took the girl's chin and locked eyes.

"If someone comes for us before I get back, try to stall them." She glanced at a wall clock. "I probably got twenty, thirty minutes." She picked a gossamer outfit from the closet and hurried off.

The bathroom window was small, an awning-type with a crank-to-open handle, but Nicki was narrow-hipped. And she was a trained black belt athlete. She hung the little lacy nothing on a hook on the back of the door, ready to don when—(*if*)—she returned in time.

She climbed onto on the toilet bowel, spun then handle to maximum opening, and removed the screen, dropping it to floor inside. She sucked in a breath, grabbed the sill, and facing the ceiling, hoisted herself up, head first through the opening. This style window was going to make this a tight fit. *Very* tight.

Half-way through her hips, slim as they were, still wedged too snugly. Backing in a bit, Nicki twisted her body on an angle and tried again.

Just enough to clear and... goddammit. Her jumper snagged on a protruding screw head, stalling her progress. She wiggled and twisted but couldn't proceed or retreat.

I'm fucking stuck! Two precious minutes fled by with no progress, and her arms were tiring. She was about to try again when the sound of male voices froze her. Swiveling her head, she spied two men, black-clad, and carrying AK47s. She never expected guards patrolling the grounds in such a remote local.

Nicki held motionless, taking quiet, shallow breaths as the men passed below. If either looked up, she was toast. They paused as one lit a cigarette and exhaled a plume of smoke, his head tilted back. Though his eyes were focused away, any motion by a woman, stuck half out of a second-story window, might catch his peripheral vision.

Her arms vibrated from the strain of holding her position as she struggled to remain silent. Then, still talking softly, the two guards started off. Nicki exhaled a soft gasp of pent-up breath as she watched them about to disappear around the corner of the building, but then one of the men paused.

"Did you hear something?" He tugged the other's sleeve.

"No, what? Ain't nothing to hear out here but the birds and the bugs."

"No, I heard something else back there. Sort of a hiss." He started back, his head on a constant swivel.

"C'mon, Jake. It was probably one of those big snakes. I seen two in the last few days." He glanced at his watch. "It's break time, and I need a cold one. Tromping around in this heat and humidity is a fucking bitch."

"Yeah, but I'm pretty sure I heard something..." He stopped directly under where Nicki hung, half out of the window.

I'm screwed. No way that other guy's not gonna see me.

But he was looking down, adjusting his cartridge belt. "C'mon already. You're chasing ghosts."

"Yeah, okay," Jake said. "I don't see nothing." He strode back toward his partner. "Let's get outta this fucking heat." They turned the corner and were finally gone.

Nicki relaxed and shook out her cramping arms as her jackhammering heart slowed back to a normal beat. She grunted and shook her head, trying to dispel frustration.

Gotta get moving, or I'm gonna run out of time.

She gritted her teeth, gulped a breath, and rammed forward with all her strength, finally rending free with the sound of ripping fabric. The violence of her thrust hurled her through the opening, plummeting downward headfirst. Quick reaction painfully hooked the sill with the back of her knees and prevented an upside-down crash to the ground and a disastrous blow to the head.

Damn, that was close.

She hung for a moment, catching her breath and steadied her nerves. Then she jack-knifed up, thanks to strong abs and superb flexibility, and snagged the sill with her hands to draw her feet through the window. Lowered to her full length, she dropped the last foot to a small ledge. A second drop from there put her on the ground.

She crouched, panting, glanced up, and hoped she could return the way she'd come... if she didn't get caught first. She heard the shower above go on. Kiesha was going through the motions to get ready.

Good girl.

Her eyes scanned the other building, just a hundred feet away. Olga's room was on the opposite side from their dormitory. Nicki had gotten a peek at its door as they'd departed for the main house. With no one left to tend to, Olga had followed them to their new quarters, so, hopefully, it'd be vacant.

Gotta be a window there, too. Nicki stayed low and scampered through waist-high swamp grass toward the back of the other building. Half-way there, rustling in the grass froze her.

Who the hell else is sneaking around back here? She dropped to one knee. *Fight or flight?* Neither was a good option, and—

Holy shit!

She lurched back, landing on her butt and shimmying backward. The head of a twelve-foot-long python reared up, beady, onyx-black eyes riveted on her, its red tongue darting in and out. Nicki barely stifled a scream. She *hated* snakes, and these monsters had taken over the Everglades, decimating its natural wildlife.

Her heart thundering in her breast, she drew her feet under her, ready to flee, guards be damned. The reptile studied her for a moment, then began slithering toward her, its huge head bobbing and weaving. She scrabbled around, desperate for a stick, a rock, or *anything* to defend herself with. She couldn't split without being seen.

Too late! The creature arched back and struck.

Nicki threw up her hands to no avail, because the beast had latched onto a large rodent, maybe a possum, which cowered close by in the grass. The struggling animal in its jaws, the apex predator receded into the deeper grass to enjoy her meal.

Nicki sucked in a couple of ragged breaths, knuckled tears from her eyes, and rolled into a crouch. For the second time in six-minutes, she had to rein in her galloping heart. Breathing normalized, she scanned the area, head cocked, listening for any other movement, but found none. Precious minutes wasted. She had to get moving or she'd never succeed. She rose on wobbly legs, her heart still working over her ribs, and again started for the other building.

She reached the corner and slipped along the wall toward where she envisioned Olga's room to be. There, a conventional double-hung window. She eased to its edge and peeked in. Olga's bedroom, and as expected, it was empty.

Nicki scoured the interior through the glass: a queen-size bed, double nightstands, an overstuffed armchair, and a small dresser with a TV on top. She spied a VCR and a stack of tapes atop the dresser.

Her internal clock said she'd spent over ten minutes to get here, so she had to hustle. Her eyes again swept the area and she listened for any motion or sound, but heard nothing but the chirp of insects. Returning her attention to the window, the screen came off, and she studied the lock, easily opened if she had a knife or thin piece of metal. Unfortunately, she did not.

She scoured the ground, ever mindful of possible patrolling guards, and searched for something she could use, finally coming up with an eight-inch twisted piece of perforated metal strapping. Not great, but it might do, but another two minutes spent.

Voices again!

Nicki dropped flat, thankful her green jump suit wouldn't stand out against the grass. She held her breath as two guards strolled by. How could they miss her, not fifteen feet away? The knee-high grass was her only cover. Busy in conversation, they never glanced in her direction, and a minute later, they were gone.

She sat up, wondering how much her heart could take? Her breathing getting back to normal, she addressed the piece of metal, which she straightened and flattened between two scavenged stones, making more noise than she wanted. Finished, she tried to insert it between the upper and lower window frames.

Too tight.

She again rubbed the metal between the stones, attempting to remove any burrs and thin out the aluminum strap. A second try, and although snug, she forced the strip into the opening.

Ideally, this was done with a thin, steel blade. All she had was a too-thick, not so rigid piece of aluminum, and it wasn't working very well.

Nicki sighed, and checked again for danger. Seeing no one, she went back to work.

Been at least seventeen minutes. I'm running outta time and if I can't—Shit!

She'd moved the latch about halfway and then the strap cracked. She drew it out and ripped off the damaged piece, cutting her index finger in the process.

Goddammit, this has gotta work, and NOW!

She wrapped the bleeding digit with a tissue and repositioned the metal near the lock, but with only about six inches left to work with, it was a struggle.

Frustrated, she thumped the frame with a fist... and the lock popped open!

Sonofabitch! About time.

She eased the sill up, listened but heard nothing, so she climbed through. One step and a pause.

Damn! Now what?

She glanced down and saw her shoes were caked with sand. She sat, removed them, and clapped them together out the window, making more noise than she wanted, then left them balanced on the sill.

Nicki strode to the dresser and scanned its top. No gold tube. A quick examination of the dual nightstands proved fruitless. Precious minutes flew by with no success. She paused and listened. They may already be looking for her.

She shrugged, then hurried into Olga's bathroom and searched the counter and sink top. Nothing. A peek into the medicine cabinet was fruitless.

Where the fuck did she put it? I don't think she had it on her. Rifling the cabinet drawers was unsuccessful. Dropping to her knees, she opened the two doors under the sink, but only found bottles and a box of bandages. She snatched two bandages and covered her wounded finger, which had bled through the tissue she'd wrapped it in. She didn't want to leave blood stains on the carpet that may expose her visit. The tissue and wrappers went down the toilet.

~ 47 ~

Returning to the bedroom she paused, hands on hips, and once again scanned the room. There, a small jewelry box she'd missed, by the TV. She flipped it open and there, nestled among a pearl neckless and some broaches, was the glint of gold: the missing tube.

Nicki plucked it up, snatched off the cap, and wound the stem, raising the lipstick. She gulped air and prayed she wasn't too late, and that the battery was still good. She receded the lipstick, capped it, and returned it to the box.

Back in the bathroom, she snatched a handful of toilet paper, and hurried to the window. The sand she'd brought in on her shoes was quickly wiped up. Not perfect, but hopefully, not noticeable either.

She raced back to the bathroom to flush it down the toilet, then froze. Voices, and the click of the door lock. Olga was coming! Nicki's eyes swept the room. If the Russian hulk came in, she was a goner.

"Tell Rex I be right back. I do something first to fuck with that cocky bitch." Her words were followed by a nasty chuckle.

Shit! Now what? I could try to kill her and make it back undetected. She shook her head. *Not much chance that'll work.*

She glanced at the tub and shower curtain. *My only chance.* She tiptoed over and slipped inside, quietly adjusting the flower-decorated plastic screen, and squatted behind it, ready to spring up and do battle if necessary.

The matron rummaged around in the bedroom, and Nicki prayed she would find whatever she was looking for and leave.

"Ha. Here it is. I gonna piss her off, big time." A moment later, she lumbered into the bathroom and paused in front of the sink.

What the fuck is she...

Oh, shit! The window's still open and my damned shoes are sitting on the sill. If she notices that...

Nicki shuddered. If they killed her, she'd still managed to activate the tracer, so all wouldn't be entirely in vain. Not much solace if she were dead.

"Now, what's that bitch gonna think of this?"

Nicki shifted quietly and peeked around the curtain. Olga was admiring her reflection, an act of hubris, holding Nicki's gold lipstick tube, the pale pink gloss smeared across her lips.

Sonofabitch! She'd used it! All the danger she'd embraced to bring the law proved unnecessary. Nicki shook her head, making a silent chuckle. Olga was sure to notice the window when she left.

"Okay. Now I go and rub in the salt." The matron pocketed the tube and turned to leave. She paused, cast her eyes around the room, hands on her hips, shrugged, and exited.

Nicki was quickly out of the tub and at the door, gripping a ceramic bottle of bodywash as a club, ready to pounce. She peeped around the jamb in time to see Olga going through her door with never a look around the room. The open window had gone unnoticed.

A pent-up breath hissed between her lips, and she slumped against the doorframe, shaking and slick with sweat.

"Damn, that was close," she mumbled, then, despite her tension, chuckled at the irony of events.

She shrugged, strode back to the bathroom to flush away the sandy toilet paper, and was out the window, closing it behind. No way to lock it, but Olga would probably think she'd left it that way. She slipped on her shoes and scurried back toward her window.

"Hey, you!"

Oh, shit, now what?

She froze and turned. It was one of the guys who worked at the dorm she'd just left.

"What are you doing out here?" He strode up to her, arms crossed. "You're supposed to be in the main building, getting ready. We got clients coming any minute."

"Sorry. I've been cooped up so long, I just wanted a look around the island."

"Yeah, well, it's not allowed." He grabbed her arm. "Let's find Rex, and see what he says."

He started to draw her after him, and she pulled back. She might talk her way out of this and just suffer some discipline... or he'd kill her. She couldn't chance it.

"Wait." She yanked free, and as he turned, she delivered a hard blow to his windpipe with the back edge of her flattened hand. He staggered, choking, gasping for breath. She snatched his shirt and smacked the heel of her right hand hard against the bottom of his nose, driving the cartilage back into his brain—a kill shot.

Nicki caught his limp body, glanced around, and seeing no one else, carried him into the tall grass. She hesitated, then hurried through a copse of trees and found the water of the swamp. She dumped the body in a bed of reeds.

Still no one around, so she raced toward the window to her new room. She'd been gone way too long, but whatever happened now, at least the signal was going. Hopefully, help was on the way.

She arrived at the wall and glance up. No commotion, so maybe her absence hadn't yet been discovered. She gathered into a crouch and leaped, snatching at the lower ledge.

Yow! The stab of pain to her injured finger was far worse than expected, and she lost her grip, tumbling to the ground.

Shit, that hurt!

The bandage was gone and the wound bled profusely. She sucked off the blood, heedless of grime, and fished out a spare binding and rewrapped it.

Gotta get moving, and come up with a story if I'm caught.

Nicki studied the wall and realized its rickety feature provided possible hand and footholds. Mindful of her painful finger, she worked her way high enough to grab the first ledge and lever up.

Hugging the wall, she pulled to her feet. Head craned back, she studied the windowsill, about a foot beyond her reach. Normally an easy jump, but coming from a narrow ledge with minimal purchase complicated things. A missed grip would drop her a good ten feet, with likely injury. A cut finger could be accounted for, but scraped shins or a sprained ankle would be harder to explain.

She sighed, gritted her teeth, and made the leap. Her left hand snagged the sill, but she dangled precariously until able to make purchase with three fingers of the right. Gulping a breath, she began the pull up, and hoped getting back through would be easier than getting out.

Then she heard voices coming from her room.

Fuck! Hold 'em off, Kiesha, 'til I make it inside.

She'd wiggled half-way through the window, still a tight fit, when the voices got louder.

"She's in the bathroom, getting cleaned up." Kiesha's voice was strained. "Give the girl some privacy."

The locked door rattled, sending goosebumps across Nicki's back as she struggled for entry. Suddenly freed, she surged through the opening and tumbled to the floor with a thump.

"What's going on in there?" A woman's voice.

"Slipped on a wet floor," Nicki rasped. "I'm okay."

"Well, get ready. I'll be back in a few to prep you. One of the bosses will be by soon to inspect you guys, and you wanna be ready."

"Okay. Thanks. We got it." Nicki exhaled a pent-up breath and perched on the toilet.

Well, no matter what happens now, the signal's gone live... if the battery is still good. All we can do is hope.

Exhausted, she lurched to her feet and went to the door to see how Kiesha was holding up.

Then she needed a shower.

~ 48 ~

Al Warner pushed away from his desk and rose, tossing a file he was reading onto its scarred oaken surface. The conundrum was, while he loved controlling murder investigations as Chief of Detectives, he hated being chained to a desk so much. He relished field work, hunting crazy killers, bringing them down. He grunted and paced around his office, one hand tracing the X-shaped scars on his skull above his right ear, hidden under a mop of curly dark hair.

He'd scrimmaged with seven world-class baddies in the past five years and had luckily come out alive each time, but bringing down those loonies was his calling... the thing he lived for. And now he was tussling with number eight, and they had one of his detectives.

Something's gotta pop...

He jerked to a stop and spun around as his door clattered open and Jack Harris burst into the room.

"We got it. Boss. We got it!" He was breathless, his face flushed.

"Got what, Jack?" He grabbed the smaller man's shoulders, yanking him to a halt. "What are ya talkin' about?"

"Unger's tracker went live about fifteen minutes ago. I just got word from—"

"Settle down, Detective, and tell me what we know." Warner's heart raced as he fought to stay calm. It was about time!

"A sheriff's Cessna picked up the signal somewhere over the northern 'Glades just east of the Collier County line."

"They get a fix on it?"

"Working on it now. They sent a second plane to try to triangulate the location." He rubbed his hands together. "The signal is kinda weak, but they're working on it up in Tech."

"Okay, I'll head up there now." He retrieved his shield and Glock. "You get Olvida and the team fired up." He paused just outside his door as Harris hurried by.

"Jack, contact whoever is on point with SWAT. We're gonna need one of their teams, too."

"On it, Boss," and he disappeared through the doorway.

Warner scanned the bullpen. Four detectives still at desks. He started for the door and the stairway up to Tech.

"Beck," he yelled over his shoulder. "You're with me."

"Coming, Boss." The detective jumped up from his desk and trailed after Warner who was already taking the stairs two-at-a-time.

Warner shoved through the half-glass paneled door and spotted three officers plying keyboards and staring at monitors. He strode to Chuck, the department's head guy, hunched over his computer. Warner lay a hand on his shoulder.

"What d'ya got?" He glanced at the screen, displaying a Google Earth view of a desolate swampland.

"Still triangulating, but the signal is pretty weak. Gotta be in that general area, though." He nodded at the display. "We're scanning for any kind of structure."

"Any roads or even trails in the area?" Warner drew over a chair and perched on its edge.

"Nothing I've seen, Boss. Looks like the only access would be airboats. Not sure you could get in there with a conventional craft." He clicked at his keyboard. "I'm going to see if I can get a real time satellite image." He glanced at Warner. "The BAU team gave me the codes the FBI uses."

Warner nodded and withdrew his cell phone. "Shit! It's

out in the middle of Hell-and-gone."

He hit auto dial. Harris answered on the third ring.

"I got SWAT on the other line, Boss."

"Okay. We might need a chopper and their team to rappel onto the scene. And contact Fish and Wildlife. Looks like we're gonna need a few airboats with their pilots to get us out there." He glanced again at the monitor. "This place is gonna be in the middle of nowhere, and I wanna hit 'em from the water and the air simultaneously." He straightened and rubbed the back of his neck.

"No tellin' what kind of resistance we're gonna run into."

"On it, Boss, soon as I set up SWAT, I'll get onto F and W."

"Okay. If we can we pinpoint the location, we'll organize the strike." He disconnected and turned to Detective Beck.

"Dean, see if ya can find Major Conklin. He heads the Organized Gangs squad, and I worked with him when we took down those terrorists last year. We may need some of his guys for this strike."

"You expecting heavy resistance?" Beck began paging through his Contacts list on his phone.

"This looks like a big, well-organized operation. Bound to have some muscle on hand. I ain't takin' any chances." He turned back to the Tech supervisor.

"C'mon, Chuck. I need a positive fix. What d'ya got?"

"That's the area. This is real-time satellite images now." He gestured at the display. "Not much there, other than a few deserted islands surrounded by swampland."

Warner studied the screen. "What's that?" He pointed toward the largest one. "Looks like some sort of structure." He tapped the man on the shoulder.

"Can ya zoom in?"

"Yeah, I think so." He began working the keyboard. The image blossomed until that one scant piece of land filled the screen.

"Looks like two shacks fallen into ruin. Doesn't seem a likely—"

"Look." Warner hovered a finger close to the glass. "Ain't that a pier or some sorta dock?"

"I guess, but it's also pretty rickety." He glanced at Warner. "How could they run what you suspect's going on in that—?"

"'Cause that looks like an airboat on the beach." He caught his breath. "And *there,* someone just walked out of that smaller structure." Warner sprang up, still staring at the monitor.

"Airboats, and people moving between dilapidated buildings!" He spun toward the door.

"We *got* 'em, goddammit. Get me the GPS coordinate," and he was flying down the stairs, Beck hot on his heels. He dialed Harris.

"We got the bastards, Jack." He rushed into his office. "Get it teed up. I want the SWAT commander in my office in thirty, and Conklin on the phone." He grabbed a Kevlar vest from the closet.

"Tech'll have GPS coordinates for us." He glanced at his watch. "We got five hours 'til twilight, and I'm guessing it'll take at least three to get the teams on site. I want everyone locked and loaded and ready to go in no more'n sixty minutes."

"I'm on it, Boss, double-time. I promised Unger we'd have her back. I just hope the hell she's still safe."

They disconnected and went about the hurried business of planning a takedown of... what? They weren't really sure who or what they'd confront, but whatever it proved to be, Warner and his team would be right in the middle.

As usual!

~ 49 ~

As Maggie entered the lounge, she peeked over her shoulder. No sign of Sam or Hoek. She continued inside and spotted José behind the bar, polishing glasses. She gave him a come-hither nod before settling at her usual table.

He stowed four glasses and a furtive glance confirmed they were currently alone. He approached, trying to look casual but there was a nervous shuffle to his feet.

"Hey, Mags, how're you feeling?"

"Pretty good today, José." She patted her distended belly. "The kid's really warming up for a career as an NFL kicker, though." They shared a soft chuckle.

"What'll you have today?" He squatted beside her and lay a hand on her belly, his back toward the doorway.

"You up to making a break for it now, kid?" he whispered. "Gotta go soon, or it'll be too late."

"As ready as I'll ever be, I guess," she mumbled, barely moving her lips. Her eyes held his as he rose.

"I'll have a tonic and lime," she said aloud. "Join me when you're free and we can play some gin."

"Coming right up." He turned toward the bar. "I'm actually free now, so I'll bring the cards."

Maggie nodded, eased back in her chair, and winced as her active fetus tried to kick a fifty-yarder. Her lips morphed from a gentle smile into a grim clench, and tiny droplets bloomed in the corners of her eyes.

She'd agreed to this assignment for the hundred grand and a chance to get back on her feet, and now they were about to throw it away. Were these people really so dangerous, or did José just have an active imagination? Maybe his way to get close to her?

She shook her head and gave an almost silent groan. Despite her search for normalcy here, she *knew* José was right. The whole thing with Charlotte stunk. She'd overheard enough to know soomething was really rotten there.

But could these people actually have *killed* her and used the baby to blackmail some widow, as José said? And if they had, was she next? She shivered, goosebumps cascading down her spine.

She was jolted back to the present as José arrived with a tray, carrying two glasses of clear effervescent liquids, and a deck of playing cards. He settled beside her rather than across the table, so their backs were to the open doorway to the lobby.

"Are you sure about this?" she asked.

He nodded and lay his hand atop of hers.

"It seems so extreme." She glanced at him from the corners of her eyes. "To commit murder and blackmail..."

"People will do a lot for a million bucks, Maggie." He dealt two stacks of ten cards each and slid one in front of her. "I heard Hoek bitching to Sam yesterday that the widow they're blackmailing has gotten some influential guy involved, but they still expect to get paid."

"Jesus! I still can't believe it." Fingers slippery with sweat struggled to control her cards.

"Believe it, Babe." He sorted his own hand and drew one from the stack. "Also heard they've got another one lined up and they're looking for another volunteer."

"Volunteer? You mean someone like me?"

"Yeah, I guess. Probably not nearly as sweet as you, though." It was a feeble attempt to defuse tension.

She shivered, vacantly studying the fan of still unsorted

cards, clutched in her fingers, her mind a kaleidoscope of disparate thoughts.

Can these people really be so dangerous? Wicked enough to murder for money? She shook her head. *Yeah, I guess it's done all the time.* She glanced up, finding José's eyes riveted on her. *But if they are so evil, can we even get safely away?*

She absently sorted her hand, drew one from the deck, and discarded another, as she voiced that last thought to José.

"I got a plan I think's gonna work. You're gonna have to be sly and brave, but I think we can pull it off...today, right after lunch."

"Today?" The word a hissed squeak. "I'm... I'm not ready—"

"We can't delay, Mags." His fingers brushed across hers. "There's nothing to keep you here. Nothing to do before we split. The longer we wait, the harder it'll be, physically, for you." He peeked over his shoulder to verify they were still alone.

"You might have to move fast, and your little field goal kicker will make that tougher the longer we delay."

She sighed and plopped down her cards. "What do I have to do."

"Wear sneakers, and if you got pants that still fit, that would be best." He collected the cards and set them aside. "That metal drink container of yours, the one with the screw-on top, filled with some cold water, if you can manage it. Dress as if we're going for one of our walks."

"So, how's this gonna work, José?"

"Here's what I thought of." He leaned closer, his voice a whisper. "It's simple, but we gotta be precise..."

Three minutes later, all the details covered, Maggie struggled to her feet. *He's right. I'm not exactly nimble now, and this is gonna take some quick footwork.*

"Okay," she said, loud enough for possible eavesdroppers to hear. "I'm going to change into something more comfortable for our afternoon walk. See you after lunch."

He rose and nodded, winking, and she waddled off, exaggerating her clumsiness. If they were really going to do this, she had to wrap her mind around it. Get psyched.

She whined softly under her breath. *Say goodbye to those thousand Franklins, if they were even real. How am I gonna manage this kid, if it's all a hoax? Will I have to raise it?*

Going back to a strip club wouldn't cut it. If they got away safely, would she be with José afterwards? She hoped he'd become as fond of her as she was of him.

Time would tell.

~ 50 ~

Nicki sighed as she watched Kiesha dry off after her shower. Her obsidian skin, firm boobs, and small waist over a taut butt and shapely legs would make her a frequent pick here. She hoped the girl could keep it together until help came... *if* they picked up her tracker beacon.

Nicki sauntered into their parlor and opened the closet door. She stepped back, hands or her hips and couldn't help but admire the rack full of clearly expensive and very erotic outfits. The one she snatched without looking, prior to her foray out the bathroom window, was too small.

She hesitated, then selected the least revealing ensemble, a blue one-piece body suit, cut low in front and high on the sides, accented by a diaphanous robe of sheer, see-though silk. It was for Kiesha, and she hoped it might keep her out of the limelight compared to the rest of the very revealing duds.

She glanced over her shoulder as her new roommate entered, wrapped in a towel.

"Here." She hoisted the outfit on a hanger. "This seems like it might work for you." She nodded toward the closet. "It's about as demure as there is in there."

The girl accepted the hanger, rotating it as she inspected the scanty nothings. "Jesus, I'll look like a whore in this."

"That's their idea, hon." Nicki pulled the girl to her and wrapped an arm around her shoulder. "You're one of the few here who *wasn't* a hooker prior to being snatched. The clients are coming to this joint looking for a high-class babe."

The girl sank onto the loveseat, the clothing puddled on her lap, tears streaming down her cheeks. "I... I don't think I can do this. It's... it's..."

Nicki settled beside her and took her hands.

Poor kid. Can I give her hope that we're gonna be rescued... if someone picked up that tracker signal?

She studied the girls face, then set her jaw, making what could prove to be a dangerous decision. She put her hand under Kiesha's chin, raising the girl's eyes to hers.

"Look. I'm gonna tell you something that's... that's dangerous for you to know. Dangerous for *both* of us. It's to give you hope and something to hang onto, but if you let this out—even hint at it—we'll both be killed out of hand."

"Oh god!" She pulled back and swiped the moisture off her cheeks. "Tell me! Tell me. I feel so lost." Her eyes stayed locked on Nicki's.

"I'm an undercover cop." Her voice was a bare whisper. "I got snatched on purpose to try to locate this place. A tracker signal was finally just activated—"

"A signal?" Her eyes flared and one hand covered her mouth. "How—"

"Shhh." Her head was on a swivel. "They could have the room wired." She glanced back at the girl. "My lipstick tube. That's where I went, to Olga's room, to activate it." She peeked over her shoulder at a knock on the door.

Shit! "Help's on the way," she whispered, "but it may take a day or two for them to organize—" She stopped as the door opened, admitting Sheri. Nicki rose, eyes narrowed, and she hissed from the corner of her mouth, "Tell *no* one, or we're dead."

"Hi, guys." The blonde stepped into the room. "I'm back to see how're doing, getting ready for your debut." She picked the hanger from Kiesha's lap. "This is nice." She handed it back. "But whatever you wear, nothing's gonna hide your assets from the johns." She folded her arms across her barely covered breasts.

"You gotta get your head around what's gonna happen, and get prepared. Either Boss Rex or the witch, Morgana, are gonna stop by in ten or fifteen, so you better be decked out and dolled up. They got a boat full of clients arriving soon, and they'll want you downstairs, ready to entertain."

"We just got here." Kiesha fought off tears.

"I know, and it's a tough deal, especially for you, not being a working girl, but it is what it is." Sheri stroked Kiesha's raven hair. "You gotta be an enthusiastic lover to whoever picks you, or you're gonna end up floating face down somewhere out in the 'Glades."

"Jesus!" Kiesha dropped her head in her hands.

"It could be worse... a lot worse." Sheri perched on a chair. "The guys, and occasionally girls, mostly treat you like a girlfriend. The bosses here don't allow any rough stuff." She crossed shapely legs. "If you're lucky, you'll find a regular, who may even bring gifts." She displayed a Rolex watch. "Not much use here, but it shows he cares. If they're really hot for you, they can pay to keep you exclusively theirs, but that's rare."

Kiesha sighed and clenched her jaw. She had to get through this until Nicki's cavalry arrives. "What about condoms?"

"No condoms." Sheri made a wry chuckle. "The johns pay top buck for the full girlfriend experience."

"No *condoms?* I don't want to get pregnant."

"None of us do, kid." She sighed. "You had a physical exam over there?" She nodded toward the other building.

"Yes, but—"

"Knocked you out, didn't they?"

"Yes." Kiesha nodded. "but—"

"And they poked a little hole in your belly, right?"

Another silent nod from both women.

Sheri rose. "And that's when they tied your tubes."

"*What?*" Said in unison.

"A pregnant girl is of little use to them. At least they don't seem to take out your ovaries. Probably too much recovery time. Tied tubes can be undone, but what diff does it make?" She started for the door.

"You're never getting outta here no how." She paused at the entrance. "Get prepped. You're up for inspection any time now. Better not screw up your first time outta the box." And she was gone, closing the door behind her.

The two women looked at each other, eyes wide. Nicki shook her head, and moved toward the closet, looking for her own outfit. If—no, *when*—rescue came, these bastards were going to pay. She glanced at the other girl.

"Hang onto the fact that help's coming, Kiesha," her voice again a whisper. "Picture your hottest boyfriend and take your mind there. Make love to him in your head and you'll be okay." She studied the girl. "Don't fumble the ball when we're near the goal line."

I just hope Jack Harris and his team are on the way. I can get through this, but I'm not so sure about this poor, innocent babe.

Ten minutes later, as both girls finished up lipstick and eye liners at a well-stocked make-up table, a tall, fit-looking, fortyish guy strode into the room. His navy-blue suit, cuff-linked shirt, and red-striped preppy tie, seemed out of place out in the middle of a steamy swamp. The lips of his heavily tanned face tilted into a crooked smile as he appraised them.

"Ahh." His gaze swept over Nicki, and then he turned to Kiesha. His fingers under her chin raised her eyes to his.

"Even better than I hoped." Grasping her upper arm, he drew her to her feet, his pink tongue darting across his lips.

"You're too fucking gorgeous to share with some vacuous dilettante." He leaned down and kissed her, molding her to him.

After a moment of fluttering indecision, her long arms circled his neck, and remembering Sheri's admonishment and Nicki's advice, she sent her mind away and responded with forced passion.

His head tilted back, his eyes sparkling, and his tongue swiped his gloss-stained lips.

"*Fantastic!*" He took her hand and started toward a bedroom. "I'm gonna keep you for myself. You're the first babe here that's lit my fire. So fucking exotic!" He glanced at Nicki, still perched at the makeup table.

"You. Get downstairs and make some guy happy. Five new clients just arrived. Ebony, here..." He stroked her cheek. "That's your new name, hon. Ebony." He looked back at Nicki, who'd started hesitantly toward the door.

"Anyway, Ebony and I are gonna have our own party here, so stay away. Ask Morgana to send up a bottle of champagne. And tell her we're gonna have to find one more replacement for my new mistress. We'll move her stuff over to my suite later." He caught Kiesha's eyes.

"You're not gonna make me regret this are you, Ebony?"

Her hand on the back of his slicked dark hair, she pulled him down for the sweetest kiss she could muster, her eyes closed. "Never."

He mistook her sigh for pleasure, rather than the resignation that fired it.

If Nicki's rescuers never show, this has gotta be better than servicing a bunch of different guys. She shuddered and ground her teeth, accepting the inevitable. *If he treats me right, I can do this.* She dropped her gaze and blinked away tears pooling in her eyes.

If I'm stuck here forever, I gotta try to find a way to love this guy, or at least pretend to, or I'll never survive. Like Stockholm syndrome. If we do get out of here, that'll be a different story. It's gonna be easier to hate him than love him, that's for sure.

The bedroom door closed behind them as they kissed, tongues darting, fingers teasing explorers. Pelvises plastered together, she felt his hardness. He began peeling away her outfit, his lips cruising across her raven skin, tweaking a nipple and sending unexpected goosebumps galloping down her back. She was quickly naked and his clothing shed.

He slipped onto the bed and pulled her atop of him, his fingers and tongue busy wanderers.

Jesus, I gotta do this.

Her eyes closed, she responded with faux passion she hoped he didn't recognize as forced. Heeding Sheri's advice, she put her body on autopilot, her thoughts spiraling away to happier times.

If help didn't come, this would be her life.

Make the best of it, and survive.

No home, no school, not the modeling career she'd sought. No, this was sexual slavery.

Survive, and hope for a better day.

Survive!

~ 51 ~

Warner hurried through the doorway of Conference Room Two, a manila folder in hand. His eyes swept the six people seated around the rectangular table as he settled in a chair at one end.

"I just finished up with SWAT Commander Kontos. He's organizing a six-man team and talkin' to the Coast Guard about using their Blackhawk rescue 'copter."

"They don't have anything of their own for this, Boss?" Harris asked.

"Nothin' with the range, carryin' six men, I guess. It's gonna be about seventy-five miles from the SWAT heliport to what we believe is the target." He leaned forward. "We'll call 'em ta depart when we're about thirty out so they don't have ta hover outta range 'til we can get there in airboats." He looked at Detective Olvida.

"And what *is* the skinny on those airboats, Ralph?"

"Been working on it, Boss." He glanced at his Android. "Fish and Wildlife's only got one operational at the moment, and he can only carry three of us with gear."

"That ain't enough." He glanced at Special Agent in Charge, Pauletti. "I know our FBI friends wanna be there, and I especially like havin' Agent Yeager handy with her long gun skills." He nodded to her. "She's saved my ass at least twice in the last couple of years." Warner shifted his gaze to Agent L'Shawn Swift.

"I expect you're eager to see if your niece is there, too."

The agent nodded. "You bet your ass." His face drew into grim lines.

"So, we're gonna need either a bigger boat, or at least two

more of the standard ones."

"I figured that." Olvida paged through screens on his tablet. "I contacted Everglades Tours. They got a big boat they use for sightseers that'll handle up to eight. The owner is an ex-state trooper. He knows the 'Glades better'n anyone, and he'll be gung-ho to drive."

"Ex-cop or not, he's a civvie now. He gonna be willing to sign a waiver, Ralph?"

"Yeah, I'm pretty sure. He's helped law enforcement before, running down poachers."

"Okay, so we're gettin' the boats and 'copter. What about logistics." Warner glanced at the digital wall clock. "We're on the clock here."

Detective Beck clicked a video remote, lighting up an eighty-inch wall-mounted TV. The screen filled with an image of the Everglades—an area so wild and vast that the U.S. Army had never been able to catch and conquer the Seminoles that hid there during three mid-nineteenth century wars, making them the only Native Americans never to surrender.

"Here's an aerial view of Big Cypress, where our target is located." He hovered an electronic pointer over the subject island. "There are the two big shacks and a dilapidated pier."

He indicated a section of shoreline. "Airboats can run up on the beach here, but there doesn't appear to be anywhere a 'copter could set down, Boss."

"I suspected that." Warner rose and walked to the flat-screen and pointed at the open beach. "First thought was an amphibian bird that could drop down close to shore, but that chopper is in service in the Gulf." He turned to face the group.

"Commander Kontos said his team will rappel down close to shore and wade in. Usually SWAT's the first guys in, but they'll be exposed, comin' down the rope, so they'll wait to swoop in as soon as we hit the beach." He glanced again at the wall clock.

"No tellin' what, if any, resistance we're gonna meet, but I suspect an outfit as apparently sophisticated as this is gonna have some serious muscle handy." He hooked a thumb in his pocket.

"We got a time line to launch this op, Jack?"

"Fish and Wildlife's got a dock on the Tamiami Trail about thirty miles out." He motioned to Beck who zoomed the image out to enlarge the area."

"Okay." Harris rose and pointed to a spot along the Trail. "There's the Fish and Wildlife dock and their building. They'll have their boat there within the hour." He pivoted toward Beck. "How about your guy, Dean?"

"I talked to Neal McKeane less than an hour ago. He's servicing the boat, and he'll bring it down, but it's currently in Palm Beach County. Won't be here until near dark."

"Shit!" Warner studied the aerial map, then returned to his chair. "Gettin' too late to mount an op tonight, anyhow. Let's get it teed up to go at first light. I want everybody locked and loaded and at the dock by six-thirty a.m. Full Kevlar and your M-4s with extra mags."

His eyes caught Agent Yeager.

"Ina, I'd like ya to set up in the bigger boat when we storm the beach, to provide overwatch with your 50-cal, in case this devolves inta a full-out war."

"Always a pleasure watching your six, Detective. I hope I don't have to save your butt for the third time, though."

They both chuckled, then everyone stood, gathering their notes, and headed for the door.

Warner drew next to Agent Pauletti. "Kinda quiet in there today, Lon."

"Not much to say, Detective." He patted Warner's shoulder. "You seem to have all the bases covered." He paused.

"Now we've just got to execute without losing anyone... this time."

Warner nodded. "It's never easy to lose one of your team... especially the boss. How're ya holding up?"

"Made my peace with it, Al. The job goes on. I hope I'm not being overconfident, but I doubt we'll run into anyone on this op as diabolically deadly as the Shadow."

"Me either." Warner patted him on the back as they parted. "That was a once-in-a-lifetime killer. We'll cue up in the parking lot here at five and then caravan to the launch site."

"Okay. We'll all be there. See you then." He waved as he headed for the door.

"Try ta get some sleep, Agent. I expect it's gonna be a busy day."

"Copy that, Detective." And he was gone.

Yeah, sleep. Never easy on the eve of a big op.

Well, Eva would be there, and she was a calming influence for him.

He turned toward his office to retrieve his jacket and gun.

~ 52 ~

José exited the storeroom and glanced around, searching for signs of Maggie. He shrugged, then retrieved his car keys from a cubby under the bar and tried to ease the hardened planes of his face.

Relax! If Maggie wasn't in sight, he presumed she was ready. He damned well hoped so because they had only one chance at this, and now was the time. He grabbed his peaked cap and strode toward the front, hoping to avoid Sam.

As José approached the outer doors, Hoek's Lieutenant appeared from his office, intercepting him before he reached the exit..

"Where are you heading, José?"

"Gonna run into Sweetwater for supplies." He dangled his keys. "Need to stock up on soft drinks, and most of the bar snacks are just about gone."

"Really?" Sam scratched his head. "I thought we loaded up on that stuff about two weeks ago."

"Yeah." José forced a chuckle. "But no accounting for a pregnant woman's hormonal needs. Maggie vacuums that stuff up like a Hoover."

In reality, the bar man had been slowly discarding the snacks each day, and three-fourths of a bottle of gin had gone down the drain.

"Hang loose while I go check the storeroom."

"Okay." It was harder each time to get away from this joint, and Sam wasn't about to make it any easier today. José shoved his hands in the pockets of his cargo pants and leaned against the door jamb as his boss started for the lounge.

José tried to remain calm as he reviewed the details of

their plan to flee this luxurious prison. He'd slipped out last evening and hidden a few of his and Maggie's valuables in his car, along with a couple of outfits for each to carry them over until they got settled somewhere safe.

He wondered if Maggie would even *want* to set up with him once they got away and she had the baby. Had she fallen for him as hard as he had for her? He hoped so.

José hadn't quite figured what to do about that infant, either. It really wasn't theirs... *hers*... and he didn't know who the father was. They'd worry about that if and when they escaped. Right then, getting away safely was their top priority.

"Okay." Sam's voice broke through his thoughts. José pushed away from the wall and faced the man as he approached.

"Looks like you could use a refill. Don't be too long."

"Shouldn't take long. Twenty minutes each way, and maybe an hour to shop. I oughta be back in time for hors d'oeuvres." He slipped through the door and hurried around to the small parking lot at the west side of the building.

Arriving, he beeped off the alarm of his silver Toyota Corolla and slid inside, quickly firing up the engine. He lingered as the eight-year-old car's a/c wrung heat and humidity out of the air. He scoured the side of the building, concentrating on the outside access door of the kitchen, but Maggie was nowhere in view. Too early for her, anyhow.

He sighed and shifted into gear. If she'd chickened out, there was nothing more he could do. He just had to decide, if she had, should he buy the required supplies in Sweetwater and come back, or just bug out to save his own ass and leave her to fend for herself.

He groaned softly as he pulled in front of the building, knowing that wasn't an option. He parked as planned, just west of the entrance, then killed the engine and exited the car, keys in hand.

Sam stood on the portico, arms crossed, watching.

"Forgot my wallet," José said as he started up the walk.

~~~

Maggie crouched as best she could and peered through the crack of the slightly ajar kitchen outer door. She'd heard José talking with Sam, and now he'd gone to get his car.

She peeked over her shoulder at the cook, who kept glancing at her as she diced vegetables for the evening meal. Maggie straightened and said she was just awaiting José for their afternoon walk.

"Joining him from the kitchen is easier," she explained.

She turned her head at the crunch of gravel. His car idled by and turned the corner toward the front of the building. She waved at the cook and hurried into the brightly sun-lit yard, pulling the door closed behind her.

Maggie's heart galloped inside her chest, and her hands shook as she eased up to the corner of the mansion and peered around the side. José had stepped out of his Toyota and started toward the front doors. That was her que to move.

Bent as low as her bulging belly would allow, she shuffled quietly up behind the small sedan and hunkered there, near the passenger-side rear door. The car was between her and the building, so she prayed she was hidden from any curious eyes.

Her sweat slickened palm rested on the rear door's handle. The signal to slip in would be José's return, to allow minimal time for anyone to spot her inside. She fidgeted in place, anxious and shivering.

What will happen if they catch us before we can get away? If José's right about how dangerous— She spotted her accomplice exit the house, talking with Sam.

José had to separate from him if this were to succeed.

Their conversation didn't seem heated, but Sam had a hand on José's forearm, impeding his departure. The longer they delayed...

"Where's Maggie?" rang out from the house.

"Oh, shit!" she muttered.

Miles Hoek, trailed by the cook, strode around the building from where Maggie had just come. She pressed closer against the car, hoping not to be seen, but it looked like they were blown.

"Where's Maggie?" Hoek yelled again. "Clara," he gestured toward the plump cook who struggled after his hurried approach, "said she snuck out the side door, looking very nervous."

"José!" Sam reasserted his grip on the young man's arm. "What's going on here?"

José's struggle to get free seemed futile.

"What are you trying to pull?"

Maggie rose from alongside the car and edged toward its front.

"Maggie!" José's voice was strident, full of pain and frustration.

She stood, uncertain what to do, tears filling her eyes. They'd failed, and things were surely going to get bad, if what José believed was true.

"Maggie!" Terror and panic were there now. "Here," he screamed and hurled his car keys toward her, landing at her feet.

"Go, Maggie, go." He spun around and delivered a left hook to Sam's jaw, dropping the man like a felled tree. The restraining grip broken, he pivoted and charged Hoek.

"Go, baby, go. Get away now or it'll be too late." Launched headlong through the air, he tackled Hoek around the waist, both men spilling to the ground.

Maggie shook her head, casting away momentary paralysis, and looked at the keys, nestled next to her foot. She bent and snatched them up, then looked at the two men tussling on the ground. A protracted groan drew her eyes to Sam, struggling to sit up.

"I... I can't leave you like this," she cried, tears now in full flood.

"Go, go! It's too late for me now." He panted, trying to keep the larger man pinned down. "You gotta... get away or this... is all for nothing."

"Sam! Stop her for god's sake." Hoek was fumbling to his feet with José still wrapped around his knees. The younger man pushed up and delivered a fist to Hoek's groin, bringing him back down, writhing in pain.

José was trying to rise, but the other man, despite his agony, had a vice grip on his ankle.

"Maggie! Please! Run for it, or all this is wasted. You gotta go, babe."

Sam was on his knees, fighting to stand. He'd be on her in a minute if she didn't make a move.

Uttering a plaintiff wail, she spun and slid into the driver seat. She adjusted the seat back to allow room for the kid-in-waiting and started the engine. Looking over her shoulder, she saw Sam lumbering toward her, a snarl distorting his face. She hit the door lock button and got the sedan in gear just as he arrived, snatching at the door handle.

Maggie hit the accelerator. Hurling curses, Sam was dragged thirty feet before being cast off. She sped down the drive to the entrance road and turned left, heading east and, hopefully, back to civilization.

My god, what a mess. What are they gonna do to José after this?

That answer came with the sound of a single gunshot.

She cried and shook so hard she could barely see as she

navigated the narrow road. Get to Miami. Find the cops and come back to rescue José... if he were still alive.

Glancing in her rearview mirror, she saw a large, black Mercedes burst from the access road, coming after her.

Oh, shit. Won't they ever let go?

She pushed the accelerator to the floor and prayed. The damned kid wasn't going to make a car chase any easier.

Tears dried, she concentrated on driving... and staying alive.

Damn it. A peek in the mirror showed the big sedan gaining on her.

José risked everything for me, so I gotta get help... and hope he's still alive.

~ 53 ~

"That should be the exit on the right, Boss."

Jack Harris gestured toward an opening in the dense growth of sawgrass that lined the Tamiami Trail canal, exposing a narrow dirt road. They were ten miles west of Sweetwater, and four miles since the last sign of civilization—a classic old southern manse house, set well back from the road.

Warner guided his vehicle, the first in a caravan of three black Chevy SUV's, onto the path and across an earthen dike over the canal. His fingers found suddenly itching X-shaped scars over his right ear. This was not far from the location of his near-death encounter with his first serial killer, the Baby Butcher, just four years before. He shook his head, glanced at his watch, and concentrated on the road before him.

"The boats are finally ready to go, Jack?"

"Yep. Talked to McKeane before we left. He arrived at nine last night, and the Fish and Wildlife boat was already on site."

"Okay. We really need that big boat." He glanced at his detective. "Remind everyone, cell phones only. These perps could be monitorin' the police bands." He peeked at his rearview mirror and saw the other two SUVs close behind.

"Same with the chopper. Cells only, unless they're talkin' to Air Traffic Control."

"Copy that, Boss. They all know the drill."

They rounded a massive live oak and drew into a clearing bordering a marshy backwater canal peppered with reed and broad hyacinth leaves. Two airboats, one very large and the other suited for three or four persons, were beached on the shoreline.

Warner pulled as far as possible into the clearing and killed the engine. The other SUV's rolled up behind him, disgorging five of the FBI's BAU agents and Miami Detectives Beck and Olbredo.

Everyone had assembled at Miami-Dade headquarters just after dawn. The entire BAU team was there except for Harry Ashkin, who stayed behind to make room for Agent Swift. The newest member of the BAU team had more skin in the game. Ten was the maximum the two airboats could safely handle.

Warner, with Detectives Harris and Olvida, exited their vehicle and gathered with the rest of the team near the two boats. Most carried M4 assault rifles as well as their hand guns, plus extra magazines and clips. Agent Ina Yeager hefted her Barrett 50 sniper rifle.

Warner scrutinized the group. "Everyone in Kevlar?"

All nodded.

"Harris, I want vests and helmets for the boatmen."

"On it, Boss." He retrieved the gear from the back of their SUV and delivered it to their two boat operators.

"Okay, here's the drill as I see it." Warner faced a semi-circle of his crew. "Harris, Olvida, and I will take the lead in the smaller boat, which is faster." He turned to Agent Pauletti.

"Your team, along with Detectives Beck and Olbredo, will ride in the bigger boat. We'll form up just outta their range to coordinate with the SWAT chopper." He paused. "Usually, we follow SWAT's lead in an assault, but they'll be too exposed while rappellin' from the chopper if we meet any fire, so we're gonna have ta secure the beach to give 'em cover."

His eyes found Agent Yeager. "We got no idea what kind of resistance we'll meet, so I'll want Ina to remain in the bigger boat to maintain overwatch."

"Got it." She nodded.

Warner laid his hand on Harris' shoulder. "Jack, you'll stay in the smaller boat to corral any runners."

"Shit." Harris grimaced.

Warner faced the smaller detective. "Look, partner, I know you always loved the action, but this is your first field op since I almost lost ya to the Shadow." He squeezed the man's shoulder.

"Wouldn't be surprised if you're one of the busiest guys in the op. Let's see how it goes when ya get your feet wet again." He turned back to his team.

"Okay, let's saddle up and get this thing in gear. Olvida, notify SWAT command we're on the way. Accordin' the GPS, our ETA is thirty-five minutes."

Five minutes later, the two boats, fully manned, had skidded off the shore and were accelerating down the narrow canal toward the open wilderness of the Florida Everglades.

Ten hearts raced with the roar of spinning props and soaring crystalline spray. Warner hated charging into a situation without knowing what to expect, but they had no choice.

It could have deadly results, as it had, not many months ago in their action against the Shadow, but this was another one of those times, and there seemed no other option.

~ 54 ~

Maggie's foot was to the floor after José's sedan surged over a dike crossing a canal and skidded left, onto a main road, heading, she hoped, east. Her head swiveled right and left, taking in waterways bordering the highway.

The Tamiami Trail?

She'd been blindfolded on the way out, but that's what it looked like. Of course, there were several roads in Dade County that ran alongside canals, but this sure looked like the one that transected the south end of the state. She glanced at the instrument display and spotted an "E," confirming her direction.

Good! At least I'm headed toward Miami. She peeked at her rearview mirror and shivered as the black Mercedes trailed her.

Shit! Are they really gonna chase me out here?

She'd eased up on the accelerator after steadying on the road, but stomped down again when the black sedan appeared. The small Toyota sprang forward with surprising energy. Glancing again at the mirror, Maggie was unsure if her pursuer was gaining on her.

Who the hell is that? Probably Sam.

Droplets trickled from the corners of her eyes. That they were so panicked at her escape... that she even *needed* an escape... lent credence to José's fears for her safety.

José! José! Did he die to save her? She gritted her jaw, determined not waste his sacrifice.

Another glance in the mirror confirmed the Mercedes was closing. If they caught up, no way her modest vehicle could defend itself against that big, black brute. She would have to rely on a long-ago experience, when her stock-car racing brother showed her the move.

She scanned the road ahead but saw no traffic. If this was the Tamiami Trail, it was mostly pretty remote, crossing the southern end of the Everglades. Traffic was usually light. She grunted and concentrated on getting the most she could out of the Toyota, but a peek in the mirror showed the big sedan gaining on her.

Where's a cop when you need one?

That thought ignited another one. Trying to stay centered on the road, she reached over and popped the glove box. Her bulging belly made maneuvering difficult, and the kid took that moment to practicing tap dancing, which complicated things.

Her fingers found then edge of a smooth, thin rectangle, but she couldn't get a grip on it. She pressed as tightly as possible against the steering wheel and finally made purchase on its slick surface.

As she retrieved her prize, she realized she'd momentarily lost control, and the car had wandered onto the shoulder, mowing down sawgrass and lurching toward the canal. Maggie jerked back in her seat and dropped the cell phone on her lap, applying power and fighting the wheel.

The sedan skidded sidewise and fishtailed along the edge of the bank, its rear tires nearly hunkering over dark water before the growling front wheels pulled it back toward the road.

Shit, that was close.

She shivered, slick with sweat and covered with goosebumps, but was able to regain the narrow highway and leap ahead. A quick glance confirmed that her fumbling had allowed her pursuer to make a substantial gain... probably no more than a hundred feet back now.

She gasped a couple of deep breaths, then fumbled to power up the cell phone José had stashed in the car the previous night. The Android lit up, went through its startup sequence, and beeped. The task of keeping the accelerator floored, staying on the road, and finding the phone's keypad was almost more than she could handle.

Finally! The twelve-digit display appeared, and she hit three numbers: 9-1-1.

Nothing happened! She lifted the phone to her eyes.

No bars!

Damn! Now what?

She sensed the chase car almost on her tail. It looked like it was going to be up to her. Eight years since she'd been taught the "duck and bump."

Only got one chance to get it right.

The size difference between the two vehicles would make it more than just challenging. And a fetus doing the jitterbug was damned distracting.

Her pursuer was on her now. The Mercedes was edging along her driver's side. The bigger, heavier vehicle could lean against her little sedan and force it off the road, across twenty feet of shoulder, and into the canal. She'd figured they didn't want to do that and endanger losing the infant. Maggie was of no value to them, but apparently her baby was another matter. It was the only scenario in which she had a chance to survive.

Maggie kept one eye on the road and the other on her sideview mirror. Then the black monster was alongside, and the time had come. She glanced over and saw Sam, as she'd expected, at the wheel, looking very grim. He waved at her, a pistol in his hand, signaling her to pull over.

Maggie waved back, then hit the brakes hard, the car's automatic skid control avoiding a spin out. The Mercedes shot ahead, and she accelerated again just as Sam slammed on his brakes. Maggie roared up as the other car fishtailed and timed a perfect clip to its right bumper. The bigger car slewed, lost traction, and spun off the road, heading for a canal.

Maggie shot by and glanced at the driver who was frantically trying to control his vehicle. She was unsure if he made it into the canal, which was her hope. Regardless, he was going to be out of action long enough for her to get away. At least that was her fervent hope.

As she raced east, she exhaled a held breath, sighed, and forced herself to relax.

Now if I can only...."

"9-1-1. What is your emergency?"

Maggie giggled softly. She'd moved into an area with cell reception, and the phone had dialed itself. She took a breath and spoke.

"I'm in a Toyota Corolla eastbound on the Tamiami Trail, being chased by a guy in a black Mercedes who wants to kill me and steal my baby." She spotted a small sign along the road.

"Just past mile-marker 27." Her words breathless and ragged. "The other car skidded off the road, but I think he's gonna be coming again soon."

"Try to stay calm and keep going," the woman on the phone said. "I'm contacting the sheriff, and he'll have a patrol car out there in a few minutes. You're not far from a sub-station."

"Okay." Maggie's voice cracked. "But tell 'em to hurry. I don't feel safe, and I think they've killed my boyfriend."

"Two sheriff's cars are on the way. Please stay on the line until they arrive."

"You bet." She whimpered. "I'm eight-months pregnant, and my baby's really kicking up a fuss."

She put the phone on speaker, laid it on the passenger seat, and started to sob, all tension bleeding away. She looked up the road, drawn to the pulsing sound of a fast-approaching siren, and then spying flashing red and blue lights of a sheriff's cruiser.

"Thank God," she muttered, and pulled to a stop on the narrow shoulder. As the black and white vehicle slid to a halt beside her, its rooftop light bar flashing but siren stilled, Maggie dissolved into a full-blown, hiccupping bawl. Her hands to her face, she let loose her tension and fear, a waterfall of tears cascading across her cheeks.

She was safe, but what of José? That gunshot she'd heard may mean he died to protect her.

"Miss?" A sheriff's deputy stood by her door.

"Huh?" She blotted her eyes and found a tissue to wipe a runny nose.

"You the one who called 9-1-1?" He looked up as a second car rolled in.

"Oh, yeah. Geeze, thank god you got here." She panted, trying to control her breathing and slow her thundering heart.

"You said someone was trying to kill you?" He ran a hand over the crumpled hood of the Toyota. "A car accident?"

"Yeah. No." She sighed, back in control. "There's a guy in a black Mercedes back there a couple of miles or so, who was trying to run me off the road." Her lips ticked into the barest smile. "I got him instead."

"Why did he want to do that?" The deputy nodded to the new arrival, signaling him to drive west and look for the alleged perp. Turning back to Maggie, he asked, "Why do you think he was after your baby? That's what you told the operator."

"That's a long story, one not filled with facts as much as suppositions."

"Okay. Follow me back to the station and you can make a statement. Then we can sort things out."

"But my friend. He was shot back at that big house, about ten miles back."

"You saw the shooting?" He removed his hat to wipe a perspiring brow.

"Well... no, but I heard it as I escaped."

"Escaped?" His hat replaced, he'd produced an Android and was taking notes. "You were a prisoner there?"

"I... I'm not sure. I went there willing to have this baby, but then—"

"Look." He pocketed the tablet. "This isn't the place to do this. With no hard evidence, we can't go barging into this place, wherever it is, without a warrant or probable cause." He glanced up as the other patrol car returned and parked.

The officer exited and strolled over. "Black Mercedes sedan, three miles back, half in the canal. No sign of the driver. I called for a tow truck."

"Okay. So, let's all go back to the station while we try to straighten this out." He turned to Maggie. "You'll make your statement, and then we'll see what's the next appropriate action." He started for his cruiser.

"But what about my friend, José? He may be hurt, or even dead."

"Like I said," he looked over his shoulder, "we'll get your story and then see what we can do. Without any hard facts, we're going to need a warrant if we're going to do anything more than pay a social visit."

"You gotta do something!" she wailed, tears coming again.

He paused and pivoted back, hands on his hips. "Tell you what. I'll send Deputy Consil," nodding at the other man, "out there and see what he can see, within our constraints. Where is this place?"

Maggie sighed. "Big mansion on the right side, set way back from the road. Maybe eight or ten miles." She rubbed her eyes. "I'm not sure how far I got before I stopped here."

"Okay. Deputy Consil will go and check it out. We'll learn what he found when he rejoins us at the station." He opened the door of his cruiser.

"Now, follow me, and well get this all sorted out."

Maggie shook her head, sighed, and pulled out behind the patrol car, going east, as the other deputy took off to the west.

Moisture again leaked from her eyes. What had happened to José? She ran a hand over her belly, the infant quiet for the moment. And what's the future for this baby? Whose was it, and did they even know it existed?

Maybe there would be answers at the house, once the police started an investigation.

~ 55 ~

Warner glanced at the other boat, nestled against a sprawling bed of reeds, its engine idling. His boat drifted quietly, fifty feet away, as he awaited a call from SWAT Commander Kontos, relaying their position.

There'd been some confusion between SWAT and the Coast Guard as to would pilot the Blackhawk chopper, but it was the Coast Guard's bird, and they insisted their guy fly it. It got sorted out, and after a twenty-minute delay, the SWAT team was on the way.

Warner's phone vibrated in his hand. A text message popped up: "Six mikes out."

He activated the voice recording button: "Keep coming. We'll be on the beach in three minutes." He pocketed the phone and waved to the other boat.

"We go in three minutes. Check weapons and vest, and follow the plan." He looked at Agent Yeager.

"Ina, I'm countin' on you keeping shooters off SWAT when they're comin' down the rope."

She nodded and held her Barrett 50 sniper rifle high and pumped her arm.

Warner gave her a thumbs-up, looked at his watch, and raised his arm, twirling his index finger.

"Fire 'em up. No unnecessary heroics, and cover each other's sixes." He gestured at the boat's pilot.

"Let's go."

He popped the clip from his M4, checked the load, reinserted it, and chambered a round. Harris and Olvida did the same, their jaws set in hard lines.

Engines on each boat roared to life, spinning huge, caged propellers, thrusting the crafts forward. They skimmed across the reeded wetlands, arcing around a small cluster of islands, beyond which lay their target, just a one-minute run from where they'd lay hidden.

~~~

Morgana stood on the stoop just outside the door, one hand shading her eyes.

"Rex." She turned, gazing back into the lounge, looking for her partner. "A boat's coming." She squinted back across the swamp, confounded by the glare.

"No! Two boats, and one's big and full of people."

Rex appeared beside her and scanned the approaching crafts, still a quarter-mile away. "We expecting any more clients today?"

"No." She grabbed his arm. "And they don't look to be dressed like our people, either."

He grunted and snatched a radio from his belt. "Security, *everyone,* armed and on the beach. We've got uninvited visitors." He pivoted and rushed inside, hauling Morgana with him.

"Organize the staff and keep our people under control. And tend to our guests. Get them to the panic room and then ready to use the escape route back to their boat."

"Oh, god." She clapped a hand over her mouth. "You think it's the cops?"

"I don't know how they found us," Rex retrieved an AK47 from a weapons locker, "but we'll know for sure in less than a minute." He pocketed two extra clips. "Now move!"

Morgana hurried into the lounge where their five guests and six of the girls all stood motionless, their faces filled with confusion. She began barking orders, reverting to a well-practiced drill, prepared for this exact possibility.

Six black-dressed security guards, each armed with semi-automatic rifles, were taking up positions in the yard as the staff from the smaller building hurried by.

~~~

Nicki took the steps three at a time and raced to her room. She burst through the door and spied Kiesha, sitting on the bed, surrounded by her few new possessions. She'd been crying.

Nicki bounded to her side. "They're coming. C'mon, we gotta move."

"Who's coming, Nicki?" Kiesha rose from the bed. "The cops?"

"Yeah, I think so."

She sped into the bathroom, searching for the more modest clothing they'd arrived in. If this was Harris and his team, she didn't want him to see her like this, dressed as a concubine. She located both their outfits in a trash bin and brought them back into the bedroom.

She peeled off her flimsy outfit and donned the jumpsuit she'd worn in the other building, and Kiesha started to follow.

"My tracker beam must have..."

She was cut off by the rattle of gunfire. Her head snapped up at the boom of a big, automatic weapon, firing from the roof. It went silent after a ten-second burst, followed by a thump.

~~~

Warner's team skidded ashore in their airboats and hit the ground running. As planned, the two boats backed fifty feet into the marsh and set up support positions as a half-dozen armed men poured out of the larger building.

The *whump, whump, whump* of a fast-arriving helicopter shook the ground, raising clouds of sand.

"Spread across the beach and take cover." Warner hit the ground as their opponents, also seeking cover, opened fire.

"Suppression fire," he roared. "Protect the SWAT team."

The first of those repelled down from the chopper, hovering fifteen feet above the surface. Warner, Olvida, and Agent Swift emptied their first clips, then scrunched against the ground at the rattle of return fire.

A ricochet off a small rock inches from Warner's face spew sand in his eyes, momentarily blurring his sight. These shooters were no amateurs. Blinking away tears, he squinted, picked a target, and squeezed off a four-shot volley. The black-clad guy pitched sideways and went down.

Agent Swift raised to his elbows and fired a burst from his rifle, then grunted and dropped to his side. He grimaced, then gave a thumb's up, and picked a slug from his Kevlar vest.

The air suddenly reverberated from the roar of a heavy automatic weapon, its slugs pounding the sand in front of him, then whistling over his head, followed by a yelp of pain behind him.

"Jesus! A machinegun?" Warner's eyes swept the building and spotted the shooter on the roof, just as he pitched backward, and the gun went silent. Warner glanced toward the shoreline and spotted Agent Yeager sprawled across the larger airboat's bow, plying her sniper rifle.

"Saved my ass again." He grunted and returned his attention to the Tangoes in front of him, who were making a spirited stand.

"Looks like we're gonna have ta fight this out to the end," he muttered, snapping in a fresh clip into his M4.

He scanned the beach and saw most of his team effectively pinned down, trying to return fire. Peeking ahead, he saw another enemy crumple to the ground, a black hole in his forehead. Agent Yeager seemed to be doing most of the heavy lifting with her 50-cal sniper rifle.

His people on the beach had to keep up suppression fire and survive, while she cleaned up.

~~~

Nicki peeked into the second-floor hall and spied pull-down stairs, deployed to a hatch in the ceiling. Tentatively ascending, she and poked her head through the opening. A thirty-caliber machine gun sat on a tripod. Its operator was sprawled on his back, a large black hole on his forehead. She scampered up and disengaged the long belt of cartridges, and threw it and its ammo case off the roof.

She peeked over the eave and surveyed the gun battle raging in the yard. The brothel's security was engaged with the police team, and four SWAT members who had just repelled down from a Blackhawk chopper. One of their members lay crumpled on the ground, probably a victim of the gunner who lay dead beside her.

She watched, mesmerized as another one of the house's guards flew backward, the rear of his head disintegrating from a big bore slug. A moment later, a third pitched down with a similar wound.

Her guys must have a sniper somewhere, picking off the baddies, one at a time. That's who apparently got the machine gunner. Probably that BAU agent, Yeager. She had the rep.

Nicki slipped down to the floor below and found Kiesha, also changed into her more modest togs.

"C'mon, let's get downstairs." She took the girl's hand.

"The cavalry has arrived." She towed Kiesha after her as she hurried to the first floor.

The room was bedlam, with the staff trying to maintain order. She surveyed the scene, looking for Rex and Morgana, when she staggered from a blow between her shoulder blades. Nicki stumbled but caught her balance and spun around. Olga loomed, arms raised, a snarl on her face.

"Where the fuck you think you're going, slut," she snarled.

"Where ever I want, bitch."

Nicki stepped forward as Olga shook a fist. The detective ducked under the swing and drove a fist into Olga's gut, surprised at the hardness there, probably a girdle. Unfazed, the Russian slammed her joined hands down on Nicki's shoulders, driving her to her knees. Gasping for breath, she spun away and struggled to her feet.

More wary now, they circled each other, and then Olga attacked, both arms flailing. Dodging aside, Nicki lashed out and landed a vicious kick on the bigger woman's leg, just above the knee. The joint buckled but didn't give, and Olga grunted and then lunged, folding Nicki into a bear hug. The detective's arms were pinned, her face mashed between the woman's massive breasts.

With her nose and mouth buried in Olga's flesh and her ribs about to crack, she struggled for breath. Nicki fought to rotate her arm, and cupping her fingers, managed to dig her nails into the brute's thighs and rip flesh.

"Uhhh! Bitch!" Olga snarled, "I'm gonna break your back."

The Russian adjusted her grip, snarled, and tried to bite the detective's ear. Her struggles gave Nicki a moment to shift position, freeing one leg. She raised it enough to stomp hard on the arch of the matron's foot, and Olga howled, her eyes flaring as big as quarters.

The woman's clutch weakened. Nicki arched her back, shoved with her elbows, and managed to wiggle free. She gasped for air, crouched, and brought the heel of her hand up hard under Olga's jaw, snapping her head back. The matron moaned and the light went out of her eyes.

Nicki stepped back, sucked in a welcome breath, and fired a powerful karate kick to her massive abdomen, and Olga tumbled backward, crashing across a table and slamming to the floor, the back of her head smacking down.

The girls cheer resounded through the room, and Nicki, still panting, managed a smile, then shouted, "C'mon, ladies. Let's take this place down." She pumped a fist. "We're *free!*"

The four-man staff was quickly overrun by screaming women, venting their anger and frustration. Sheri leaped upon the back of one, wrapping her arms around his neck as Tanya kicked him in the crotch. The other staff were on the ground as several women pummeled them.

The bartender snatched a taser gun from under the bar. The blonde who'd welcomed Nicki grabbed a heavy crystal snack dish and hurled it at his head, splitting his forehead and taking out one eye. He crumpled to the floor without a sound.

Nicki steadied her breathing and scanned the room, searching for the two bosses, Rex and Morgana, but they'd disappeared.

Meanwhile, the war being fought outside had wound down, so she scurried to the front door, hoping her guys had survived intact.

~~~

Jack Harris' eyes were drawn from the melee on the beach to movement in the sawgrass. And then he spotted a big airboat up the shoreline, partially obscured by tall grass. He motioned to his boatman.

"Put me ashore, and try to block that airboat over there." He pointed to the large, twin-engine vessel.

"Ain't gonna be easy," the F & W officer mumbled. "That beast's five times my size."

Harris scrambled off his craft and moving in a crouch, scurried toward the other boat. His M4 was ready for action, and he wasn't going to hesitate to use it if met with armed resistance. He'd been shot before, but the last time was almost the last time ever. He was lucky to be alive and back on the job, and this was his first trip back into the field.

He knelt, weapon ready, as six men and a woman, all bent low, hurried into the open, headed for the big airboat. Harris twitched as that craft's twin engines fired up at the approach of the group. He hadn't realized a boatman was aboard, and that careless mistake could have been deadly for him.

He grunted to himself. *The boss is right. I'm outta practice.* He pivoted to cover both the boat and the perps.

"Hold it, folks." He brandished his automatic rifle. "No one's going anywhere."

The seven pulled up and milled around nervously. The tallest man started to reach around his back.

"Don't try it, bub. I got an itchy finger on this trigger and I'm not afraid to pull it." He squeezed off two shots into the dirt at their feet.

"Oh, my god," one man whined, his hands thrust out in the "stop" motion. "This can't be happening." He glared at their apparent leader. "You promised we were protected here, Rex. That we'd be *safe*." He swung to the woman.

"We'd be safe." Tears ran across his cheeks. "You promised!" He slumped to his knees. "I'm ruined." He waved at his companions. "We're *all* ruined."

"Relax," their leader said. "We've got impeccable connections. We'll fix this."

All eyes snapped toward their boat as its engine roared to full power, sliding backward off the bank. The operator had apparently decided it was time to go, passengers or not.

"Hey!" Harris swung his rifle as the airboat spun and started away. He fired a warning shot but it kept going, gaining speed, slipping past the smaller F & W craft. In another moment, it would be gone, but Harris was reluctant to open up on the guy, who was probably no more than a glorified taxi driver.

His attention was drawn to the tall guy and the woman, trying to edge away.

"Hold it!" He brought them under his gun. "No one's going anywhere." He cocked his head and realized the gunfire on the beach had ended.

Their larger boat had just come aground, and Agent Yeager stepped ashore, still toting her deadly sniper rifle.

"Looks like the battle's over, folks, so let's get back to the building and see what's what."

His prisoners, shoulders slumped, staggered ahead, many weeping, as they made their way toward the buildings.

I hope Nicki Unger is okay. I'm going to have a hard time, if anything happened to her. She'd taken this undercover gig at Harris's urging, so he bore a strong mantle of responsibility if she'd suffered in any meaningful way.

~ 56 ~

Maggie hunkered over the table in the interview room, head in her hands, weeping softly. What a surrealistic day, trying to escape, and then José... What *happened* to José? Sacrificing himself for her... and then the gunshot.

Did they kill him?

That sweet and wonderful guy who tried to rescue her... from what? His fear for her life seemed more well-founded than she had been willing to believe... until they shot José and then tried to run her off the road.

Something nefarious was going on with the baby she carried, but she had no inkling what that might be. From what José said, there was some sort of blackmail...

She glanced up, her thoughts interrupted as the door opened and a man entered. Maggie blotted her eyes with a tattered tissue and sat up, her palms on the metal table.

"Hello, Ms. Bagwell. Sorry to keep you waiting like this." The Latino officer settled in a chair across the table from her.

"I'm Sheriff's Detective Torres, based in Miami. I got here as quickly as I could." He studied her for a moment. "From what little briefing I've received, sounds like you've been through a ringer. Want to tell me about it?"

"José?" Maggie interlaced her fingers. "Do you know what happened to my friend, at the house?"

"Not yet." He eased back in his chair. "We're still waiting for the deputy who went out there to check back." He withdrew a Samsung tablet from his jacket, laid it on the table, and tapped a few keys. "Meanwhile, why don't you tell me what you know, and how you're involved with whatever was going on out there?"

Maggie sighed and ran a hand through her fiery red hair.

"About nine months ago I met this guy, Brett, who basically offered me a hundred G's to be a surrogate to carry some rich guy's kid. I guess the dad was someone famous because it was all hush-hush." Her fingers caressed her belly, sensing the infant's first activity since she'd arrived.

"Anyway, he brought me to this big old, secluded mansion..."

And over the next ten minutes, she spun a tale of her last eight months in seclusion. Winding down, she massaged her eyes, sighed again, and dropped her hands into her lap.

"That's about it, Detective. I'm about six weeks to term, but José heard them say they were taking the baby early, like they did with Charlotte, and engage in some sort of blackmail with the wife." She paused, eyes rolled up, searching memory. "Widow, actually." She nodded. "Yes. He said *widow,* not wife." She searched Torres's face. "I don't get it. If she's a widow—"

"This other girl, Charlotte?" The detective scrolled back through his notes. "Was the wife they were contacting about the child a widow, too?"

"Hmm." Maggie stroked her chin. "Yes, I think so, and the woman was reluctant to pay. We heard she had an influential friend who was advising her..." She swiped away tears.

"That's when José began worrying about our safety, because they were so unguarded in front of him. And I heard some of it, too. No way would they let us live to tell our story. They were planning—" She was interrupted by a knock at the door, and a deputy entered.

"Steve's back," the deputy said.

Torres rose. "He found the house?"

"Yes. He said—"

Torres waved him to silence and turned to Maggie.

"Excuse me, Ms. Bagwell. I want to hear the deputy's report." He headed for the door. "Shouldn't be gone more than five minutes or so." He glanced over his shoulder. "Can we get you anything? Water? A soda?"

"A bottle of water, I guess." Her eyes beseeched him. "Can't I hear what he found? José...?"

"I'll tell you everything when I return. I promise."

And he was out the door. A moment later, a deputy returned with a cold bottle of spring water.

~~~

Detective Torres finished entering notes to his Android, then looked again at the Deputy.

"You didn't enter the house?"

The man shook his head. "No warrant, and no clear probable cause. Found a black Mercedes E-450, abandoned, its front wheels in the canal, about five miles from where we picked up Ms. Bagwell." He flipped a page on a small notebook. "The big mansion was two-and-a-half miles farther down the road." He closed and pocketed the notebook.

"The place's been vacant for years until some big-bucks guy picked it up about twelve months ago. A lot of renovations went on for sixty days or so, and then it went quiet. We patrol the Trail most days, and there was very little activity there that anyone noticed, once they completed whatever they were redoing."

Torres turned to the sergeant who ran the sub-station. "We need to get a warrant, ASAP. And contact Miami-Dade's Chief of Detectives, Al Warner. He may be interested in this, if it turns out Bagwell is right."

"I've heard of Warner. He's the real deal, but he's got no jurisdiction out here."

"Normally true, but he's a friend, and told me about someone pressing Anthony Stirling's widow about her deceased hubby's 'love child' from an inconvenient affair." He shoved his hand into his pockets.

"This Charlotte Colman sounds like the paramour. Bagwell said Colman carried a kid for someone and then may have been murdered after delivering. Believe me, you want Warner on this if it's as bad as Bagwell thinks."

Torres glanced at the deputy. "No signs of anyone shot?"

"Nope. Place looked vacant. No vehicles in the drive and no apparent activity in the house."

"Okay. Get on that warrant. I got Warner's cell number. I'll see if I can reach him." He strode toward the interrogation room to report what he could to Maggie Bagwell. Unfortunately, there wasn't much new to tell her.

Especially about her boyfriend.

Warner's phone went right to voicemail, which probably meant he was in an area without reception.

Torres left a detailed message and then rejoined Maggie.

It would be a while before they knew anything definitive.

~ 57 ~

Warner and Nicki Unger lounged against the bar in the salon and watched his detectives taking statements from the women who had been captive there.

There were a lot of tears and relief at being rescued. Two of the nine gals seemed terrified at having to return to their previous lives, under the control of particularly cruel pimps. With little education no skills other than prostitution, they admitted working there, even as prisoners, was far safer than patrolling the streets. Here there was no worry about a bed to sleep in and where the next meal was coming from... and no drugs and abusive pimps.

Nicki had counseled the two, promising entry into a women's shelters where they could learn some sort of job skills, but they were still fraught with doubt.

Kiesha Swift had fallen, bawling, into her uncle's arms, and Warner had to restrain the agent from pummeling Rex. Human trafficking was a federal crime, and Special Agent Swift vowed to see a merciless prosecution of the man and his accomplices.

SWAT Commander Kontos radioed his HQ for another chopper to help ferry the victims back to Miami where more comprehensive statements could be taken, and family and/or relatives could be notified. Warner's team cleared the beach to make room for the bird to land.

Lost souls had been found, and the one upside to their confinement was, they were all clean of drugs. At least for now.

Warner hoped every effort would be made to keep them that way. Unfortunately, without guidance and protection from falling back into the hands of their pimps, many might be back working the streets, again forcibly hooked on heroin or cocaine.

Warner's eyes found the eight remaining employees of the bordello, handcuffed and seated on the floor in the back of the room, under the watchful eyes of two of the SWAT team. Four of the cabal had died during the battle, as well as one SWAT officer, who fell victim to the machine-gunner before Yeager took him out.

Five others, apparently clients caught up in the raid, clustered around a table under the watchful eye of Detective Olbredo and another SWAT officer. The detective sought their ID's, and despite locking up tighter than clams, he thought he recognized two; one a Florida state senator, and the other a Florida US House member. Detective Unger marked a third as the director of a Broward County battered women's shelter. How weird was that!

Warner pushed away and joined Agent Solto who, along with Detectives Beck, were taking statements from their captives. He touched Agent Solto's arm.

"Gettin' anything useful?"

She shook her head, hands on her hips. "Looks like the grunts are just worker bees, Detective. The queen bee and her apparent partner got nothing to say except 'lawyer.' My boss and Detective Harris are in their office, seeing what they can dig up."

She nodded her head toward the other five. "Those bastards are mum, and with no Wi-Fi, cell or Internet service out here, no way to run a search. Probably will have to wait our getting back to the city."

"Well, they ain't goin' anywhere in the meantime. People like that are what make operations like this possible." Warner scanned the room.

"So, where's this office Pauletti and Harris are tossin'?"

She nodded toward a door at the rear of the lounge. "Through there. Follow your nose. You can't miss it."

A moment later, Warner entered a room large enough to support two desks and several file cabinets. Jack Harris and Special Agent Lon Pauletti each occupied one of the desks, pouring over stacks of files.

Harris spotted his boss and sat back, his face bunched into a scowl. "You ain't gonna believe *this*, Boss."

"Believe what, Jack?"

"This joint is the headquarters of a huge network of sex playpens for the rich and famous." He brandished a stack of papers. "New Orleans, Atlanta, Charleston, Richmond, Chicago, just to name a few."

"All in remote locations and staffed by kidnapped sex slaves?" Warner strode over and took the files, flipping through the pages.

"Jesus, this is huge." He glanced at Pauletti, who nodded.

"And it's Federal, Al. Interstate racketeering." He sighed. "You know we never try to steal cases from locals, like some of our brethren, but we have no choice on his one."

"I got no problem with you takin' the racketeerin', Lon. It's way beyond our resources." He shoved hands into his pockets. "Just as long as you leave the local murders to us. We got dibs on prosecutin' these bastards for those."

"Be our guest, Detective. Those were all done in your bailiwick." He grinned. "The only hitch may be who gets first crack at them."

Warner shrugged. "Let the lawyers figure that out. I just wanna see them go down for killin' at least four gals we know of." He looked at the papers, still in his grasp. "May be evidence of even more in here."

"Possibly." Agent Pauletti returned to the desk. "One thing about people like this, they keep excellent records of everything. The Nazis were a perfect example of that."

"Okay." Warner headed for the door. "I'll leave you guys to it. I'm gonna get everything tied up out there so we can get back to Miami."

Twenty minutes later, Warner, Harris, and Olvida were skimming across the Everglades in the smaller airboat, heading for their cars.

As they stepped ashore, cell phone service returned, and Warner's buzzed, showing three texts. He paused to scan them, then grabbed Harris' arm. "Looks like we ain't gettin' back to town so quick, Jack." He turned to Olvida.

"Ralph, you take all the stuff we gathered back for analysis. Get the photos and prints of the perps and the five clients to Tech and run ID's. Looks like Harris and I got a date with the local sheriff." He turned to the shorter detective.

"We need a warrant for a raid on that mansion we passed on the way out here. You may have ta pull some strings."

"What's the gig, Boss?"

"Looks like something Charlie Seagrave was concerned with may have had legs." He tugged Harris after him.

"C'mon. Sheriff's Detective Torres is waitin' for us at the local substation." They climbed into Warner's customized Charger and took off. Warner's day was about to get a lot longer than he'd imagined.

~ 58 ~

Warner peeled his coupe off the Tamiami Trail and slid into a parking slot in front of a single-story, gray concrete-block building. The sign above the glass double doors read:

MIAMI-DADE SHERIFF, S.W. COUNTY

He and Detective Harris stepped from the sleek, black muscle car, and were instantly blasted by the drenching mid-day heat from an aqua sky lightly peppered by small puffs of cottony cumulus. They hurried through the doors, eager for the benefits of an airconditioned office.

Warner stepped to the reception desk and said, "Detectives Warner and Harris, to see Detective Torres."

"Detective Torres is expecting you." The uniformed lady deputy punched a button on her desk phone. "They're here, Detective." She nodded and replaced the receiver.

"They're in the interview room." She stepped from behind the desk. "I'll show you."

Warner and Harris followed her down the building's single hallway. She rapped on the second door, then opened it and stepped aside, signaling them to enter.

Inside, the two Miami detectives were met by the sheriff's deputy, Damian Torres, and a very pregnant freckle-face redhead whose eyes were inflamed from an apparent crying jag.

"Detective," Torres said, shaking Warner's hand. "Glad you came. You made great time."

"We were in the neighborhood, just finishin' up a case." Warner glanced again at the woman, who was edging forward. "What's this about a baby scam you thought we should be involved with?"

"Please." The woman tugged at Torres's arm, her voice choked. "We've gotta hurry."

He nodded and shook her off. "It's that case you were talking about with Charlie Seagrave last time I was in your office. The pregnant mistress looking to score with the Stirling widow." He took the woman's wrist and eased her forward.

"This is Maggie Bagwell, who just escaped from that mansion just west of here. She says she knew the woman who she thinks was reputed to be Sterling's mistress, but never was. And she's unwittingly in the same position with someone else—"

"*Please!*" She snatched at Warner's hand. "They shot my friend, José, who helped me get away, and they were gonna kill me after the baby—"

"You *saw* them shoot this guy?" Warner studied her eyes.

"Well, no-o-o, but I heard the shot as he fought with them, giving me time to drive off." She sniffled and blotted her eyes. "They chased me, but their car went into the canal and then the sheriff—"

"Deputies found the car, abandoned. One officer went to the building, which appeared vacant. We had no probable cause, based solely on her," glancing at Maggie, "unverified statement."

"Shots fired didn't provide exigent circumstances?" Warner folded his arms, eyes narrowed.

"One uncorroborated shot, lots of lapsed time, and the place looked vacant." Torres glanced at the woman.

"Anyhow, the deputy opted not to create any grounds for a claim of an illegal search. However, when I interviewed Ms. Bagwell, I immediately thought of you and Seagrave..."

"Okay. Ms. Bagwell..." Warner gestured toward the room's chairs.

"Let's sit and you tell me what you *know* for a fact, and

then what you suspect."

He looked at Harris. "Contact your ADA buddy with the friendly judge and get a warrant. Make up something that fits but will be enough to get it. Move!"

"On it, Boss." Harris hustled into the main office to make his call.

Warner returned his attention to Maggie. "So, let's hear it. Brief and to the point. Time may be runnin' out if your friend, José, was really shot."

Maggie settled on a chair, her fingers interwound on the desk, and sighed. Tears again welled in her eyes.

"I met this guy who offered me a hundred grand..."

And the tale of hope, then doubt, and finally, fear, unwound over the next ten minutes.

Before she finished, Harris had returned with a warrant, texted to his Android. The judge knew any warrant requested by Detective Al Warner was never without merit.

~ 59 ~

Warner paced in random patterns across the floor of the sheriff department's vestibule, anxiously awaiting two more deputies and the region's captain. All this delay gave the perps—if there were any—time to slip their noose. From what Maggie Bagwell said, he, Jack Harris, Detective Torres, and the two local deputies were more than enough to serve the warrant and handle any possible resistance.

He knew there might be a jurisdictional pissing contest over who was in charge. This was sheriff's territory, but Warner had more possible skin in this game than anyone. Torres already said he was happy for Warner to lead the charge, but the final decision was the Captain's.

At that moment, Warner didn't give a damn who got credit for a bust, if there were one. He glanced at his watch.

"Dammit," he muttered, "time ta go. *Past* time ta go!" He entered the office area and found Detective Torres working at a computer. Warner perched on a corner of the desk.

"Look, Detective. If that woman's right, these guys may already be in the wind. We can't lollygag here, waitin' for backup we don't need." He waved a hand across the room. "We've got five able officers here to serve that warrant and handle any trouble that comes with it." He rose. "Not to mention a possibly injured civilian who may need help. Let's go, and worry about any possible flack later."

"You willing to flout protocol and take the heat, Warner?"

"Been doin' it my whole career, Detective. I'll take the guff from up top, if there is any. What d'ya say? Let's mount up and do this."

"Okay, I'm in, but I gotta give the two local deputies a chance to opt out."

"No problem. You, me, and Harris are enough, if it comes ta that." Warner scanned the room, searching for his partner.

"And we still got our M4s from this mornin's raid, so we got plenty of fire power, if needed."

Six minutes later, the three of them, plus one of the local deputies headed west on the Tamiami Trail in a three-car caravan, with Warner's Dodge in the lead. Maggie Bagwell sat in the rear of Warner's coupe, eager to check on José, and ready to show them around, once the site was cleared.

All four men were armed and wore Kevlar. Arriving on site, Warner slid his Charger to a stop in the mansion's driveway, just before entering its circle in front of the building. Harris, in the passenger seat, scanned the front with a scope, concentrating on the windows.

"No sign of any activity, Boss."

"There's a concierge desk in the lobby, and then the lounge and bar..." Maggie said, and continued to describe the interior.

"Okay," Warner said when she'd finished, and he spoke into his cell phone, avoiding radios in case they were monitored.

"Torres, you and your deputy circle to the back. Cover any possible exits. Bagwell said there's a side door from the kitchen, too." He glanced at his watch. "Ninety seconds, and we'll knock on the front. Get movin'."

The exited their vehicles, and the two sheriff's deputies split up, trotting around each side of the huge house. Hands rested on undrawn weapons, ready for action.

Warner and Harris inspected their M4s for fresh magazines and chambered rounds. Warner checked his watch and nodded at Harris. He pulled his car up to the front.

"Let's go."

They slung their automatic rifles over their shoulders and strode to the door. When he rapped on the mahogany panel, it swung inward. He squinted at Harris, shrugged, and shoved it fully open. An open door offered probable cause for entry, and they also had their warrant.

"Hello? Police." He called. "Anyone here?" He peeked over his shoulder at Harris, then stepped inside. "We're comin' in to serve a search warrant. Show yourselves."

A scuffling noise came from the rear, and the two detectives readied their weapons. A voice rang out.

"Sheriff's deputies." It was Torres. "All clear back here, Detective."

"Clear in the front, too." Warner's eyes swung to the stairs. "Cover us while we check the second floor."

He paused at the foot, scouring the shadows above, looking for danger. He slung his rifle, drew his Glock, and began edging up, Harris trailing two stairs behind, his handgun also drawn.

A woman's voice, squeaking with tension, called out. "Up here, officers. Everyone else is gone, except for me and my patient. Hurry. Second door on the right."

Warner and Harris continued a cautious ascent. "We're comin'. I'll wanna see both hands up." Last thing he would do was rush into an ambush.

A moment later, he peeked around an open door's jamb and spotted a middle-aged woman, dressed in nurse's whites, perched on the edge of a sofa, both hands raised. What appeared to be a young man lay behind her.

"He's been shot," she said, "and needs more help than I can give him."

Warner cleared the room and then stepped closer, looking from the woman to the man on the couch.

"This is José?"

She nodded. "He's been shot on the right breast." She touched the patient's arm. "The bullet is still lodged in there. I did what I could—"

"Hang on." Warner's gaze swept the room, a den-type setting, and watched as Harris cleared the rest of the mini-suite.

"Clear the rest of the rooms on this floor, Jack, then get Bagwell up here." He glanced down at the supine figure. "I'm guessin' she's gonna want to see him. And have the sheriff call for a bus. Not sure what hospital services this area."

"On it, Boss." He scurried off, pistol in hand.

~ 60 ~

"José!" Maggie surged through the doorway and skidded to a halt beside the sofa while Warner stood by. She cradled the man's hand in hers, her eyes welling.

"Oh, José, please..." She paused as his fingers curled around her palm, barely tightening.

His eyes fluttered, and a bare smile tickled his lips. "Maggie." His scratchy voice barely audible. "You okay?"

"Yeah, thanks to you." Her words choked with sobs. "I brought the cops. Sam and Hoek were gone, though." She leaned in and brushed his lips with hers.

"Just so you're safe..." His voice faded. His breathing was shallow but steady.

"I gave him a sedative to ease the pain," the nurse said, checking his pulse. She touched Maggie's arm. "He's hanging in there. Strong young man."

Maggie mewed, brushed moisture from her eyes, and perched on the bed, holding José's hand.

"How'd ya get him up here?" Warner touched the woman's shoulder.

"The grounds-keeper carried him, then he split on his moped. I think he's an illegal, and—"

Harris stepped into the room. "A bus is on the way, Boss. And we got another body, a woman, in the kitchen pantry. One shot to the head."

"Sounds like cleanin' house."

Warner studied the nurse. "So, what's your part in this?"

She groaned. "I was clueless about their con. Just hired to care for the pregnant women."

She rechecked José's pulse, then sighed. "I objected when they wanted me to induce Charlotte two weeks early." Her eyes caught Warner's.

"It was a healthy pregnancy. No need to rush a delivery, but they insisted." She glanced back at José.

"When I still refused, they did it without me." She sighed again. "Then they disappeared."

"Who?" Warner turned her toward him. "The woman?"

"Yes, and the baby. A few days later, they were both gone. I asked, and they said Charlotte took her infant and left, but I never saw them go." She shook her head.

Warner looked at Harris, his eyebrows arched.

"Charlotte wasn't strong enough to go anywhere with that child so quickly. And, there was no car for her, anyhow." The woman shuffled her feet and adjusted her uniform.

"That's when I began suspecting things were not as they had presented them, but what could I do? I had no way to leave, either."

"And they just left you and Jose here, alive and as witnesses, before they took off?" Warner's dark eyes rivetted hers.

"That wasn't their intent." She perched on the edge of the sofa. "When Sam stumbled into the yard, all out of breath, he yelled they had to run. Cops were coming." She brushed moisture from her eyes.

"Hoek shouted for him to find 'the nurse and the cook and clean things up.' I knew what that meant, so I hid." She shuddered.

"I heard a gunshot from the direction of the kitchen, and a lot of shouting about records, and saying there was no time. Then they were gone."

"What about José? They just left him?"

"I guess they thought he was dead." She rose and

straightened her dress. "So did I, at first."

"When the first sheriff's car arrived, they reported the place looked vacant. If he..." Warner nodded at José, "was on the ground, why didn't they see him?"

"He was laying close to that low hedge along the drive."

Their attention was drawn to the warble of an arriving ambulance. Harris started for the door.

"I'll get 'em." He hustled off.

Warner turned to Maggie. "I suppose you'll wanna ride to the hospital with José?"

She nodded, still clutching his hand.

"Okay by me. Ya might wanna get checked out there, too. See how that little one's doin'." He caught her arm and drew her to her feet.

"I'll send Detective Harris up ta see ya later today. We're gonna need a complete statement, and we gotta figure out whose baby you're carryin', and what ya expect to do with it." He glanced at the door.

"Ya said there was an office?"

"Yes. Through that hallway that begins under the staircase. There's also a smaller room behind the entry desk." She paused and rubbed her eyes.

"That's where Sam usually worked if he wasn't at the desk, but from what José found out, if there's any records, they'd probably be in the one past the stairs. "

"Okay." Warner stepped back as Harris returned, followed by two EMTs toting a stretcher. After a quick check of the wounded man's vitals, they transferred him to the gurney and hurried off, Maggie trailing closely behind.

She peeked over her shoulder as she left and mouthed, "Thank you."

Warner turned to the nurse. "I know you probably feel like a victim here, but you're gonna have to come with us to the station until we get the facts sorted from the suppositions." He shrugged.

"It may take a while, but looks like there's been several serious felonies committed in this place, includin' at least one murder. One of the Sheriff's deputies will tend ta you 'til we finish up here, then we'll head back to Miami."

She sighed and sank onto a chair. "I knew this damned job seemed too good to be true. I'm probably screwed."

"Maybe your luckier than ya think. If Ms. Bagwell didn't escape and bring them law…" Warner's dark eyes held hers.

"If it turns out her fears were well-founded, then as you recently discovered, these guys weren't plannin' on leavin' any witnesses. Not alive, anyhow."

"Oh, sweet Jesus." The woman rolled forward, her head in her hands, whimpering.

Deputy Detective Torres stepped into the room. "The house is cleared, Detective. The ME is coming for the stiff, and we found the office. Surprisingly, there's lots of records there. You'll want to take a look."

"Yeah." The nurse rose. "Hoek was paranoid about being hacked, even though he wasn't on-line. He was very old-school. Everything done on paper. They sped off less than a minute before I heard a patrol car pull up, outside the drive." She glanced at Warner.

"By the time I crawled out of my hiding place and got down to the door, they were gone." She shrugged.

"Okay." Warner glanced at Torres and gestured toward the nurse.

"You take custody of her as a material witness. Harris and I'll check out the office. See what we want ta take back to Miami for a deeper dive." He looked at Harris.

"Contact the Hawk to arrange a co-op CSU scrub here

with whoever the sheriff wants to attend. I'm sure he's gonna want ta be involved." He started for the exit.

"Then join me in the office so we can see what's what and figure out what was goin' on here."

~~~

Warner perched on the corner of an antique, cherrywood desk, skimming documents they'd found in its file drawer. Harris was settled in the black leather executive chair on the other side, reviewing another small stack of folders. The only other furniture in the eight-by-ten, cypress-paneled office was a small sofa and an arm chair.

Warner grunted, then plucked up a page. "Here's the file on Bagwell's friend, Charlotte Colman." He read for a moment.

"Pretty complete background and all her medical data. Even a DNA profile." He laid the page aside. "I'll get the info to the Hawk ta run through the data base. I got a sneakin' suspicion it may match that dismembered Jane Doe."

He studied another page. "Here's the info on the invitro impregnation, and the complete follow-up on the pregnancy. And the caesarian delivery. Healthy six-pound girl... and a list of potential buyers!" He glanced at Harris. "I thought Bagwell said they were usin' the kid to blackmail a widow inta protectin' her hubbie's rep."

"I don't get it, Boss."

"Me either, Jack." He shuffled through the file and plucked out another page. "Shit. Well, this explains everything."

"What?"

"I'm pretty sure I got what's goin' on and whose baby it is, but I can't figure how they did it."

"They ID the sperm donor?"

"Not directly, but they *do* name the nosey big shot who is causin' them problems."

"Uh-huh." Harris rubbed the back of his neck, a small grin splitting his face. "Suddenly, I'm guessing that'd be Charlie Seagrave."

"Bingo. He's Stirling's friend." Warner replaced the papers, closed the folder, and set it aside. "Now all we gotta do is figure out how a dead, squeaky-clean billionaire managed to impregnate a woman he apparently never met." He chuckled. "The Hawk's gonna love this one."

"Did he ever leave samples at a fertility clinic?" Harris lifted another file. "Didn't his wife say they'd tried everything to have a kid?"

"Yeah, and that was one of the first things she checked. Every sample still present and accounted for."

"So, no hanky-panky at the clinic." Harris shrugged. "That doesn't make sense."

"Right. Where the fuck did the sperm come from? Either he was bangin' Colman, which Bagwell is sure never happened, or they lifted a sample somewhere else. It don't make sense."

"Well, maybe the Hawk—holy *shit*." Harris waved the file he was scanning.

"What?" Warner rose and circled the desk.

"I bet I just found who Bagwell's donor was."

"Yeah? Who?" He leaned over the smaller man's shoulder to read the document. Harris' finger pointed to the name.

"Evengi Sokolov?" Warner stood back, hands on hips. "The Miami Heat center? Ain't he dead, too?"

"Yeah. Beck investigated it. Drive-by shooting about eight months ago in Coral Gables. That's weird." Harris pulled at an earlobe. "Both donors *dead*?"

"And I'm bettin' both died almost immediately after supposedly knockin' up a mistress." He squeezed Harris's shoulder. "Check with the widow as soon as we get back to HQ. As I remember, this guy was another super-role model with an impeccable rep. I suspect these perps were puttin' the squeeze on his wife too, to protect that rep."

"Hmm." Warner massaged the bridge of his nose. "Did Beck investigate whether the vic was havin' an affair?"

"Never found any evidence of that to my knowledge, Boss."

"Yeah, but if true, coulda been a reason for the shootin'. Doesn't explain the need for a surrogate to have a baby, though." He looked at Harris. "Have Beck check ta see if they were tryin' ta have a kid and couldn't succeed."

Warner gathered the various files. "Meanwhile, let's get this back to the Hawk for a forensic review. I think we got the who and the what on these babies. Now we gotta work out the how."

"And tell Bagwell who the daddy of her kid is, Boss?"

"Yeah, once we verify everything." Warner ran a hand through his thick, wavy hair. "She deserves ta know. So does Sokolov's widow. It's something they'll have ta eventually sort out." He headed for the door with Harris trailing.

"I hope there's something in these papers to lead us to these bastards... and the Stirling baby. I'm bettin' there's another murder here, as well as extortion."

"Yeah. The kid may have already been sold off."

Warner found Deputy Detective Torres in the lobby.

"The crime scene's in your care, Torres." He shook the man's hand. "We've got evidence of murder and extortion to investigate in our jurisdiction, so we're headin' back to Miami. Keep me looped in if ya get a lead on the perps, willya?"

"You got it. Keep me posted from your end, too."

Warner nodded and waived as they exited the mansion. He was eager to get back to the Hawk and Forensics to see what sense they could make of this.

One way or the other, there were some evil people out there that needed to be put out of business... permanently.

~ **61** ~

Warner pushed through the swinging doors of the CSU lab and found Moe Gold, the Hawk, as he always seemed to be, hunched over a microscope.

"Got your message, Moe." Warner paused beside the man. "What'cha got for me?"

"In a second, Detective." The little forensic wizard's eye remained glued to the scope, while he jotted notes on a pad. Finally, he grunted and sat back.

"That for me?" Warner asked.

"Fiber analysis for a different case, but I *do* have several things for you."

He slipped off the stool and waved at Warner to follow him to his cluttered desk. The Hawk settled on his chair and sorted through scattered papers, coming up with two manila folders. He slid back in the chair and opened one.

"First things first." He extracted a sheet covered with symbols. "DNA comparison from the tests you recovered, re: one Charlotte Colman, and compared to that of your dismembered Jane Doe, are a match." He sighed.

"The poor girl was the surrogate mother of the Stirling infant." He handed the file to Warner. "Murder wasn't the outcome promised her, according to your Ms. Bagwell."

"Damn right." Warner leafed through the few pages in the folder. "No idea how they impregnated her with Stirling's sperm, though?"

"Always so impatient, Detective." Gold waved the second folder. "Ms. Bagwell mentioned that the man who recruited her was named Bret." He grinned. "On a hunch, I checked the medical examiner's staff." He thrust the second file at Warner.

"Bret Snider is an assistant-examiner there. You'll note on those assignment sheets he was the first from that office on both the Stirling and Sokolov deaths."

"So?"

"I suspect he extracted viable semen from both men and passed it on to your perps. He had the tools and the skill. All he needed was a refrigerated container to store the vials in, and that's normally part of their equipment at a fatality."

"Sonofabitch! Damned clever." Warner ran a hand through his curly hair. "That explains why they took the baby two-weeks early. It supported a timeline for the so-called affair and a full-term pregnancy." He chuckled.

"Eva even mentioned the baby in the photo looked small for full term." He patted the Hawk on his shoulder. "Thanks, Moe. Good work, as usual." He started for the door, then stopped.

"You worked with the sheriff's techs on a forensic sweep of the mansion?"

"Yes." He pushed away from his desk. "We're running fingerprints and whatever DNA evidence we found, but so far, nothing significant, other than confirmed IDs of Miles Hoek and Sam Gregory. We're checking on the rest of the staff, but..."

"Yeah, just hired folks for food and housekeepin', as far as I can see. Nobody but the nurse left alive to question, so I don't think we're gonna learn much there."

"I got bigger expectations comin' from Mr. Snider." Warner turned again for the exit. "Beck and I'll pay that guy a visit."

And he was out the door, hurrying up the stairs.

Warner stepped into the detectives' bullpen.

"Beck. Mount up. You're with me."

"Coming, Boss."

He hurried from his cubicle as he pocketed his shield and holstered his weapon, and followed Warner, who was already halfway down the stairs.

~ 62 ~

Warner, trailed by Dean Beck, slip into the morgue, where he'd been told the medical examiner was doing an autopsy.

Doc Carson, the ME, was explaining his procedures to Chester, one of his junior assistants. He glanced up as the detectives entered, nodded at Warner, and went back to his work.

"What can I do for you today, Detective?" he said as he removed the stomach and bowel of the corpse.

"Lookin' for your assistant, Bret Snider, Doc."

"He's off this afternoon. Can I help you with something?" He deposited the organs in a large, stainless-steel pan and turned toward Warner.

"It's about a case we're workin'. Got a minute ta talk?"

"Sure. Anything for you, Al." He motioned toward a desk and chairs as he stripped off latex gloves and went to the sink to rinse and dry his hands. Finished, he circled his desk and perched on his chair, hands folded and resting on the oaken surface.

"What can I help you with, Detective?"

"Snider. Anything unusual goin' on with him?" Warner and Beck settled on adjacent chairs.

"Hmm." He stroked the side of his nose. "Nothing I've noticed. Why do you ask?"

"He's your guy who usually goes to the scene, isn't he? The first to attend a recent death?"

"Yes. Not always, but most often. I still don't see—"

"Has he seemed ta have come into any money lately?" Warner leaned forward, eyes intense.

"Well, yes, he has. An inheritance of some sort. Not major, but apparently a decent amount. Why? Has he done something?"

"We think so. Can't go inta details 'cause it's an open investigation." Warner rose. "You said he was off today?"

"Half-day. Just left about an hour ago. Said he wanted to get an early start for a weekend in the Keys."

The doctor pushed out of his chair. "I suppose you'll want his address."

"Yeah. Just ta double-check what we got is right."

"Just a moment, Detective, while I check my records. I believe he's moved recently."

"Thanks, Doc. Then we'll be outta your hair."

Three minutes later, Warner and Beck hurried to his Dodge coupe, worried Bret Snider might already be in the wind. He'd radioed for backup, but expected to arrive first.

~~~

"Middle of the block, on the left, Boss," Beck said. "That yellow CBS ranch house."

"Yeah, and there I'm bettin' is our pigeon, packin' up his SUV." Warner swerved, lurching to a stop directly in front of Bret Snider's Toyota. Both detectives were out of Warner's Dodge, approaching the man from either side of the Ford.

"Bret Snider?" Warner said.

He deposited a carton in the hatch and stepped back. "Who's asking?"

"Detectives Warner and Beck." Both flashed their shields.

"Oh, shit." The man's shoulders sagged, and he plopped down on the rear bumper, below the raised hatch. He rubbed his eyes, and then looked at Warner.

"What's this about?"

"I think you know." Warner's eyes held his. "Accessory to extortion and murder."

"*Murder!*" His head snapped up. "I wasn't party to any murder." He groaned and wrung his hands.

"Who died?"

"Charlotte Colman. Murdered, disfigured, and dismembered, to avoid identification."

"*Charlotte*? She wasn't supposed..." He stammered to a stop. "I think I need an attorney. I got nothing more to say."

"Certainly." Warner withdrew the ever-present card. "Let me read you your rights," which he proceeded to do.

"Now, ya don't have ta talk ta me, but I'm gonna talk ta you." Warner studied the man before continuing.

"We know you extracted viable semen from both the Stirling and Sokolov bodies. And you gave—sold, more likely—them to Miles Hoek to perpetrate a scam and extortion on the widows." Warner frowned and shook his head.

"Pretty heartless way ta treat a grievin' woman. Ya probably don't know that Maggie Bagwell escaped the mansion, and Hoek and Gregory are in the wind." He paused, hands on his hips.

"Looks likely they planned ta kill her, too, once she had the baby. Save 'em a hundred grand each." He grabbed Snider's elbow and yanked him to his feet.

"Now, we're takin' ya in, and you face some serious prison time for accessory ta extortion and first-degree murder. But you could help yourself, and maybe get some leniency if ya told us where the Stirling baby is. Ya *know* your buddies are sellin' it, or have already sold it on the black market." Warner turned the man to face him.

"I don't know." Snider groaned, his eyes dropping. "Hoek owned some sort of clinic in Coral Gables on Old Cutler Road, north of Davis, I think. Maybe there."

Warner glanced over his shoulder and spied the arrival of two patrol cars. He dragged Snider to the first vehicle as a uniformed officer stepped out.

"Take him in ta bookin': accessory to extortion and murder." He shoved the weeping man into the blue's grasp.

"He's been read his rights and has asked for his lawyer. I'll send CSU up to sweep his home." He nodded at Beck.

"C'mon, Dean. We're goin' to Coral Gables."

The two detectives strode toward Warner's Dodge. They had an infant to find, if it was still alive. These bastards might try to cover their tracks, and the kid was becoming a liability.

~ **63** ~

Warner guided his Charger down Old Cutler Road, scanning the passing buildings. Mostly boutique shops and a few bistros.

"Davis Road is the next light, Boss." Beck pointed ahead.

"Yeah." Warner gestured toward a two-story, beige CBS building. "I think that must be it, ahead on the left."

"Check ta see what's up with backup, Dean." He slipped his Dodge into an open spot at the curb.

"If it's only Hoek and Gregory, we can handle it, but it he's got some hired muscle..." He paused as a tall, slim man exited the building.

"Lemme see that image of Hoek."

Warner reached for Beck's Android. A quick scan and a grunt.

"That's him, all right." He released his seatbelt and opened the door.

"Look, Boss."

A second man trailed behind, carrying a briefcase.

"That's Gregory." Beck pointed.

"Let's go. Shields visible and a hand on your weapon."

Both detectives were out of the car and approaching the two perps from both sides, as Hoek was starting to enter an Audi SUV.

"Miles Hoek; Sam Gregory." Warner's voice rang out. "Miami Police." He waved his shield. "Stay where you are, and keep your hands where we can see 'em."

The two men exchanged glances, then Hoek darted into his vehicle.

"Don't do it!" Warner growled. "I won't hesitate to shoot,

if ya try anything funny."

Hoek glared at Warner, then yelled, "Run for it, Sam!"

He fired up the engine, and the SUV leaped from the curb and charged Warner.

The detective dodged aside but caught a glancing blow from the rear fender and tumbled to the pavement. He rolled, coming to a knee, then hesitated. He wouldn't discharge his weapon in this semi-residential neighborhood.

As the Audi reached the intersection, its path was suddenly blocked by an arriving police car, and the vehicles collided, spinning onto the walk. Two women, walking dogs, barely avoided injury, and screaming, they raced away, their little pups clutched in their arms.

Warner regained his feet and hurried toward the entangled vehicles, trying to shake off a numbness in his left leg. He arrived just as Hoek extricated himself from the wreck.

"Hold it right there, bub." Warner waggled his pistol.

"I *will* shoot ya now if ya give me a reason."

The man sighed and slumped against his car. Blood seeped from a cut above his eyes. The two patrol officers from the squad car arrived, and at Warner's direction, took custody of Hoek.

Warner turned at the sound of scuffling feet and spied Detective Beck dragging a reluctant, manacled Sam Gregory behind him.

"This joker can run," Beck said, still breathing hard. "But this," raising a leather briefcase, "slowed him down. Must contain some pretty important stuff, not to just discard it."

"We'll see." Warner turned back to Hoek.

"You're both under arrest."

Hoek looked at his partner, shrugged, and sighed.

"What's this about, officer?"

"Extortion, attempted murder, murder, and probably illegal trade of infants."

Hoek glanced at Gregory, whose face was twisted into a grimace. He frowned and shook his head, then turned to Warner.

"What murder? I don't know what you're talking about."

"Charlotte Colman, for one. We used your DNA chart for Colman from your office to match it to our Jane Doe."

"You can't prove anything." He reached for the inside pocket of his sport jacket.

"Hold it!" Warner waggled his pistol.

Hoek paused. "Just going for my cell phone to call my attorney."

"Okay. Slowly." Warner watched as he retrieved his phone and dialed, talking softly into the phone.

"We got your records from the house, and two reliable witnesses: Maggie Bagwell and José Leon." Warner glanced over his shoulder as another patrol car arrived.

"José?" Sam Gregory's eyebrows arched.

"Yeah. He survived your attempt ta kill him."

He signaled to the officers from the first car to handcuff both men as Warner read them their rights. Shackled, the men were patted down, and a 9mm Heckler & Koch pistol was taken off Gregory.

"Get that to the Hawk," Warner told the officer. "They got slugs outta Leon and that cook that I'm bettin' are a match."

Everything had been recorded on the officer's body cam. There'd be no doubts of origin or chain-of-custody for the gun.

Hoek glared at his partner and mouthed "idiot."

The cops led the two to their patrol cars, guiding them, one into each of their back seats. Keeping perps separated is Police 101.

Warner turned to Beck. "Did you send this address to Harris?"

"Yep. He's onto his ADA buddy for a warrant."

Warner nodded. "We might not need a warrant, since we've nabbed a perp with a weapon." He glanced at the clinic's door.

"I'm eager ta get in there and see if we can find the infant. I hope she's still alive."

"Harris said probably thirty minutes." Beck scanned his Android. "Nothing so far, Boss."

"We need probable cause." Warner's eyes shifted to the patrol cars carrying the two perps.

"Hmm." He signaled the car about to leave carrying Hoek to wait, and strode to its rear door, yanking it open. He pointed at the man.

"Gimme your cell phone."

"What? That's personal—"

"Yeah, and you'll get it back if and when you're released." He pulled him from the back seat and patted him down, retrieving the phone.

Warner scrolled to Recent Calls and redialed the last number... supposedly Hoek's lawyer. Three rings before it was answered.

"We've got everything packed up," a throaty female voice said, "and just about to leave out the back."

"Right," Warner forced a whisper, and disconnected. He started for his car and gestured at one of the pair of patrol cops.

"Get movin' and block the south end of the back alley." He waved at Beck. "You guys cover this front entrance. No one leaves."

"On it, Boss."

With Hoek and Gregory restrained in the caged and locked rear seats of each patrol car, Beck and the two officers approached the building's front, weapons drawn.

Warner peeled his Dodge away from the curb, raced around the corner, and entered the north side of the alley. He spotted a woman, carrying a bundle, entering the rear door of a Ford Explorer. Two men already occupied the front. He thought he saw another woman in the back.

Warner pulled up fifty feet short of the SUV, angling his car cross the alley, blocking possible passage. He stepped out, his forty-caliber pistol at his side, with a round chambered. As he approached the vehicle, the two cops from the patrol car were coming from the south.

"In the car." Warner was alert for motion. "Everyone out of the vehicle, hands where we can see 'em." He paused at the corner of the rear fender.

"Nice and easy, and no one will get hurt."

The passengers shuffled around, their voices muffled.

"C'mon, the game's over, and ya got nowhere to run. The easier ya make this, the better for ya later. Give it up."

More, louder arguing inside, then the rear door flew open. A thirty-something blond woman staggered out, yanking free from the grasp of someone inside. She cradled something bundled in a blue blanket.

"Please." She started toward Warner. "I'm not with these people, whatever they've done." She waggled the bundle. "I was just here for my baby."

Warner remained cautious as she approached. A rumpled blanket was an easy place to conceal a weapon. Meanwhile, the two officers circled the Ford, its occupants under their guns, drawing out two men and another woman.

"Your baby, huh?" Warner saw the pink-skinned face of a swaddled infant. "Ya adopted the child here, didn't ya?"

The woman nodded, droplets coursing across her cheeks.

"I'm guessin' a girl, about three-months-old? Right?"

"Yes," came her hesitant, choked whisper.

"They had no right to offer ya that kid, ma'am, but I believe ya knew that by how much ya probably paid 'em."

He holstered his gun and laid a hand on her shoulder, then gently wrested the bundle free from her grasp, despite some resistance. A tiny hiccup resonated from within.

"We'll check DNA, but it's likely this infant's mother was murdered, and the child was used as a tool of extortion." He appraised the tearful woman.

"Unfortunately, you may also be guilty of participatin' in an illegal adoption, so I recommend ya hire an attorney."

The woman was probably a wealthy dupe, and Warner held little animosity toward her. On the other hand, he had a viral dislike for people like Hoek and Gregory. Murder was bad enough, but dealing in kids was no better.

He peeled away the flap of the cloth and studied the tiny, sleeping face. He smiled. He knew a couple of people who were going to be very happy to see her. He turned to one of the patrol officers.

"Get this kid to the downtown Child Protective Services clinic for a checkup. Tell 'em I'll be by later with the details."

Meanwhile, he had the probable cause he needed for entry into the clinic. A wagon was summoned to carry away the five perps, while Warner and Beck searched the building's records. They found more than they expected.

~ 64 ~

Warner exited the Child Protective Services clinic carrying a bassinette and a small denim pouch slung over his shoulder. He trotted down the five steps and met harlie Seagrave, who had just arrived.

"You got it done, Al?" Seagrave grinned as he offered his hand, shaken by the detective.

"Yep." He handed Seagrave the zippered sack. "Wasn't easy." They strolled toward Seagrave's SUV.

"CPS even brought in an expert to verify the DNA matches."

"May I take a peek?" Seagrave asked.

Warner proffered the basket as the other man lifted a corner of the blanket. Ocean-blue eyes above rosy cheeks peered up at him. The infant burped, blowing a small bubble.

"Wow! She's a beaut."

"Yeah. They just fed her, too, so it should be a quiet ride." They continued on to Seagrave's vehicle.

"Frankly, I'm surprised you got past all the red tape." Seagrave opened a back door, took the basket from Warner, and strapped it onto the seat.

"There's usually a court hearing for an abandoned child before they agree to placement," he said.

"Yeah." Warner circled to the passenger side and got in. "But I finally convinced 'em this was a kidnappin' more than an abandonment, and the product of murder."

"Whatever." Seagrave slid into the driver side and started the car.

"You did it, and believe me, everyone's gonna be happy about that. This has been a truly traumatic time." He pulled out and headed south toward residential Coral Gables.

The men rode in silence, each lost in his own thoughts.

~~~

The SUV idled to a stop before an imposing wrought-iron gate. Seagrave lowered his window, pressed the buzzer, and announced their presence. A moment later, the barrier rumbled open, and he drove up a long, curved driveway to the front of a classic Colonial, two-story mansion, complete with a columned entrance and a sweeping porch.

They exited the vehicle, and as Seagrave retrieved the infant from the rear seat, the door of the home burst open. A raven-haired, thirtyish woman took two steps onto the stoop and froze, both hands covering her mouth.

"My god," she breathed, barely more than a whisper. "Is it true?" Tears trickled across round cheeks and trailed down to the edges of her arched lips.

"It's really *his* baby? Our baby? *My* baby, now?" She held out her arms, waterworks at full flow from her eyes.

"Yes, Lois," Seagrave said, and strode to her, Warner trailing closely behind. He slipped the swaddled child into the woman's arms. "Tony's DNA. Tony's child." One of his arms circled her shoulders as she peeled away the cover to stare at the sleeping, pink face.

"The mother?" Her eyes swept both theirs.

"Dead," Warner said. "Murdered by those who intended to extort you." He sighed.

"Too bad, too. She apparently wasn't part of the swindle. Just an innocent, lured in by the promise of a big payoff as surrogate for the child."

"So, there's no one with legal recourse for custody?" She searched their faces. "She's legally mine?"

"Looks that way." Warner stuffed his hands into his pockets. "You'll need an attorney to tie up all the loose ends, but I doubt you'll have many obstacles."

"The girl had no parents who may cause problems?" She turned to reenter the house, and the two men followed.

"None we've found." Warner eased the door closed behind them. "And even if they showed up, Ms. Colman had signed a well-prepared legal doc that acknowledged she was merely a surrogate and relinquished any claim to the child."

"It's so sad that they killed her. I would have loved for her to live here with me and help raise Toni. She was, after all, the mother."

"So, you've named her?" Seagrave smiled.

"Yes. Antonia... Toni for short." Her voice hoarse now. "For her father, who'll never know her... or she him." She swiped away tears. "Middle name, Charlotte, for her mother."

"Seems pretty appropriate," Warner said. "Ya know, she wasn't the only one."

"What do you mean?" She continued to cradle the infant, peppering her face with soft kisses.

"Another young woman, promised the same deal as Colman, managed to escape their conclave. She's approaching her ninth month, and those bastards were extorting another young widow."

"But she's alive?" Lois asked

"Yeah. She escaped just in time. Apparently, they take the baby early, by Cesarean, to fit the alleged illicit affair scenario."

"Oh, sure." She settled on a beige leather sofa and signaled the men to take seats. "So, if they awaited a natural delivery—a full nine months—the man would have impregnated her *after* he died."

"Which is exactly what he did, thanks to a crooked assistant medical examiner." Seagrave stood, as did Warner.

"Anyway, we'll leave you to get acquainted with your new

daughter. I've got to get Detective Warner back to his car. I believe he's still got some work to do today."

Warner grunted assent and clapped Seagrave on the back.

"Don't get up," he said to the woman. "We can let ourselves out."

Seagrave bent over and kissed Lois's cheek.

"At least some good has come from this. Keep me posted on how she's coming along."

"You bet." The woman smiled at him. "Her godfather will be expected to participate in her life."

"Godfather? Me?" Seagrave's eyebrows arched.

She nodded. "If you're willing. You made it happen, Charlie."

"It'd be my honor, Lois." His lips brushed her cheek again.

"That's terrific, but we gotta go now." Warner tugged his arm.

Back in Seagrave's Lexus, en route to Warner's car, the detective chuckled.

"It feels good ta have a nice outcome for a change." He patted Seagrave's shoulder. "Ya know, accordin' to their files, Bagwell was actually their third gambit."

"Really?" Seagrave glanced at him. "Another dead surrogate?"

"Looks like it. Extorted another widow of a squeaky-clean celeb, two years ago. Harris is checkin' for a Jane Doe vic about then. We got the pigeon's name, so we can get the baby's DNA they gave the widow to match against any likely female deaths. We know where they sold the kid, too. Jack Harris and the widow's attorney are in France to retrieve him."

"France! Jesus! These are some callus bastards."

"Yeah, well they're done now. We got 'em for at least two counts of Murder One, two counts of Extortion, and Illegal Traffickin' in babies. Another murder and extortion indictments will certainly sweeten the pot."

"You've had a busy week, Al." Seagrave's turn to chuckle.

"Yeah. They're all that way, nowadays."

He settled back and gazed out the window, wondering how Maggie Bagwell was making out. She was scheduled to meet the Sokolov widow and talk about the kid she was carrying.

She seemed like a nice gal, so Warner hoped it would go well for her.

~ 65 ~

Maggie Bagwell stepped onto the pavered driveway as the Uber driver pulled away. She paused at the head of the entrance-walk as the SUV disappeared down the street, and stared at the huge, sprawling ranch house. Its pinkish-beige color and barrel tile roof had a Caribbean flavor.

She hesitated, suddenly unsure. She had been cleared through the security gate at the Boca Raton Polo Club, so the woman knew she was coming. The ride through this luxurious golf community was impressive: carefully manicured trees and shrubs bordering lush golf fairways, many individual upscale neighborhoods sprouting from the main road, the massive two-story clubhouse, and now the stunning estate homes of the Vintage Oaks community, each more impressive than the last.

Her eyes swung to the opening front door, revealing a tall, model-slim blonde in the threshold. Arms folded, the woman regarded the redhead, focusing on her bulging abdomen.

"So, you are the one?" She took a step and paused. "Pregnant with Evengi's child? How did that happen if you never slept with him?" Her English was perfect, with a slight Russian lilt.

"I... I..." Maggie hesitated, her eyes cast down, studying her shoes. "I was impregnated with his semen. I thought I was a surrogate for a couple who couldn't have kids."

She swiped away a tear. "That maybe there was something wrong with the wife's eggs, so they needed mine." Maggie lifted her gaze.

"I didn't know who he was or what those bastards intended." She shrugged and regained her composure.

"I was lucky to escape alive." She studied the woman.

"Well, don't just stand there." Elena Sokolov held out a welcoming hand.

"Come in, and tell me everything. Especially about your child."

"*Our* child." The corners of Maggie's lips ticked upward, then froze.

She'd never really thought of the infant as *hers* before, despite providing half its DNA. She'd expected to raise her own family, hopefully with José.

Maggie sighed, feeling she owned no claim to this baby, even after carrying it for nine months.

She forced out a smile.

"Or, more properly, *your* child, if you want her."

She lumbered up the three steps to the stoop, one hand on her belly. The fetal girl was practicing her dance steps again.

Elena took Maggie's hand, wrapped one arm around her, and ushered her inside.

"Here." Maggie laid the woman's fingers against her belly. "Feel."

She chuckled. "I think your daughter's gonna be a ballerina."

"Oh, my god!" Elena's eyes flared.

"Evengi's daughter!" She hugged Maggie.

"How is this miracle possible? You must tell me the whole story. Every detail." Tears coursed across her cheeks.

"Is it really possible to a child of my lost lover to cherish in his absence? A child to help keep his memory alive?"

She leaned over and her lips brushed Maggie's cheek.

"You are an angel from heaven, Ms. Bagwell. An angel!"

"Please." Maggie smiled and squeezed the woman's hand.

"It's Maggie. We have too much in common now to be Ms.

Bagwell."

Elena guided her into a large den, and Maggie shuffled toward a leather armchair.

"Let me off my feet, and I'll tell you what I know."

She settled back on the seat and sighed as her hostess perched on a nearby, gold satin upholstered loveseat.

"So, where should I start? As far back as how I came to Florida, hoping for a new life?"

Elena nodded and leaned forward as the story of Maggie's hopes, frustrations, rekindled hopes, and then fears, slowly unfolded.

~~~

A Latina maid brought iced tea and chocolate-chip cookies as she talked. After twenty minutes, often peppered with questions from the widow, Maggie sat back and sighed.

"So, that's about everything. The crooks who extorted you to preserve your husband's good name are all in jail. Detective Warner said his case seems iron-clad, especially with José's and my testimony." She grinned and rubbed her stomach.

"This baby should make her bow in less than four weeks, so I've gotta find a good OB. Hoek had me monitored by a nurse, so everything should be on track."

"You'll do nothing of the kind." Elena rose and caught Maggie's chin with her fingers, raising her eyes.

"I will find the finest doctor in Boca, and you'll have our baby here. I will arrange every detail."

"*Our* baby?" Maggie struggled to her feet. "She's *your* baby, Elena. Evengi's daughter."

"You *are* her mother, Maggie. Bring here is a blessing. I do not insist, but if you wish to be in her life, you can live here and help me raise her. It is not uncommon today for a child to have two same-sex parents. She will be *our* daughter."

"Geeze, I don't know." She ran a hand through her fiery hair. "I never expected... I hoped to have a life with José..."

"The man who helped you escape? You are in love?"

"Yep. He's nearly recovered from his gunshot wound. I thought we'd find a little place..."

"Ridiculous! You will both live here, if you agree. To be close to your daughter." She took Maggie's hand.

"Come, let me show you our guesthouse. A bedroom, a den, and a kitchenette." She smiled at the redhead, and with an arm around her shoulders, gave her a fierce hug.

"You will want for nothing. Evengi's contract with the Heat requires them to pay his sixteen-million-dollar annual salary for two years, should he be injured and unable to play." She sighed, eyes filling with moisture.

"Unfortunately, death is the ultimate injury." The widow's eyes again leaked tears.

Elena led Maggie through French doors and onto a courtyard patio. Beyond a sparkling blue, kidney-shaped swimming pool, lay the large, three-room guesthouse.

It seemed Maggie's dreams of a new life were taking a strong upturn after all.

~ 66 ~

Warner parked his Charger on the drive because Eva's Jag was in his one-car garage. He beeped the alarm and carried several folders up the stairs and into his townhouse.

The odor of roasted tomatoes, garlic, and oregano wafted out to him: Eva's home-made pasta sauce. He pursed his lips, salivating.

"That you, darling?" she called from the kitchen.

"Yeah." He headed toward her. "Pasta tonight, huh? Smells yummy."

"Yes, Detective." She turned from the stove, wiping her hands on a dishtowel, and grinned. "Your deductive talents are in top form."

He dropped the stack of folders on the table and folded her into his arms, savoring a warm kiss.

"So, if you're home at a normal dinner time," she leaned back and studied his face, "it must mean your current cases are pretty well tied up."

"You can read that in my face, huh, Doctor?"

"It helps to be so familiar with the patient." She chuckled. "Can you tell me about them?"

"Yeah, the two major ones are outta my hands now. The perps have been charged, so they're in the Fed's and DA's ballparks."

He ran a hand through her auburn hair and planted another kiss before releasing her.

"Finish whatever ya have to do here, and I'll be in the den, reviewin' these files. Come in whenever you're done, and I'll give ya all the skinny."

"Okay." She stroked his cheek, then turned back toward the stove. "Ten minutes, max, before the sauce is finished. The pasta's already cooked, and salads are made."

"Great. Didn't realize how hungry I was."

"So, we can talk during dinner, if you prefer." She gathered up a large mixing spoon and was busy over a pot.

"Sounds like a plan. Anything I can do ta help?"

"Nope. Table's set and everything is ready to go, soon as the sauce is finished. I'll call you when it's ready."

"Okay."

He gathered his files and started toward his den.

"I'm gonna have a Scotch. Ya want anything?"

"Not at the moment, Al."

~~~

Ten minutes later they settled at the kitchen table, salads plated and steaming bowls of linguini and tomato sauce perched in the middle. Warner munched on a bite of Romaine and licked his lips.

"Homemade dressin', too, huh?"

She nodded, chewing some salad.

He chuckled. "When did a shrink have time to become a great cook?" He reached across the table and touched her hand. "You continue to amaze me."

"You ain't seen nothing yet, buster." She grinned and winked.

"So, tell me about your cases." She skewered a forkful of greens.

"Yeah, well, ya know most of what was goin' on. Usin' the info we gathered at the brothel, the FBI has rolled up seven similar ops around the South and Southeast, plus Chicago and

Cleveland."

"All staffed by snatched prostitutes, like here?"

"Pretty much. I understand there were a few like Kiesha Swift, but most were streetwalkers. Sixty-four girls, overall."

"My god!" Eva sat back, palms flat on the table. "That's huge!"

"Yeah, but that's only half of it." His salad eaten, Warner heaped pasta onto his plate and slathered it with large dollops of tomato sauce. Aromatic garlic rolls perched in a small bowl.

"They also found ledgers full of johns, and even a few janes. They know who some are, and got the techies workin' on decodin' the others." He rolled a forkful of linguini and ate it, chewing slowly.

"Almost all so-called elites: senators, congressmen, big business execs and CEO's. The names are staggerin', and the Fibbies plan on prosecutin' who they can ID for aidin' and abettin' interstate sex trafficin'." He rolled more pasta.

"It's gonna ruin a lotta careers." He sampled a garlic roll, licked his lips, and leaned back.

"And the money! Wow!" Warner shook his head. "Agent Pauletti told me they've confiscated over a dozen accounts worth well over twenty-million."

"Jesus! So, the girls?" Eve searched his face. "What about them?"

"Funny thing about that." Warner shook his head and took another bite.

"They were pissed at bein' snatched, and glad ta be rescued. They feared for their lives and survived by toein' the line, but on the positive side, they're all drug-free, and most said they were well-fed and healthier than they've been in years. We're offerin' councilin', so maybe most won't go back ta hookin'."

"I hope so. I've been assigned to work with them, but few

have any job skills, or even GED's. These are emotionally fractured girls with little self-esteem. Prostitution is all most have ever known. Simple clerical or food service jobs don't seem to hold much interest for many of them.

"A few have talked about joining high-end escort services, now that they're clean of drugs." She shrugged. "It's a sad thing, but some of those girls *do* make a lot of money."

"Interestin'. So, I heard Detective Unger and the Swift girl are havin' their tied tubes reversed soon. And strangely," Warner winked and grinned, "someone has managed to get each of those workin' girls ten grand, possibly from an undisclosed account."

"Nice, but I wonder how long that'll last them?" Eva said with a sigh. "Few of them ever learned to save."

"Too bad, 'cause that could get 'em started back on the right track, if they try." He rose to clear the table, their plates cleaned of everything but some red pasta sauce stains.

Eva retrieved two bowls of tiramisu from the fridge, and they returned to the table.

"No wine with dessert, Babe?" Warner's eyebrows arched.

"Not today, lover. Too many calories after a pasta dinner and this dessert." She handed Warner a bowl and fork.

"So, what about Maggie Bagwell? She should be due any day." She nibbled at a forkful of the creamy treat.

"Yeah, well, she met with Sokolov's widow who offered her the chance ta move into her guest house and help raise the kid, kinda like a co-parent. Far as I know, that's goin' along fine."

They dropped into silence and finished their rich dessert. Warner studied his fiancée and wondered if something was going on with her. She seemed preoccupied.

He sighed and folded his hands over his belly, contented. A great meal with the woman he was about to marry. Hunger slaked now, and passion would be on the plate later.

He wondered how he'd gotten so lucky.

~ 67 ~

Warner eased back in his leather desk-chair, hands clasped behind his head. His crossed ankles rested on the corner of his unusually uncluttered desk as he ruminated.

With both major cases closed at his end, he had only two open-and-shut murders on his plate, and those were in the hands of his detectives.

Warner stretched, arms his overhead. It lucky things had mostly worked out so well, but the brutal deaths of Charlotte Colman, the female cook at the mansion, and the SWAT officer lost on the raid in the 'Glades, were unacceptable thorns in everything else that had come up pretty much roses.

Lois Stirling's life had taken an upturn with the arrival of her deceased husband's child... especially since the baby girl really wasn't the product of infidelity. It was a nice treat to inject a package of joy into an otherwise shattered life.

Maggie Bagwell was doing the same for Elena Sokolov, and was doubly sharing in that happiness. José Leon was out of the hospital and into Maggie's loving arms, and they would be part of another little girl's life.

To Maggie's surprise, Hoek had apparently put her hundred-grand fee into an escrow account, so she had the stake she needed to start her bakery. She'd sent Warner an invitation to their wedding.

Warner chuckled as he sat up and picked up an action report.

Only Eva knew he had conspired with Special Agent Lon Pauletti to appropriate one of the bordello's accounts and use it to compensate the various victims. It took some convincing, but Pauletti, who wasn't above "independent thinking," finally agreed. Cash like that usually disappeared into a government's General Fund, to be wasted somewhere else.

Warner contacted a CPA he knew whose ethics could be compromised for a five-percent cut, and the money disappeared behind a magic curtain that only a very determined forensic sleuth might uncover. The funds were anonymously doled out. Each kidnapped prostitute, and Kiesha Swift, were beneficiaries to ten-thousand-dollar trusts, and Maggie Bagwell got her hundred grand.

So, everyone was happy... especially Al Warner. Besides the satisfaction of closing two major cases and the apprehension of some really vicious perps, he had discovered what was on Eva's mind.

It didn't even take any detective work. That "perp" made a happy confession.

The stick had turned blue, confirmed by her OB.

He was seven months away from becoming a father.

The End

If you enjoyed **Taken**, the 6th Detective Al Warner novel, the author would appreciate you leaving an honest review at Amazon, Goodreads, Bookbub, or any other readers' blog sites.

And if you haven't read any of the first five, 5-Star rated novels in the series: **Death's Angel, Born to Die, The Prom Dress Killer, White Death,** & **Sniper,** you will want to learn how Detective Al Warner's previous adventures got him to this place, and how he became *The Hero of Miami.*

Become a Detective Al Warner fan.
All of George A Bernstein's books may be found at:
http://amazon.com/author/georgeabernstein
Contact the author at: suspenseguy@aol.com

Here is brief synopses of **Death's Angel,** the 1st Detective Al Warner novel, if you'd like to start at the beginning.

Death's Angel
Available in print, Kindle, and Audio

The second serial killer in less than a year is prowling the streets of Miami, systematically snuffing out some of South Florida's most beautiful young women. Detective Al Warner is just back on The Job, fully recovered from a bullet wound that cracked his skull during a deadly chance encounter with another madman.

Warner is in the best physical shape of his life, but his days are laced with headaches and his sleep fraught with terrifying dreams. Lack of rest clouds his usually laser-sharp mind but that doesn't slow his single-minded hunt for this new killer.

Warner and the FBI's BAU become more frustrated as each new death provides plenty of evidence it's the same Unsub, but no new clues to his identity. They learn the killers name, Angie Dedios, and eventually realizes it's really "Angel de Dios" . . . the Angel of God . . . but they are helpless as more beauties die with no new leads as to this deadly "angel's" real identity.

Then Warner's love, Sharon Clark, becomes a target for this madman, and Warner must stop him before she becomes his 8th victim. Only chance brings them all together in one final deadly dance of terror.

Available at: http://amazon.com/dp/B00P2V63X0

Taken

www.ingramcontent.com/pod-product-compliance
Lightning Source LLC
Chambersburg PA
CBHW020734250626
47155CB00003B/743